"Victoria Malvey adds a fresh voice and new verve to the genre."
—*Romantic Times*

Praise for the enchanting novels of Victoria Malvey

A MERRY CHASE

"Malvey delights with her charming characters and witty situations, and the many plot twists add a dash of spice and suspense to this romantic chase."
—*Publishers Weekly*

"You'll find yourself enjoying every minute. . . . Ms. Malvey's new historical novel is delightful, delicious, and delectable. Her intelligent, witty characters are easy to like and their comical antics bring a quick smile and genuine laughter. Don't miss the fun."

—*Rendezvous*

TEMPTRESS

"Victoria Malvey gives classic romance a fresh and exciting new voice."

—Teresa Medeiros, author of *The Bride and the Beast*

ENCHANTED

"A delightful and alluring romance. This is the kind of tale that brightens the day and brings back memories of first crushes and the wonderful feeling of falling in love."

—*Romantic Times*

"Written with skill and humor—a delight to read. . . . A compelling story about the endurance of love."

—*Rendezvous*

"An enthralling tale of mystery and intrigue. Splendid."

—*Bell, Book & Candle*

PORTRAIT OF DREAMS

"A new star has burst upon the romance horizon. Victoria Malvey's *Portrait of Dreams* [is] a sensually sweet tale of love found and fought for. The spark that makes a book a bestseller is present on every page of this beautiful story. FIVE STARS."

—*Affaire de Coeur*

"Heartwarming and tender—a truly unforgettable story."

—Julie Garwood, author of *Heartbreaker*

Books by Victoria Malvey

Portrait of Dreams
Enchanted
Temptress
A Merry Chase
Fortune's Bride
A Proper Affair

Published by POCKET BOOKS

VICTORIA MALVEY

A PROPER AFFAIR

SONNET BOOKS
New York London Toronto Sydney Singapore

This book is a work of fiction. Names, characters, places and incidents are products of the author's imagination or are used fic-
titiously. Any resemblance to actual events or locales or
persons, living or dead, is entirely coincidental.

An *Original* Publication of POCKET BOOKS

A Sonnet Book published by
POCKET BOOKS, a division of Simon & Schuster, Inc.
1230 Avenue of the Americas, New York, NY 10020

Copyright © 2001 by Victoria Malvey

ISBN: 0-7434-1883-2

First Sonnet Books printing May 2001

10 9 8 7 6 5 4 3 2 1

SONNET BOOKS and colophon are trademarks of
Simon & Schuster, Inc.

Cover art by Steven Assel

Printed in the U.S.A.

To Steve

You're still the one.

A PROPER AFFAIR

1

A true lady never displays her emotions in public.

Quoted from *A Lady's Guide to Proper Etiquette*,
written by Lady Cassandra Abbott

London, England
May 1836

"That corset needs to be tighter."

Cassandra Abbott felt the muscles between her shoulder blades knot at the sound of her mother's voice.

Lady Darwood swept into the bedchamber, moving to stand in front of her daughter. "If you are going to fit into your gown, Cassandra, you must cooperate, my dear."

"But I am," Cassandra protested lightly, unable to draw a deep breath with the binding garment entrapping her body. "I don't believe the corset can be any tighter."

"Nonsense." Waving two fingers, her mother instructed, "Now exhale deeply."

Ignoring the throbbing in her head, Cassandra obeyed her mother. Tightening her hold upon the bedpost, Cassandra released her breath as the maid cinched the corset in another precious inch.

Lady Darwood nodded in satisfaction. "Perfect!"

Perhaps she looked perfect, but Cassandra seriously doubted she would be able to draw another breath. An inappropriate giggle rose to her lips as she imagined her mother's reaction if she were to fall onto the bed in a dead faint. Still, years of training made her swallow both her laughter and her protest.

Drawing in a shallow breath, she forced a smile onto her face and released her white-knuckled grip on the bedpost.

Lady Darwood reached up to pat her silver-streaked golden curls. "That's better, isn't it?" She smoothed her hands down her own tightly bound waist. "No price is too high for fashion, Cassandra. A lady should always look her best."

Even at the price of breathing? Cassandra wondered, yet she held her tongue. Instead she lifted her arms as the maid draped the gown over her head. "Will Lord Linley be escorting me to the Perths' ball or are we to meet him there?"

"Neither, as His Grace is unable to attend the affair," her mother replied, perching on the edge of a chair.

Stunned at the reply, Cassandra twisted out of the maid's grasp to face her mother. "But our engagement announcement appeared in today's paper, so it is expected that we are seen together this evening."

"Expected perhaps, but not required." Lady Darwood pursed her lips. "I must say, Cassandra, that I detect a note of displeasure in your voice. It is very unappealing."

Displeasure? Lord, if that was all her mother heard in her voice, she'd managed to hide the panic overwhelming her. Ever since her parents had informed her they were accepting Lord Linley's suit, Cassandra had been fighting the urge to scream a refusal. The one meeting she'd had with her affianced, a gentleman old enough to be her grandfather, had terrified her. Pushing away that horrid memory, Cassandra concentrated on her conversation. "Forgive me," she said, hoping her voice didn't sound stilted. "The unexpected news that my affianced will not be attending Lady Perth's ball caught me unawares."

Remaining silent for a moment, her mother stared at her. "Why do I get the feeling that there is something else troubling you?" Finally, Lady Darwood sighed as she rubbed at her forehead. "You're still apprehensive about marriage to Lord Linley, aren't you?"

Cassandra couldn't hold back her reply. "He's so much older than I . . . and he seldom comes to town. Once we marry I fear I shall be left to molder on his estate . . . and no one seems to know much about—"

"That's quite enough, Cassandra!" Her mother rose from the chair. "I understand you have concerns, but you must trust in your father and me." Stepping forward, she lay a hand upon Cassandra's cheek. "When have we ever led you astray?"

"Never," Cassandra conceded, knowing that it was true. All her life she'd followed her parents' advice, believing they knew what was best for her. Indeed, Cassandra knew that accepting the guidance of her parents was the natural order of life . . . and without order, there is nothing but chaos. Still, a part of her wondered how her parents could possibly be right in this matter. After all, how could she marry a man who repulsed her with his shaking hands, wrinkled skin, and fouled breath? Still, years of good breeding overcame her fears. Surely her parents, who were older and wiser, knew what was best for her. . . . So, being a proper daughter, she must trust in them and believe that their advice would prove sound.

"Then you must trust us in this as well," her mother said softly.

Ignoring the clenching in the pit of her stomach, Cassandra nodded once. "I will, Mother. You know what is best for me."

Satisfied, Lady Darwood gestured toward a box that lay upon Cassandra's dressing table. "His Grace sent over these jewels for you to wear this evening."

Cassandra stood frozen as the maid retrieved the box and opened it for her. Gazing down at the ugly, garish necklace made of thick knots of yellowed diamonds and clunky lumps of gold molded to resemble leaves, Cassandra felt her dread deepen.

Helplessly, she looked at herself in the mirror as the maid settled the weight of Lord Linley's gift around her neck. Her reflection revealed a perfectly gowned, slender young lady with her light brown hair caught up in a classic style . . . a young lady whose blue eyes were clouded and dull.

"Isn't it lovely?" gushed Lady Darwood, moving to stand behind Cassandra. "You should pen His Grace a note on the morrow to let him know of your pleasure with his gift."

Drawing as deep a breath as her binding corset would allow, Cassandra forced a polite smile onto her face. "Of course I shall," she assured her mother softly.

Praying she wouldn't pass out, Cassandra followed her mother from the room. As she stepped into the drawing room, her father rose to greet them.

"My dears," he said with a wide smile, "how radiant you both look this evening."

The little knot at the base of Cassandra's neck eased as her father wrapped her in an embrace. "You always say that," she teased.

"Only because it is true." Her father squeezed her once more before stepping back. "I consider myself most fortunate to have such a beautiful daughter."

"Your beautiful daughter was expressing concern over our choice of husband," Lady Darwood said as she walked toward the mirror to adjust her necklace. "But she knows she can trust us to do what is best for her."

The warmth in her father's gaze soothed Cassandra's still jittery nerves. "That's my girl," he crooned in a soft voice. "Your mother and I only want to see you happy."

"I know," Cassandra reassured her father as she leaned up to press a kiss onto his cheek.

With a pleased smile, her father offered her his arm. "We should be off to the Perths' affair." As Cassandra tucked her hand into the curve of her father's arm, he patted her fingertips. "Be certain you save me a dance, young lady."

"Of course, Papa," Cassandra replied, feeling lighter than she had in two weeks. "Anything for you."

* * *

"Are you interested in some company, my lord?" Glancing up, Bryce Keene sipped at his brandy as the voluptuous blond strumpet swayed closer to him. Leaning down, she whispered into his ear. "I've heard of your wicked ways."

"Oh, have you now." Wrapping an arm around the strumpet, Bryce pulled her down upon his lap. She was a perfect example of the attractive whores provided by Madam Bouvier in her house of ill repute. "And just what have you heard, my beauty?"

The woman pressed her lush bosom against Bryce's chest. "That the Marquess of Towle knows how to pleasure a woman."

Bryce ran a finger along her creamy flesh. "It is my mission in life to never leave a lady wanting more," he assured the strumpet with a laugh.

She cooed prettily as she shifted even closer. "How about a demonstration, my lord?"

"As much as I would undoubtedly enjoy to do precisely that, I'm afraid I have other obligations that demand my time at this moment."

Her full lips twisted into a pout. "Are you certain you can't spare an hour?" she whispered, tilting her head to lick at his earlobe. "I promise to make it worth your while."

"Of that I have no doubt," he agreed, settling his hands upon her waist. "Perhaps on my next visit I shall have more time to give you proper attention."

"Be certain to ask for Nicole," she said in a disappointed voice. "I'll be looking forward to your call."

Assisting the pretty Nicole to her feet, Bryce patted her backside as she sauntered away.

"I can't believe you passed up that morsel," Jonathan Conner, Earl of Dunham, remarked as he sank into the seat across from Bryce.

"Regretfully," he assured his friend. "Unfortunately, I've other obligations."

"And you are undoubtedly exhausted from your earlier play with those two over there," Jonathan added, gesturing toward two curvaceous brunettes Bryce had bedded earlier in the evening.

"Hmmmm," he murmured with a smile.

"You do seem to prefer those dark beauties."

"Indeed, I do," Bryce agreed, thinking of Francesca, the woman he planned to wed. "They have more fire."

"Especially when you take them on two at a time."

"True enough," Bryce returned readily. "One alone would have drained me, but the two of them together . . . well, it left me nearly exhausted."

Jonathan snorted derisively. "Not to the point where you would have passed by the lovely Nicole if you weren't so bullheaded in your determination to attend the Perths' horrid ball."

Bryce had to laugh at his friend's astuteness. "Perhaps, but it is a moot point, as my mother specifically requested that I attend Lady Perth's affair this evening. The esteemed hostess is one of my mother's oldest and dearest friends."

"I still say it will be horribly dull," Jonathan remarked as he straightened his cravat.

"No one says that you must attend with me."

Jonathan responded to Bryce's remark with a

smile. "That's quite true." His demeanor brightening, Jonathan leaned forward in his chair. "What do you say to meeting at Barrow's Gaming Hell in a few hours?"

Lifting a shoulder, Bryce agreed easily. "I'll probably need something to revive me after the ball and a game of dice just might do the trick."

"I still don't see why you feel compelled to comply with your mother's request." Jonathan chuckled softly. "It's not as if you never disappoint your parents."

"Indeed not," Bryce replied with a bitter laugh. "Disappointing my parents is something at which I excel." Hell, all his life he'd met with nothing but his austere father's disapproval. And his brother, Clayton, was an exact replica of his father . . . right down to his censure.

So why was he going to Lady Perth's ball? Bryce knew when his mother asked him that she half-expected him to disappoint her, but for some odd reason he didn't want to prove her right. Though he might enjoy annoying his father and brother, making them bluster at his antics, Bryce hated to cause that look of bewildered hurt to settle into his mother's eyes. Lord knew, he caused it to happen often enough, so if he could avoid that look by whiling away an hour of his time at Lady Perth's dull affair, it was well worth the price.

Thrusting to his feet, Bryce straightened his vest. "Since I know my parents expect me not to appear at Lady Perth's, I've decided that I simply must . . . just to prove them wrong," he remarked broadly, not wishing to expose the real reason behind his desire to attend the ball.

"Who knows? Perhaps you'll give the old boy apoplexy when he returns home."

Bryce snorted with a laugh. "This just might do it."

"Why aren't you dancing, Lord Towle?"

With an easy smile, Bryce bowed to Lady Perth. "I have been waiting for you, my lady," he replied smoothly.

A girlish laugh, more befitting a lady twenty years her junior, escaped his hostess. "My goodness, no one will ever be able to say that the Marquess of Towle is anything less than a perfect . . . charmer."

"Ah, for a moment I thought perhaps you might refer to me as a perfect gentleman." Bryce pressed a hand against his chest. "Such a blatant falsehood would have stunned me."

Swatting her fan lightly against his arm, Lady Perth chided, "You make light of a most grievous occurrence, my lord. I've often heard your father and even your elder brother bemoan the fact that you pursue . . . less than desirable pastimes."

"A rake to the core," he admitted with an unabashed grin. "I fear it is to be my fate."

"Than I shall pray for divine intervention, sir, as you are far too entertaining a fellow to spend the rest of your life alone, lost in devilish pursuits."

"Alone?" he queried, lifting his brow.

Flicking open her fan, Lady Perth gazed at him unblinkingly. "Why, of course, my lord, for no proper lady would be interested in accepting an offer from a scoundrel like yourself . . . even if you are the second son of a duke." She shook her head. "I fear there are far too many suitable lords for a young lady to choose from before any eager mama would cast her eye upon you, Lord Towle."

"Despite my . . . how did you put it? Ah, yes, my charming manner?" he teased her.

"A dissolute rake may indeed be most charming, my young lord, but if the coffers are strained and the title stained, you shall have a most difficult time convincing a steady-minded lady to marry you."

But he didn't want a steady-minded lady. No, he wanted Francesca, Bryce thought, as he gazed out over the simpering society misses who paled in comparison to his dark beauty.

"You are undoubtedly correct," Bryce murmured in return, knowing that Francesca, with her hot-blooded spirit, would laugh at Lady Perth's assertions.

"You realize I only say these things to you because of my dear friendship with your mother." Snapping her fan shut, Lady Perth leveled a stern look at him. "If she weren't touring the Continent at the moment, I'm quite certain she would be saying these things to you. However, because of her absence, I shall have to stand in her stead."

Lifting his hostess' hand to his lips, Bryce pressed a kiss to the back of her fingers. "Most generous of you, my lady."

"Don't believe for an instant that you will be able to wriggle out of this conversation, my lord," she said in a voice colored with amusement. "I believe that what you need is the support and guidance of a wife."

Grinning down at her, Bryce shook his head. "I

fear it is far too late to guide me. Besides, marrying a lady who would harp at me is hardly my desire. I would much rather marry someone for whom I feel a grand passion."

"Passion fades quickly," Lady Perth retorted. "Yet a solid marriage to a well-bred lady remains constant, creating a steady, comfortable life."

Boring year after boring year. Bryce couldn't help but smile over that thought. However, to his hostess, he replied smoothly, "Your argument bears consideration."

With a firm nod, Lady Perth accepted his concession. "Now all we need to do, my lord, is choose a perfect lady for you to court."

Feeling wary, Bryce tried to extricate himself from the conversation. "While I appreciate your offer, my lady, I believe I shall be able to choose—"

"It is my *pleasure* to help you," Lady Perth said, cutting off his protest. Rising onto her tiptoes, she began to search the crowded ballroom. "Who would be your match?" she murmured softly.

Praying she didn't find anyone suitable, Bryce found himself remaining by her side, trying to devise a method to escape Lady Perth's unwanted assistance. If only he could explain to his hostess that he was madly in love with Lady Francesca Milford, then none of this polite posturing would be necessary.

But he'd vowed to Francesca that he would keep their engagement a secret until the end of the season. While he didn't understand why her parents insisted upon it, he accepted their request nonetheless. Though he felt a need to blurt out news of their engagement whenever he saw Francesca dancing and flirting with all of the youngbloods who constantly seemed to be surrounding her, Bryce held his tongue, taking comfort in the knowledge that, in the end, she would belong to him.

Suddenly, he became aware of someone tapping him on the shoulder. "Lord Towle?"

Thrusting away his thoughts of Francesca, Bryce redirected his attention onto Lady Perth. "Forgive me, my lady, I was woolgathering."

"So I surmised, since I called to you no less than three times." The tartness in her voice made him smile. Lady Perth sounded just like his mother whenever she was annoyed with him. "We're addressing a most serious issue, my lord, so your utmost attention would be greatly appreciated."

Bryce bowed his head in deference. "While I understand you only wish to help me, perhaps this evening isn't the best time to choose—"

"Ah, there's a wonderful lady." Lady Perth nodded her head toward the hallway.

Curious, Bryce leaned forward to see who Lady Perth considered his match. He nearly stumbled when he saw none other than the epitome of the perfect Englishwoman.

"Lady Cassandra Abbott?" he rasped, astounded that Lady Perth would ever consider him a good match for such a tight-laced prig.

"Of course. Lady Cassandra would be the perfect choice," Lady Perth returned, her voice filled with conviction.

Regaining his composure, Bryce continued to

gaze at Lady Cassandra. "But you have just finished chiding me for my vices, and it is well-known that Lady Cassandra values propriety above all."

"It is for that precise reason I feel she would be a fine wife for you, Lord Towle. A lady such as Cassandra Abbott would encourage you to turn from your vices."

Harping at him until she drove him from his home, Bryce thought with certainty. Instead of trying to dissuade Lady Perth, he offered another possibility. "My preference lays in another direction, my lady."

Curiosity burned in Lady Perth's gaze as she looked up at Bryce. "Really? To whom do you refer?"

"Lady Francesca Milford has captured my eye," he admitted. "With her exotic Spanish looks and bold spirit, I feel she would make an excellent wife."

For a long moment, Lady Perth stood there silently, her eyes wide and her mouth open. Finally, a laugh burst from her. "A fine jest, my lord," she said as she dabbed at the corners of her eyes. "Lady Francesca indeed. Any gentleman unlucky enough to marry that one will have nothing but uncertainty and mayhem in his life."

"You've forgotten to mention excitement," he added.

Slowly, Lady Perth shook her head. "With your youth, I'm quite certain you believe an exciting life is what you seek, but you must trust me in this, my lord—excitement can be most wearying and, as you age, holds little appeal."

"At two and twenty, I understand what I desire in life, Lady Perth, and I assure you it is not suffering through unceasing lectures on proprieties."

Glancing back at Lady Cassandra, he held in a shudder.

"You are quite mistaken if you believe life with Lady Cassandra would be unpleasant." A side of Lady Perth's mouth quirked upward. "She is a charming lady."

"I'm certain she is," Bryce conceded without hesitation. "I never questioned her gentility." *Only her lack of spirit,* he added to himself.

"I should hope not." Lady Perth's voice rang with indignity. "After all, she's the leading authority on feminine grace."

"Ah, yes, her book." How could he have forgotten? The paragon of virtue had written a tome about the etiquette that should be observed by all young ladies. In other words, a *rule* book. This time, he couldn't hold back his shudder.

"Lady Cassandra is most accomplished for someone only eight and ten." A sigh escaped his hostess.

With her light brown hair, blue eyes, fair complexion, and cool nature, Lady Cassandra was indeed the quintessential Englishwoman. The perfect English rose.

However, he'd always found roses to be dreadfully plain little flowers.

Now his Francesca, with her flashing dark eyes, long black hair, olive skin, and fiery nature, was closer to a lily, exotic and brilliant. Watching Lady Cassandra make her way across the room, he felt a spark of guilt for comparing her so unfavorably to his Francesca.

After all, Lady Cassandra had been raised to believe in the strictures and dictates of a rigid society . . . and she obviously saw no reason to question the rules. He shouldn't judge her so harshly. Most men, he knew, would find her immensely appealing, but he wasn't one of them.

As she approached their hostess, Lady Cassandra smiled politely. "Good evening, my lady," she murmured smoothly. "I am honored to be your guest."

"Thank you, my dear," replied Lady Perth as she sent a pointed look toward Bryce. "I am so happy you could come."

The vapid niceties quickly bored Bryce. If only Francesca were here. . . .

"Do you know the Marquess of Towle?" Gesturing toward Bryce, Lady Perth stepped back until Lady Cassandra faced him.

"I believe we've been introduced," Lady Cassandra said in her polite little voice. "How do you do, sir?"

"Very well, my lady," he murmured as he accepted her outstretched hand. Bending down to place a kiss upon the kid glove covering her hand, Bryce couldn't resist the urge to bedevil her. Slipping his index finger along her palm, he stroked the bare flesh of her wrist.

A small gasp broke from Lady Cassandra, but she allowed him to finish kissing her hand. He couldn't hold in a smile when he realized she was far too much of a lady to ever create a scene in public. Still, the slight flush on her cheekbones told of her annoyance. Before Bryce could continue to tease her, the string ensemble began to play.

As the strains of a waltz filled the room, Lady

Perth clapped her hands together. "My favorite dance," she murmured softly.

Turning toward his hostess, Bryce held out his hand. "I would be pleased if you would honor me, my lady."

Lady Perth clasped his fingers and squeezed once. "You delightful boy," she said with a smile. "I fear I'm far too weary at the moment for such an energetic dance."

The gleam in Lady Perth's eyes made him wary.

"However, I'm certain Lady Cassandra would do you the honor." The expression in Lady Perth's wide eyes was one of innocence as she reached for the younger lady's hand and placed it within his grasp. "Isn't that correct, Lady Cassandra?"

For one moment, Lady Cassandra's polite expression slipped away as she looked at him, revealing her inner thoughts. From that one glance, Bryce knew she'd rather dance with a toad than with him. As quickly as her mask had slipped, Lady Cassandra smoothed out her features. "Unfortunately, I am . . ."

". . . unable to resist such an invitation," Bryce finished for her with what he hoped was a wolfish grin. The devil had prodded him into replying for her. My, my, wouldn't the prim and proper Lady Cassandra Abbott be absolutely scandalized to dance with a disreputable rake!

Like all missish society debutantes, she'd been taught from birth to avoid men like him. Hell, she'd probably been raised to believe a rake would carry her off to slake his lust without so much as a by-your-leave. So, now he was left with only one choice . . .

. . . to prove her right.

With a chuckle, Bryce tugged the prim Lady Cassandra Abbott onto the dance floor.

The cad hadn't even waited until she'd refused the dance. No, indeed not. Instead, he'd pulled her onto the dance floor and into his arms as if she were a sack of potatoes to be tossed about at his will. Very well then, Cassandra thought with a sniff, he'd left her no choice; she must suffer his vulgar manner. Still, she vowed she would not stoop to his level; she'd remain the lady.

Her skirts flew out as he twirled her around the room. "Excuse me, my lord, but the waltz is normally done in three-quarter time."

"Perhaps," he replied as he flashed her another of his wicked grins, "but it's far more entertaining when done at a faster pace, don't you agree?"

His blatant disregard for proprieties stunned her. "I most certainly do not."

As he tilted his head to the side, a lock of his thick, sandy blond hair fell across his forehead. Pulling her an inch closer, he grinned wickedly at her. "Come now, Lady Cassandra, doesn't a spirited waltz heat your blood?"

Stumbling at the vulgar remark, Cassandra managed to regain her balance, vowing to suffer silently through the remainder of the dance. She refused to exchange insults with the cur.

After a few moments of silence, Bryce squeezed her hand. "Cat got your tongue?"

Though a retort rose to her lips, she settled for glaring at him.

"Not speaking to me?" He shook his head, making a tsking sound with his tongue. "Poor Lady Cassandra being forced to dance with a cad like me."

Tilting up her chin, she looked away, refusing to give him the satisfaction of an answer.

"Tell me something, my lady," Bryce began, pulling her even closer until her breasts were pressed against his chest in an alarming fashion. "Isn't it rather dull to sit around observing proprieties all day long?"

Struggling to create distance between them, Cassandra hissed, "Release me this instant!"

"Not until you answer my question," he countered with a bedeviling light in his eyes.

"No!"

His fingers began to stroke her back, making her heart race. "No *what*, Lady Cassandra?"

Willing to do anything to make him cease his torment, Cassandra answered his question. "No, I do *not* find it dull observing proprieties, my lord, for it is those very same rules that provide structure to our society."

Lord Towle yawned in response.

Anger began to simmer within her. "Think on it, my lord. If everyone were to behave in the outrageous manner you seem to prefer, Lord Towle, our entire civilization would tumble into disarray."

"Ah, but I'd wager there wouldn't be a dull moment in the fall," he retorted with a chuckle.

"It seems the sole purpose of your life is to seek amusement, my lord." She lifted her chin. "However, I leave such foolish pursuits to you, for I prefer following the rules of polite society."

"How utterly dull."

Hearing the pity in Bryce's voice, Cassandra defended her beliefs. "Not dull at all, my lord. I shall marry well, have children, enjoy a life of privilege and social acceptance, then slip quietly into old age with grace." She sighed dramatically. "Poor, pitiful me to wish for such a comfortable existence."

"You forgot to mention that you shall go quietly mad while catering to the whims of society." His fingers tightened upon hers. "Haven't you realized yet how very demanding society can be?"

"I have not found it difficult to meet society's expectations," she returned swiftly. "Perhaps you find society so demanding because people expect you to behave as a gentleman, yet you cling to your ill manners."

"*Ill manners?*"

"Come now, Lord Towle. You must admit that your manner is most offensive, sir," she replied tartly.

"And your manner, my lady, is most . . . challenging." His gray eyes sparkled with devilish intent. "You make a man wonder what it would take to unlace your overly tight corset."

She tilted her nose upward. "I assure you, my lord, that you shall never uncover that secret."

"Yet another challenge," he murmured as he tightened his hold upon her waist.

Panic skittered along Cassandra's spine at the maelstrom of emotions that assailed her at the intimate touch. It was most improper for Lord Towle to hold her so close . . . yet it was also somehow . . . stimulating. Shamed by her disgraceful thoughts, Cassandra tried to shift away from him. "I did as you asked, my lord. Now I must insist you release me," she murmured, pressing her hand against his shoulder in an attempt to shift away from him. "My affianced would not approve."

"Affianced?" He rolled the word over his tongue. "I had no idea you were engaged to be married. Who is the lucky gent?"

"The *gentleman* in question is Lord Linley," she replied tartly.

"*Linley!*" he exploded in astonishment. "Good God, the man's old enough to be your grandfather!"

Though Lord Towle's comment reflected her own misgivings about the match, she nonetheless defended her parents' choice. "He is a duke of the realm and a most suitable match."

"Suitable match? I suppose so, if you don't mind that your groom is too feeble to walk down the aisle without the aid of a cane."

Regardless of the fact that Lord Towle's prediction was quite accurate, it would hardly do to agree with the churl. "It is inappropriate to speak of my intended with such disrespect."

Shaking his head, Lord Towle looked at her with a steady gaze. "I daresay, Lady Cassandra, you demonstrated a shocking lack of respect . . . for yourself . . . when you agreed to such a foolish match."

His quiet remark stung her. "*You* have the nerve to speak to *me* of respect when it is well-known that you waste your days in . . . in useless pursuits and spend your money on frivolous . . . pastimes?" she said coldly. "When you have overcome your own multitude of shortcomings, my lord, *then* you may speak to me of respect. But until that time, I refuse to listen to any advice you offer."

Lord Towle's serious expression gave way to yet another devilish grin. "Now that wasn't a very polite thing to say, was it, Lady Cassandra?"

For the first time in her life, Cassandra couldn't control the fury that rushed through her. Tearing herself from Lord Towle's grasp, she stood facing him in the midst of the dancing couples. "You, my lord," she began, trembling with anger, "are a despicable cad."

Gasps echoed around the room before the last syllable of Cassandra's pronouncement faded. Ignoring the astonished gazes fixed upon her, she spun on her heel and walked away . . . leaving the offensive Lord Towle standing in humiliation upon the crowded dance floor.

It was her first public outburst.

And it would be her last, Cassandra vowed, as she left the room. All she needed to do was to avoid the horrid Lord Towle in the future.

2

If a lady acts in accordance with the dictates of polite
society, she is ensured a happy, prosperous life.

Quoted from *A Lady's Guide to Proper Etiquette,*
written by Lady Cassandra Abbott

Seven years later

"I have a rather indelicate matter that I need to
discuss with you," Lady Darwood said as she
glanced around the parlor of Cassandra's dowager
house. "Though I must confess that I am far from
comfortable with the topic."

Setting down her teacup, Cassandra smiled en-
couragingly at her mother. "There is no need to feel
uncomfortable, Mother. After all, we are family."

Lady Darwood patted her hair. "Family or not, it
is always vulgar to discuss one's financial status."
Straightening in her chair, she took a deep breath
before admitting, "Your father has run up quite a
gambling debt and I've come to ask you to cover
the markers."

Stunned, Cassandra could do nothing more than
stare open-mouthed at her mother. Finally, she
managed to choke out, "But I'm destitute."

A frown darkened her mother's expression.

"Destitute? How could that be? You are the Dowager Duchess of Linley."

"All that remained of Alfred's estate was the entitled portion that automatically went to his son. My husband's personal fortune was exhausted during our marriage," Cassandra explained, trying not to sound as bitter as she felt.

Sagging back against her chair, Lady Darwood pressed a trembling hand against her forehead. "Then we are doomed."

It took all of Cassandra's restraint to refrain from scoffing at her mother's melodramatic statement. "Have you considered all of your options?"

"What options do we have?" her mother countered as her hand dropped into her lap. "Everything of value has already been sold. We were only a few steps away from debtor's prison *before* these new debts arose."

Rubbing her fingers across her temple, Cassandra tried to think of a way to help her parents. "I wish I knew how we could raise some money for you."

Her mother looked around the elegant parlor. "There are quite a number of valuables in this room alone," she pointed out.

"Unfortunately, they all belong to the current Duke of Linley," Cassandra said quickly. "I am allowed to stay on in the dowager's cottage because of Randolph's good will. I could hardly repay him by selling his property without his consent."

"No," Lady Darwood agreed reluctantly. "I suppose not."

Leaning forward, Cassandra clasped her mother's

hands. "Have you asked to borrow the funds from any of your friends?"

Lady Darwood jerked backward in surprise. "Cassandra! I'm shocked you would even suggest such a thing," she exclaimed. "Imagine begging money from our friends. Why, the very idea makes me flush with humiliation."

"Far better to be humiliated than imprisoned," Cassandra returned bluntly.

Her mother blinked twice. "My goodness, Cassandra. That was a rather unrefined remark."

"I'm sorry if you find my manner a bit coarse, Mother, but I believe we should be concentrating on securing money rather than upon my manners."

"Or lack thereof."

Her mother's response struck a raw nerve. "Pardon me if my manners are growing shabby, but I'm beginning to question why I placed such value upon them in the first place."

"What?"

For a moment, Cassandra thought her mother might actually fall into a faint. "It's the truth. Where have manners gotten me? Where has following the rules of polite society gotten me?" She spread her arms wide, gesturing around the room. "A life that depends upon the generosity of others. The only thing I own in this room is my dress." Lifting her skirt, she stuck out her foot. "Even these slippers were placed upon the duke's account."

Her mother's eyes widened. "You allowed a man who was not your husband to purchase footwear for you?" she asked with a gasp.

Cassandra sagged against her seat as the utter

ridiculousness of the conversation struck her. Her mother was destitute, facing the loss of her home, yet she was worried over who purchased her footwear.

Holding in her sigh, Cassandra said softly, "There is no point to answering that question. I have no desire to argue with you, Mother."

"I know," Lady Darwood sighed, patting Cassandra's hand. "You really *are* a good daughter."

Cassandra shook her head in exasperation. "The way you said that makes it sound as if you'd had some doubt."

"Well, the—"

"Please don't, Mother," Cassandra interrupted, not wishing to hear the rest of her mother's comments.

"Very well," her mother said primly. Rising, she brushed out her skirts. "It's past time I return home, anyway. I need to make certain your father doesn't take it into his head to recoup his losses through gambling and get us even deeper into debt as a result."

Accompanying her mother out into the foyer, Cassandra kissed her upon the cheek and bid her farewell. The moment the door clicked shut behind her mother, Cassandra felt the urge to scream, to run, to kick, to do *anything* that would ease the tightness in her chest.

She'd followed the rules all of her life and look where it had gotten her—left to molder on this estate. Frustration built inside of her as Cassandra strode down the hall, through the library, and out the glass doors to the rear lawn. Driven to escape her disturbing thoughts, she continued to stride across the manicured lawns and along the edge of the woods.

Finally, she slowed her steps and sank down onto a log that lay across the footpath through the woods. How had her life come to this? she wondered as she leaned forward, resting her elbows upon her knees. If she had some funds of her own, she could re-enter society, attend parties, enjoy life . . . have friends again. Lord, she was so terribly lonely. But unfortunately, she'd been left penniless after many trying years of marriage to a rigid, old man. Now, she didn't even have the ability to help her parents.

Unless she was able to devise a different manner in which to secure funds for them, Cassandra knew she'd be forced to beg mercy from the duke. A shiver ran through her at the very thought of approaching Alfred's son for aid. Randolph had made it very clear that he was being more than generous by simply providing a home for her and that she wasn't to expect more. Still, with her parents' well-being at stake, she had to try.

A gasp broke from Cassandra as she felt something pounce onto her lap. Looking down, she found herself face-to-face with the ugliest cat she'd ever seen in her entire life. The cross-eyed little fellow meowed plaintively at her, then sat back on his haunches.

"Well, hello there," Cassandra murmured, petting the mottled gray, white, and orange fur. "Where did you come from?"

Purring loudly, the cat nudged his head against her hand. The unhesitating affection he showed her touched Cassandra. "You are a sweet thing, aren't you? I wish I could take you home with me, but I think . . ."

What did she think? That the servants would frown upon her bringing a mongrel animal into the cottage?

Why should she care if they did?

Stroking her hand over the cat's soft fur, Cassandra considered the idea. It was far past the time when she should do what was right for her . . . regardless of the reaction she might receive. And at this very moment, what she wanted more than anything was to bring this sweet animal into her borrowed home.

"How would you like to come home with me?" she asked cheerfully.

The cat stood and rubbed his head against her chin in response.

Laughing, Cassandra realized that she would now have something in the dowager cottage that truly belonged to her.

With a spring in her step, she carried her new friend home.

Sitting in the dark, silent room, Bryce wondered how his life had come to this end. He'd come to bid his niece good night, only to discover her missing, and the candle had long since sputtered out as he'd waited for her to return.

He was, Bryce decided, utterly unprepared to raise a headstrong miss who had recently lost her parents. At the thought, a wave of grief washed over Bryce. Elaina wasn't the only one who'd lost someone in that accident. He'd lost his brother as well.

Closing his eyes against the pain, Bryce realized that he would give anything to have Clayton back, that if given another chance, Bryce would make different choices. And he would have made peace with his parents before their sudden death. Bryce clenched the arm of his chair as fresh pain swept over him. How could he have known his parents would die of consumption within a year of their grand tour? God, he had so many regrets. Indeed, if given the opportunity to turn back his life, he would have chosen a far different path.

Instead, he found himself here, alone in the dark, waiting for a willful chit to return home, praying that it wasn't too late to save her from herself. As he shifted in the chair, the book he'd been reading fell to the floor. Bending down, he retrieved the leather-bound volume, turning it over in his hands. He'd been reading the book, searching for some answers on how to curb his niece.

A Lady's Guide to Proper Etiquette by Lady Cassandra Abbott.

Memories of the prim Lady Cassandra filled Bryce, making him remember how Lady Perth had once urged him to consider her for his bride . . . and how he'd scoffed at the idea. Not exciting enough, he'd sneered.

But now he wished he could turn back the clock and follow Lady Perth's advice.

Instead he'd foolishly followed his heart, marrying the wild, exciting Lady Francesca Milford. He'd thought their marriage would be the stuff of dreams, but it had turned out to be the stuff of nightmares instead. Within the first month of their marriage, his beloved Francesca had taken a lover, cuckolding him in his own home. Still, he'd believed her tearful apology . . . only to discover her in bed with yet another man a few weeks later.

In an instant, she'd killed his love for her, forcing him to admit to himself that he'd made an awful mistake. Soon thereafter, he'd withdrawn from society, unable to look at the young bucks and wonder if they'd been with his wife, unwilling to watch her shame the family name.

Rubbing a hand against his forehead, Bryce remembered how Francesca's behavior had only deepened his father's disappointment in his youngest son. Why couldn't Bryce control his own wife? his father had demanded. Yet, Bryce *had* tried to control Francesca . . . only to fail miserably. How did one contain a whirlwind?

Bryce still didn't have any idea, he realized, as he looked around his niece's room, for if he did, surely he could manage Elaina. He saw the wildness inside of her, the same wildness that had driven—and ultimately destroyed—Francesca.

Slamming the book onto the table, Bryce thrust to his feet and began to pace the room. He'd be damned to Hell and back before he'd allow his niece to follow in Francesca's path. What he needed to do was to figure out a way to guide Elaina, to devise a—

His thoughts broke off as he heard a sound from the open window. Standing utterly still, he watched one leg swing into the window, then another, until Elaina backed into the bedchamber. His chest tightened as he took in her mussed hair and rumpled clothes.

"*Where the devil have you been?*"

A shriek broke from Elaina as she spun around, a hand pressing against her chest. "You scared me half to death!"

"Good," he ground out. "Then we're even. Now tell me where you've been—unescorted, I might add—until dawn?"

Her chin lifted mutinously. "Out."

"That answer is unacceptable."

Lifting one shoulder, she gave him a dry look. "It's the only one I have."

He shook with the effort it took to control his anger. "Very well, then. You are confined to your room until you decide to tell me where you were all night."

"You can't order me about! You're not my father."

Groaning, Bryce pressed two fingers against his temple. "I'm well aware that you are my niece, not my daughter, but I must once again point out, Elaina, that I *am* your guardian . . . which gives me the right to tell you exactly what to do."

"This situation is insufferable, not that *you* seem to mind." She tossed him a hard glare. "I'll wager you're happy that my father died, since he left you with the title of duke."

"Good God, Elaina, have you no decency?" he ground out, unable to hold back his anger. "You are speaking of my *brother.* To imagine I wished him dead is far too vile to even—" Bryce broke off his rebuff as the emotions he'd struggled to suppress for months arose within him. Turning away from his niece, he stuffed his shaking hands into his pockets. Lord, didn't she understand that he would give *anything*, anything at all, to have Clayton back? How ironic it was that he'd long bemoaned his brother's heavy-handed advice, and now he'd like nothing more than to hear it.

Still, how could he expect a sixteen-year-old girl who suffered from the loss of her parents to understand, to even *want* to understand?

Taking a deep breath, Bryce turned toward his niece once more. The defiant cast of her expression didn't bode well for any hope that she would listen to him. "I understand that you—"

"You don't understand anything!"

Through clenched teeth, Bryce forged onward. ". . . are having a difficult time right now and I would like nothing more than to be completely sympathetic to your situation."

Propping her hands upon her hips, Elaina thrust out her chin and sneered at him. "Then why aren't you? Before my father died, you were the only one who understood me, the only one I could talk to," she said, her voice cracking on the last word, "but now . . . you're just like he was."

All of his anger died at her admission. Holding out his hands, Bryce stepped forward to clasp Elaina's shoulders. "You can still talk to me."

"No, I can't," she retorted, shaking free of his grasp. "You used to tell my father to be more understanding with me, to be more patient, but now you're the one who is always yelling at me."

Bryce's hands fell to his sides. "Because now I'm responsible for your well-being, Elaina."

"You mean now you're my keeper."

Bryce felt ill at the betrayal he saw in her eyes, but he knew he had to stand firm. He had no choice . . . because he loved her and he knew what would happen if he didn't curb her wildness now. Before Clayton had died, Elaina had always been mischievous, always getting into scrapes, but nothing like her actions now. Indeed, her escapades had grown wilder, even dangerous at times, since she'd come to live with him. A shudder ran through him at the thought of his niece repeating Francesca's mistakes.

Trying one more time to reach his niece, he said, "Please try to understand, Elaina. I wish we could go back to the way things used to be, but everything has changed and I'm now responsible for—"

"—making me as miserable as my father did," she finished coldly. "After my parents died, I thought living with you would be wonderful, that you'd be understanding." She shook her head. "How wrong I was."

With her skirts sailing behind her, Elaina marched from the bedchamber into her dressing room, making quite the dramatic exit. Slowly, Bryce sunk down into the chair he'd claimed for his vigil. Resting his forehead against the palm of his hand, he came to one inescapable conclusion.

The situation was completely out of control.

A chill raced along Cassandra's spine as she stepped into her late husband's study. Memories of how Alfred had berated her publicly for failing to produce a child, of how he had confined her to her room whenever she had gotten upset, of how he had subjected her to his horrible fumblings in the bedroom.

Shivering, Cassandra reached out a hand to steady herself. She brushed aside the unwanted memories of past humiliations, forced a smile onto her face, and curtsied to Alfred's son, the current Duke of Linley. "My lord."

Randolph stepped closer as she rose. "How delightful to see you, Stepmama," he murmured, using the moniker that seemed so ridiculous since he was twenty years her senior. Lifting her hand, he pressed a kiss upon the back of her fingers.

Nearly flinching at the feel of his wet mouth against her flesh, Cassandra ignored the clenching of her stomach as she tugged her hand from Randolph's grasp. "I appreciate you receiving me."

"Naturally," he replied smoothly. "You are family, after all." Walking toward the door, he shut it softly and twisted the key, locking them in the privacy of the study. "Now we can be certain we will not be disturbed."

Unease flittered through her. "There is no need to lock the door, Your Grace."

Lifting his brows, Randolph stared at her. "I believe your missive mentioned it was a delicate matter you needed to discuss with me."

"Indeed, it is," she agreed, pressing a hand to her throat. "But it is still highly improper for us to be alone together in a locked room."

He offered her a sly smile. "Ah, but no one will ever be the wiser. After all, you know better than most that my father's servants are very tight-lipped."

That was true, Cassandra thought, remembering all the times the servants had witnessed ugly scenes between her and her husband and yet never uttered a word. "Very well, then," she said, firmly ignoring the unsettling feeling inside her. "I came to ask you for a rather substantial loan."

"Really?" Randolph strolled toward her. "Just how substantial?"

As Cassandra named the sum, the duke's pale blue eyes widened. "My, my, Cassandra, that is quite a lot of money."

Her fingers curled into her skirts. "I know, Your Grace, and I wouldn't ask for such generosity if the situation weren't dire."

Running his fingers through his thinning blond hair, Randolph stared down at her.

At his continued silence, Cassandra began to feel desperate. "I understand your reluctance, Your Grace, but . . ."

"I'm not reluctant to come to your aid," he interrupted as he moved closer. Lifting his hand, Randolph stroked his index finger along the curve of her jaw. "I'm simply wondering what you will give me in return."

Cassandra blinked once. "Pardon?"

A low chuckle escaped Randolph. "Come now, Cassandra. Surely you weren't expecting me to give you such a large amount of money without some form of compensation."

Jerking her face away from his touch, she stumbled backward, coming up against his desk.

"Your address is overly intimate, sir," she replied sharply.

His eyes narrowed. "If I grant your request, I plan on being a good deal more intimate than that, my pretty Cassandra."

"I am your *stepmother*," Cassandra gasped, appalled at his suggestion.

"It is best to keep these things in the family," he replied with a chuckle. "I inherited my father's title, his wealth, his lands. Why not his wife as well?"

"You are *already* married, sir!"

"What has that got to do with my proposal?" Disbelief gathered in his expression. "You thought I was proposing marriage? Good God, no! I only wish to enjoy your . . . sweets in exchange for my future assistance." He ran his finger along the lace edging of her sleeve. "It is a fine offer."

Slapping his hand away, Cassandra drew herself up to her full height. "Your offer deeply offends me," she said stiffly, "and I will not stand here and be insulted—"

"You will if you wish to continue to live off my generosity."

Gasping, Cassandra sagged against the desk. "You cannot turn me out onto the streets."

"Why not?" Randolph asked with a shrug. "If I announce that you made improper advances toward me and I could no longer tolerate your presence upon my estate, I'm quite certain people will be most sympathetic to my plight."

"I shall tell them the truth." Determination filled her as she lifted her chin and met his gaze. "I shall tell your wife," she pronounced triumphantly, knowing she had him cornered.

Folding his arms across his chest, Randolph rocked back onto his heels. "She won't believe a word you say," he said with a laugh. "Millicent despises you."

It was true, Cassandra knew, for Millicent had often expressed her loathing. From what Cassandra could gather from Millicent's ugly accusations, she'd vehemently opposed Alfred remarrying, afraid that he might sire another son, a second son who would inherit some of the entitled lands.

"And even if my wife *does* believe you, she would be even more eager to have me toss you out of the cottage with nary a farthing to your name." His smile made shivers race along her flesh. "Now can you see the wisdom of my offer?"

Struggling for breath, Cassandra shook her head. "Why?" she asked softly. "Why are you doing this now? I've lived in the dowager cottage for months and you've never once made an improper advance."

He grasped her upper arms, propelling her closer until she was pressed against his chest. "Because my wife kept a close eye on me. But now that she is with child, she's focused all of her attention on preparing for the baby . . . conveniently leaving me to pursue my own pleasures." He rubbed his cheek against the top of her head. "And, my dear stepmama, I do believe I shall find you most pleasurable."

"*No!*" Using all of her strength, she tore herself out of Randolph's grasp. "I shall never agree to your vile proposal."

His expression hardened into a mask of cold

fury. "Then pack your bags, for you are no longer welcome on this estate." Turning on his heel, he went and unlocked the door. "Now get out."

Gathering her pride around her like a protective cloak, Cassandra glared at Randolph. "With pleasure," she replied tartly. Striding out of the manor house, Cassandra hurried across the fields to her cottage. Standing on the edge of her garden, looking at the house that had been her home for the past six months, she pressed a trembling hand against her stomach.

What in the name of Heaven was she going to do now?

"I'm at a loss with my niece," Bryce admitted to Jonathan.

"How so?"

Glancing around White's, Bryce ensured no one could overhear their conversation. "Her behavior is unacceptable." He leaned forward. "Last night, she came home after dawn . . . unescorted."

Jonathan's eyes widened. "Most inappropriate," he agreed.

"And that was merely the last in a long line of indiscretions." Sighing, Bryce thrust his hand through his hair. "I've tried everything to make her understand that she will destroy herself if she destroys her reputation, but she refuses to listen to me."

"Then you need to find someone who will take her in hand."

"Like who? Elaina is far too old for a governess."

Jonathan shook his head. "I wasn't speaking of a

servant, Bryce. I meant it is time for you to take a wife."

"I've already had one, thank you," he ground out as harsh memories of Francesca filled him. "I have no desire to experience marriage ever again."

Setting down his snifter, Jonathan drummed his fingers against the arm of his chair. "Come now, Bryce. You need to be reasonable. I know better than most the trouble you had with Francesca, but not all women are like her."

"You mean some of them are truthful, patient, and possess that elusive quality of faithfulness," Bryce retorted dryly.

"That is exactly what I am saying."

"If I find the need for companionship, I'll purchase a hound."

"One who will help curb your niece's wild tendencies?" Jonathan asked pointedly. "You might not wish to consider marriage again, Bryce, but if you want to help Elaina, I don't see that you have many other options."

Though the very idea made his gut tighten, Bryce forced himself to consider the suggestion. What his friend said was true enough: If he married a lady of refinement, she would provide a good role model for his niece. Yet, how could he bear to marry again?

"I don't know if I could take another wife," Bryce admitted in a low voice.

"Of course you could." Jonathan spread his hands wide. "You married Francesca for love, but that wouldn't be the case this time. Indeed, you would logically consider all of your choices and then pick the lady that best suits your needs. If you choose carefully, you can be assured that she will act in a manner befitting a duchess. As for you, your emotions wouldn't be involved, so there's no risk of becoming distraught even if she turns out not to be a perfect match."

Turning the idea over in his head, Bryce began to warm to the notion. "That's certainly true. And it would be most convenient to have someone to keep Elaina from plaguing me."

"Indeed, it would." Smiling, Jonathan leaned back in his chair. "If you choose wisely, Bryce, your marriage would be a most proper affair, my friend."

Lord, he liked the sound of that. Bryce nodded slowly. "I believe you're right, Jonathan. A cultured bride might be exactly what I need to set my life in order."

"Now the only trick will be finding one who will suit," Jonathan replied with a laugh.

A proper wife, Bryce thought, turning the phrase over in his mind. The perfect lady would be refined, decorous, and charming. In essence, she would epitomize a well-bred Englishwoman, following all the rules he'd read in that book last night, the one by Lady Cassandra Abbott.

Suddenly, the years slipped away and he remembered holding the prim Lady Cassandra in his arms, waltzing her around the room as she lectured him on the necessity of following the rules.

A side of his mouth quirked upward. "Do you remember Lady Cassandra Abbott? Now, she would meet my needs perfectly. She is, after all, the perfect English rose, a most proper young lady." He lifted a shoulder. "Too bad she married Linley after her first Season."

"Hadn't you heard? She's a widow; Linley passed on a few months back."

Straightening in his chair, Bryce stared at his friend. "A widow? Are you certain?"

"Absolutely," Jonathan said firmly. "I would be hard-pressed to forget Linley's son crowing about his good fortune." A look of disgust darkened his expression. "Imagine rejoicing publicly over his father's death. Poorly done of him."

But Bryce didn't hear the rest of what Jonathan was saying; all of his thoughts were concentrated on one notion. The proper Lady Cassandra was again eligible for marriage.

He remembered all too well how he'd laughed at the idea of wedding someone as dull as Lady Cassandra, how he'd dismissed Lady Perth's words of caution regarding Francesca. Well, he'd paid the price for his folly. He would never make that mistake again.

3

A true lady never makes a decision in haste.

Quoted from *A Lady's Guide to Proper Etiquette*,
written by Lady Cassandra Abbott

*L*ooking around the gaily lit ballroom, Cassandra couldn't believe that only two weeks had passed since her horrid scene with the duke. It felt like another lifetime.

"Your Grace," exclaimed Lady Perth as she stepped forward to press a kiss upon Cassandra's cheek. "What a delightful surprise."

"Thank you, my lady," Cassandra murmured, smiling fondly at the older woman. "It was most kind of you to invite me."

Patting Cassandra's hand, Lady Perth shook her head. "You are always a welcome guest in my home . . . especially since I haven't seen you in ages. Your parents must be delighted to have you stay with them. After all, you've been gone from society for far too long. It was very naughty of Linley to carry you off to his estate, then hide you away."

"Indeed." A small shiver ran through Cassandra

at the thought of those long, difficult years. "Very naughty of him."

"And I was so sorry to hear of your loss, my dear Lady Linley." Lady Perth clucked her tongue. "To be a widow at such a young age is a travesty."

No, the travesty was being married for so long. "Thank you," Cassandra returned, keeping her thoughts to herself.

"Still, your loss is our gain, for it is wonderful to have your company once again. I'll wager your parents are overjoyed to have you visiting."

Lady Perth's heartfelt sentiments tugged at Cassandra, for she knew it was only a matter of weeks before her parents lost everything. Then all three of them would be searching for a new home. Sweeping a hand down her cheek, Cassandra thrust the frightening thought away as a gentleman joined them.

"Good evening, Lady Perth," he murmured, his voice low and smooth, as he bent to press a kiss upon the elderly woman's hand.

"Lord Towle," Cassandra murmured breathlessly as she watched him straighten, his sandy blond hair gleaming in the candlelight. He cut a fine figure in his immaculate attire. The years hadn't touched his features except to deepen the dimples on either side of his mouth.

He turned his piercing blue gaze upon her and flashed her that wild smile that had affected her so long ago. "Lady Linley," he said softly, making Cassandra catch her breath all over again. Lifting her hand, he pressed a kiss onto the back of her glove. "It has been far too long."

"For all of us," Lady Perth added, her avid gaze

darting between them. "Since you've been gone for so long, Cassandra, you might not have heard that Lord Towle has inherited the title and is now the Duke of Amberville."

"It is unfortunate that such an honor can only be gained by losing someone you love, is it not, Your Grace?" Cassandra murmured softly.

For the life of her, Cassandra couldn't understand the odd light in Lord Towle . . . *no*, she thought, mentally correcting herself, *in Lord* Amberville's *eyes*.

"I am touched by your concern," he replied after a moment. "You are quite correct, my lady. I loved my brother very much."

"I'm so very sorry," she said quietly.

For a brief moment, Lord Amberville's expression reflected his raw grief, then, in the next instant, his features smoothed. "I appreciate your sympathy. It's still difficult to believe that my brother and his wife are gone . . ." he replied, his tone of voice reflecting a small measure of his distress. ". . . leaving behind their daughter."

"Oh, the poor girl," gasped Cassandra. "How difficult it must be to have lost both parents. How old is the child?"

"Ten and six."

"A most difficult time for a young lady to lose her mother," Cassandra commiserated as she released Lord Amberville's arm.

"It most certainly is," he agreed with a nod. "And I fear I am woefully unprepared to provide her with the guidance she needs."

Knowing of the duke's wild past, Cassandra tended to agree with him. Still, her honest opinion was not what he needed to hear now. "If you tell her of your affection and provide a stable life for her, I'm confident you will be fulfilling her needs."

Lord Amberville's look of immense satisfaction baffled Cassandra. "I had a suspicion you would know what to do for her." He nodded firmly. "After all, you are the expert when it comes to raising proper young ladies."

"I wrote a book on etiquette, Your Grace," Cassandra corrected him. "There was no mention on how to deal with the loss of loved ones."

"True, but there is comfort to be found within structure, is there not?"

Comfort within structure? This sentiment from a man who had embraced the dark pleasures of life? "For many, that is correct," she replied finally.

"I strongly believe my niece would benefit from structure," Lord Amberville replied.

Now she understood, Cassandra thought as a tiny smirk played upon her lips. While he might revel in freedom from society's dictates, his niece would not be afforded such luxury. "If you feel so strongly about the matter, than I suggest you seek a matron to sponsor your niece and guide her through the intricacies of proper behavior," Cassandra said, feeling a bit sorry for the girl already.

A side of his mouth curved upward. "Splendid suggestion, my lady. I shall do precisely as you recommend."

Lifting her hand, Lord Amberville pressed another kiss upon her fingers, then repeated his gesture to Lady Perth who had been watching their exchange closely. With a bow, he departed, leaving Cassandra to watch after him.

"My gracious." Waving her fan, Lady Perth cooled down her reddened face. "I could practically see the sparks flying between the two of you."

Cassandra couldn't contain her surprise. "Sparks? Between Lord Amberville and me?" She laughed softly. "I fear you are mistaken, my lady. If I remember correctly, Lord Amberville was always drawn to ladies who were more . . . exuberant than I."

"True, but the years have changed him." Lady Perth sent her a pointed look. "Or perhaps I should say his late wife changed him."

"Late wife?" Cassandra asked, unwillingly drawn into the conversation.

"He married Lady Francesca Milford a few months after your marriage to His Grace." Tipping her fan in front of her face, Lady Perth leaned closer. "Lady Francesca always was a wild sort and marriage didn't change her one measure. Since you didn't come into town, you never witnessed the rows they had that first year of marriage." She shook her head. "Their disagreements were fierce and far too public for anyone's sensibilities. After a while, Lord Amberville no longer attended social functions, but his wife still came, behaving in a most outrageous manner."

Cassandra couldn't help but feel a sense of empathy with Lord Amberville. After all, she too had suffered through an ill-fated marriage. But at least she could take comfort in the fact that her humiliation remained private.

Glancing around, Lady Perth added, "When she died in the boating accident on the Thames, she was sailing with her latest lover, the Earl of Hammond." She sighed heavily. "If that weren't enough, Lord Amberville faced the loss of his brother soon afterward and became guardian to his niece." Lifting her brows, Lady Perth fixed a steady gaze upon Cassandra. "There is much to admire about a man such as Lord Amberville."

"Undoubtedly so, and I'm certain most ladies feel the same." Smiling pleasantly at Lady Perth, Cassandra excused herself and hurried off to the ladies' chambers. Lord, save her from matchmakers!

From his position near the staircase, Bryce kept his gaze fixed upon Lady Linley as she made her way across the ballroom. Her calm, compassionate nature greatly appealed to him after having suffered through Francesca's fiery personality. Cassandra Hampsted, Dowager Duchess of Linley, would suit his needs perfectly.

"I saw you chatting with Lady Linley," remarked Jonathan as he came alongside Bryce. "And from the smug look upon your face I'd say the meeting must have gone quite well."

"I will offer for her in the morning," Bryce informed his friend. The declaration felt right. Indeed, he'd examined this decision from all angles for the past two weeks. This time he wasn't going to make a rash mistake. No, this time he was approaching the entire business of marriage with his head instead of his heart.

Jonathan's brows flew upward. "Really? Don't you think you're rushing things a bit?"

"Not at all," Bryce returned. "You must remember, Jonathan, that this match will not require a courtship. I plan on making a logical proposal to the lady, outlining how mutually beneficial a marriage would be to both of us, and, hopefully, she will agree to my proposal."

"How convenient," Jonathan drawled dryly.

"Well put." Bryce nodded firmly. "A marriage of convenience is precisely what I plan on offering."

"You're not planning on bedding her then?"

"Don't be ridiculous, Jonathan. Of course I am."

Grinning, Jonathan murmured, "And as Lady Linley is most attractive it will not be a hardship."

"Don't be crass," Bryce retorted. "What I meant is that though the marriage will be one of convenience, I also desire an heir." A side of his mouth quirked upward. "And as I've yet to hear of another method to accomplish that goal . . ."

Laughing, Jonathan clapped a hand upon Bryce's shoulder. "Point well-made. Still, I wonder if the lady will agree with your pragmatic approach to marriage. Most women wish to be wooed."

Satisfaction settled in Bryce. "That's true, but from all accounts, Lady Linley is a sensible woman who will see the logic in my proposal."

"So you believe she will marry you simply because you're a duke now?"

"Not at all. She'll marry me because she won't be able to afford not to." Bryce smiled at Jonathan's surprised expression. "Before I even sought out the lady, I looked into her current situation."

For a long moment, Jonathan simply stared at Bryce, then he broke into laughter. "I see you are determined to approach this in a most businesslike fashion," Jonathan finally said.

"Of course," Bryce agreed readily. "As I had not seen the lady in years, it was only prudent of me to ensure she was still all that I remembered."

"So I take it there were no skeletons rattling around in her closet?" Jonathan murmured with a laugh.

"Not a one," Bryce replied. "However, I did learn that Lady Linley was left virtually penniless after her husband passed away as his entire estate was entailed."

"Which is why you are convinced that she will acquiesce to your proposal without protest," Jonathan concluded accurately.

"Precisely. And if regaining her financial status weren't incentive enough, I've also uncovered the fact that her father recently suffered some rather large gambling debts." Crossing his arms, Bryce rocked back on his feet. "Naturally, I shall offer to purchase her father's markers and gift them to her as a wedding present."

"You romantic devil," Jonathan retorted, shaking his head. "Are you planning on calling upon her tomorrow then?"

"No. I shall have my man-of-business call upon her to make the offer."

"*What?*"

"I fail to see why that would surprise you. If you consider the delicate matter of offering to pay off her parents' debt, you would agree that it isn't a proper topic of discussion between us."

"While she will undoubtedly feel uncomfortable

discussing her dire financial situation with your agent, I'm positive she would be utterly mortified to discuss it with you," Jonathan agreed immediately.

"My point precisely." Nodding firmly, Bryce smiled at his friend. "Approaching this entire matter in a straightforward, unemotional manner is best for everyone concerned."

Descending the staircase of her parents' townhouse, Cassandra realized her ears still rang with her mother's laments about their dire future. All morning Lady Darwood had cried over the loss of their house, their lifestyle, their position . . . and, worst of all, Cassandra knew her mother was right.

Taking a calming breath, Cassandra stepped into the front parlor. "Mr. Jacobson?"

"Your Grace," he murmured, bowing to her. "Thank you for agreeing to see me."

After reading Mr. Jacobson's intriguing note stating that he was Lord Amberville's man-of-business, she'd been far too curious to even consider turning him away. Settling into a chair, she gestured toward the chaise opposite her. "Please make yourself comfortable, Mr. Jacobson. Would you care for some tea?"

"No, thank you, my lady. If you wouldn't mind, I'd prefer to get straight to the point of my call."

Cassandra leaned back in her chair and folded her hands across her lap. "By all means, please proceed," she invited.

"As I mentioned in my note, His Grace, Lord

Amberville, bid me to call upon you in order to set forth his proposal."

Lifting both her brows, Cassandra asked softly, "A proposal of what nature?"

"Of marriage, Your Grace."

Her elbow slipped off the arm of her chair. "*Marriage?*" To Lord Amberville? Dear God, she'd only met the man twice! "Surely you are mistaken!"

Mr. Jacobson shook his head. "There is no mistake, Lady Linley. His Grace was most specific about his proposal and felt you would find it appealing in nature."

"If he truly believed that, why isn't he sitting before me now?" she returned swiftly.

Shifting on his seat, Mr. Jacobson tugged upon his collar. "Because His Grace felt that the . . . delicate nature of his proposal would be more easily received from me."

"Delicate nature?" Cassandra asked warily.

Mr. Jacobson dropped his gaze. "His Grace is offering to settle a most generous marriage price upon you if you agree to his terms."

Her breath caught in her throat at the realization that Lord Amberville was attempting to *buy* her. Before she could spit out her refusal, Mr. Jacobson continued outlining the proposal.

"His Grace's only provisions are that you remain loyal to the state of marriage, that you bestow honor upon the Amberville line, and that you guide his niece through her first Season," he finished in a rush. "In return, all family debts will be paid in full."

Her outraged refusal died upon her lips. "All my

family debts?" she asked, wondering how much Lord Amberville had uncovered about her parents' financial troubles.

Mr. Jacobson's response answered that question. "All debts . . . including those incurred by members of your immediate family."

Settling back in her chair, Cassandra forced herself to consider the proposal. Marriage to Lord Amberville would solve so many problems, but could she do it? Could she barter herself in exchange for her family's financial security? And if she refused, could she live with the knowledge that she could have prevented her parents, her beloved father, from being tossed out of their home? Tapping her fingers against the arm of her chair, she turned the facts over in her mind.

This time she would be entering marriage as a mature woman instead of a naive girl. And, Heaven knew, Lord Amberville was far more appealing to her senses than her former husband had ever been. Still, his physical attributes did not make the idea more appealing.

Yet the sadness she'd glimpsed inside of him did. She'd also been touched by his concern for his niece. Perhaps Lord Amberville *would* make an acceptable husband. Yet, how could she be certain? Perhaps she could set forth a few of her own provisions and, if Lord Amberville agreed, she would know he was a reasonable man.

"Mr. Jacobson," she began as she leaned forward, "you may relay my acceptance to His Grace . . ."

A huge smile split his face.

". . . on one condition."

She watched in amusement as wariness crept into his expression. "And that would be what, Your Grace?"

"That Lord Amberville agree to a few provisions. After all, if he is free to outline a few conditions of marriage, then I should be as well, don't you think?" she asked.

"I don't believe His Grace would mind overly much . . . if the provisions were reasonable, that is."

"I certainly wouldn't make outrageous demands upon His Lordship," Cassandra murmured. "I shall work on the provisions this very afternoon and send them around to your office."

Smiling broadly, Mr. Jacobson rose to his feet. "As soon as I receive them, I shall offer them to His Grace for review."

"Very well." Feeling a sense of anticipation, Cassandra stood to escort Mr. Jacobson to the door. "I shall await your response."

As soon as Cassandra closed the door behind Mr. Jacobson, she hurried over to the desk and began her list, choosing each and every word very carefully.

4

Ladies of breeding bow to their husband's wishes.

Quoted from *A Lady's Guide to Proper Etiquette*,
written by Lady Cassandra Abbott

"*Fifty-six provisions?*" Bryce stared incredulously down at the sheaf of papers in his hand. "Is the woman mad?"

"She didn't strike me as such, Your Grace." Jacobson rose from behind his desk. "But as I was saying, my lord, I only just received the papers a few moments ago and haven't even reviewed them myself yet. I would have called upon you to deliver them within the hour as we'd arranged."

Waving his hand, Bryce dismissed his agent's protest. "I grew weary of awaiting an answer, so I came to your offices instead." He settled into a chair. "And since I'm here, we can review these ridiculous provisions together." Lifting the top sheet of paper, Bryce read off the first request. "Number one. Her Grace will be permitted to purchase a minimum of three new dresses per month." Bryce rolled his eyes. "Number two. Her Grace will be permitted to purchase a minimum of three new hats per month." This time he snorted in derision. "My God! What nonsense!"

"Please, Your Grace, I would prefer to have a chance to review—"

"Review what, Jacobson? These ridiculous requests?" Bryce asked with a laugh as he tapped the papers. "Linley must have been a miserly old fellow if Lady Cassandra felt compelled to make such frivolous requests."

Jacobson held out his hand. "If I might see the pages, Your Grace. I would feel better if—"

But Bryce was having far too enjoyable a time chuckling over the inane requests. "Number thirty-four. Her Grace will be permitted to ride in public parks with escort." He shook his head. "Did she think I'd planned on locking her away?" Yet thinking back, he realized that Linley had done precisely that. After their wedding, Lady Cassandra had remained on the Linley estate, missing Season after Season.

Perhaps these requests weren't so frivolous after all.

"I shall certainly sign these provisions," Bryce announced as he stood and reached for Jacobson's quill. With a flourish, he signed his name to the last page of the provisions, ignoring Jacobson's continued protests. "In fact, I believe I shall return them to the lady herself."

Folding the papers, he tucked them into his coat pocket. "Excellent work, Jacobson," he said and headed out to Lady Linley's familial townhouse.

*   *   *

Smoothing down her skirts, Cassandra rounded the corner into her parents' drawing room. "Lord Amberville," she murmured, stepping forward with an outstretched hand. "How delightful to see you again."

His appealing smile stole her breath away. "My lady," he returned, keeping his gaze upon her face as he bent over her hand to press a kiss upon her fingers.

"To what do I owe this honor, Your Grace?" she asked, discreetly pulling her hand out of his all too disturbing clasp.

"Please call me Bryce." His grin widened. "We are to be married, after all."

"Are we?" Cassandra pressed her hands against her skirt to hide the fact that her fingers were trembling. "Have you seen my provisions then, my lord?"

"Bryce," he corrected, before continuing, "And to answer your question, yes. Not only have I seen your requests, but I've agreed to them as well . . . all fifty-six of them."

"I suppose you consider it quite bold of me to ask for so many provisions," she replied warily, waiting for him to argue a few of the points.

But Lord Amberville surprised her.

Reaching into his coat pocket, he withdrew the papers and handed them to her. "If the nature of your requests are an indication as to the state of your previous marriage, your requests are perfectly understandable and quite reasonable."

Clutching her papers to her chest, she murmured, "Thank you, my lord."

"*Bryce.*" His eyes crinkled at the corners with his wide smile. "I see we shall have to work on that, won't we?"

"Perhaps," she said, giving him a smile in return, "but luckily I tend to be a quick learner . . . Bryce."

He burst out laughing. "I do believe we shall get along splendidly," he pronounced finally.

"I agree," she returned, feeling more hope for the future than ever before.

A comfortable silence fell between them until Bryce finally cleared his throat. "I suppose I should be on my way," he said, gesturing toward the door.

"Very well." Oddly enough, she felt a reluctance to see him go. "However, if you'd like to stay, I could order tea for us and we could become better acquainted."

"As enjoyable as that sounds, I have a few matters I must attend to," he returned smoothly. "Such as making arrangements for our marriage ceremony."

His crisp tone seemed so at odds with his laughter of moments ago. "That is fine with me," she informed him warily. "And I shall send you my list of people who should receive an invitation."

"A list?" Bryce's eyebrows drew together. "I trust it shall be shorter than your earlier requests. I would prefer a small ceremony."

A bit of her optimism began to fade. "Naturally."

He leaned forward and pressed a kiss upon her cheek. "I look forward to our mutually satisfactory union."

Squeezing her shoulder once, he smiled at her before bowing and walking from the room. The moment he was gone, she sank down into a chair, trying to absorb the odd turn of events.

A mewing sound from the open doorway caught her attention. "Poco," Cassandra murmured, patting her lap. Accepting the invitation, the cat jumped up and began to rub his body against her.

Hugging her pet closer, Cassandra smiled as she remembered her mother's protests over having a cat, especially one that looked like Poco, in the house.

Tightening her hand around the agreement, Cassandra allowed her concerns to drift away. "We shall be very happy in our new home," she assured the cat. "After all, I have proof that the duke is an understanding fellow. He agreed to every one of my stipulations without a murmur, didn't he?"

Poco began to purr louder.

"As long as you're dry and fed, you don't care where you live, do you?" Cassandra asked with a laugh. "Let's hope Lord Amberville is as easily satisfied."

The minister, Bryce, and the few other guests all awaited her response.

Panic gripped Cassandra, freezing the two words in her throat. She couldn't do it! She couldn't marry this man who was virtually a stranger. Frantically, she glanced around the room . . . and her gaze fell upon her father. He gave her an encouraging smile and a loving look that steadied her jangling nerves. There sat the reason she had to go through with this marriage.

Swallowing hard, Cassandra finally whispered, "I do."

Without a moment's hesitation, Bryce slipped a ring onto her finger. Looking down at the gold mounted emerald, feeling the weight of the ring, Cassandra suppressed another brief flare of panic. Her new husband deserved far better than some missish female who was wary of the mere notion of marriage.

Lifting her chin, Cassandra released her pent-up breath and smiled at Bryce.

"You may now kiss the bride," pronounced the minister, closing his Bible firmly.

Oh, Lord. Cassandra fought to keep her nervousness from reflecting on her face as Bryce bent toward her. This man was still a stranger to her. She didn't know him or what he . . .

The touch of his lips upon hers disintegrated all rational thought. Tenderly he pressed his mouth against hers, sipping lightly at her lips until she instinctively parted them. Their very breath mingled, sweeter than she'd ever imagined possible. After the dry, passionless kisses she'd endured during her marriage, this soft kiss caught her unaware and left her breathless.

Before she had a chance to sink into the sweetness, to taste Bryce in return, he straightened, breaking off the kiss, leaving her wanting more. Bemused, she settled back onto her heels, surprised that sometime during the brief kiss, she'd raised up onto her tiptoes to deepen the touch.

Her fingers trembled as she pressed them against her lips while the guests erupted into clapping and cheers of good wishes.

"Congratulations to you both," boomed her father, flashing his charming grin at Bryce. "You're a welcome addition to the family."

Lord, she prayed her father was right. "Thank you, Papa."

Bryce curved his arm around Cassandra's waist and pulled her close. "We appreciate your well-wishes, sir."

Her father's smile increased. "Make that Charles," he urged, reaching to clasp Bryce's shoulder in masculine camaraderie. "We're now family, after all."

When Bryce placed his arm around her, it brought back all the curious feelings she'd experienced when he'd kissed her.

"So have you planned a holiday to celebrate your nuptials?" inquired Cassandra's mother as she joined the trio. "It's only fitting, after all."

"While that is true, I fear we shall have to postpone any traveling. I believe it is imperative that the new Lady Amberville begin guiding my niece through the upcoming Season."

The warmth inside of Cassandra drained away at his response.

"A most sensible idea," Lady Darwood replied with a nod.

And it was, Cassandra knew, but Bryce's kiss had affected her so deeply that she'd foolishly forgotten she was simply a deal successfully negotiated. Subtly she shifted from beneath his hold.

As Bryce's hand fell to his side, he didn't pause in his conversation with her parents, not even noticing that she'd broken off their contact. And why should he? Cassandra asked herself.

This marriage was a business arrangement and

she'd best remember that . . . regardless of how enticing she found his kisses.

Exhaustion weighed heavily upon Cassandra as she bid her maid good night. She'd survived the day, borne the attention, accepted the congratulations, ignored the frosty welcome from her new niece, and behaved in a friendly manner toward Bryce. But now, she could finally relax.

A sigh escaped her as she looked around her luxurious suite. Her husband certainly wasn't a miserly sort if her rooms were any indication, Cassandra thought as she slipped her wrap from her shoulders. Watercolors hung on the wall, elegant swags framed the two doors, and a huge canopied bed filled most of the room. Tossing the bit of silk upon the back of a nearby chair, she strolled over to the fire, holding her hands out to the warmth.

Lost in her thoughts, it took a moment for Cassandra to recognize the soft mewing sound. Immediately, she turned from the fireplace and began to look for her cat. "Poco," she called, receiving a meow in response. Dropping to her knees, Cassandra lifted the dust ruffle and peered under the bed.

A pair of eyes gleamed back at her from the darkness. "There you are," Cassandra murmured as she stretched a hand out toward her pet.

The sound of the door behind her clicking open startled her and she jerked her head upward, banging it against the bedframe. "Ouch!"

"I must say, my dear Cassandra, you do have a most unusual way of greeting your husband."

5

A lady accepts her situation without demur.

Quoted from *A Lady's Guide to Proper Etiquette*,
written by Lady Cassandra Abbott

Knowing perfectly well the picture she presented to Bryce with her backside pointing at him, Cassandra crawled backward in an awkward motion until she'd cleared the bed. Settling back on her knees, she rubbed the sore spot on her head as she looked up at her husband. The sight of him in his dressing robe alarmed her.

He held out a hand. "Allow me to aid you—"

"No, that's quite all right," she muttered as she grasped the edge of her bed and levered herself up into a standing position. "I'm perfectly capable of standing on my own."

His brows lifted and, after a moment, Bryce allowed his hand to drop back to his side. "I'm well aware that you are capable of the feat. I merely thought to offer you my assistance. It's one of those pesky rules I was taught on being a gentleman."

Her cheeks warmed. "It was not my intention to

seem less than appreciative of your efforts, my lord."

A deep sigh escaped Bryce. "Am I back to being 'my lord' so soon?" Quirking a side of his mouth upward, he spread his arms wide. "I'd rather hoped that since I am now entitled to stand before you in a state of undress you might see fit to address me by my given name."

"Yes . . . of course . . . It's just that you—" Breaking off her stuttering, Cassandra took a breath to rebalance the emotions tumbling inside of her. "Might I ask why you've called upon me at this late hour?"

Both sides of his mouth curled upward now in an all too enticing smile. "I should think it rather obvious," he murmured, stepping closer.

Feeling much like a rabbit under a falcon's fierce gaze, Cassandra took a step back, until she came to rest against the edge of the bed. "Under normal circumstances, it would be, but since—"

"Shhhh," he murmured, lifting his hands to cup her face. As he moved closer still, Cassandra felt the warmth from his body melting into hers, quelling any urge to protest the intimacies. "Your reticence is perfectly understandable, Cassandra, but I promise to be gentle with you."

The low pitch of his voice mesmerized her and she remained still as Bryce lowered his head toward her. Softly, he brushed his lips against hers, the feathering touch enticingly brief. A satisfied sigh escaped her when Bryce once again touched his lips to hers. This time, however, he deepened the kiss, pressing his lips upon hers, nibbling along the edge of her mouth, licking at the seam between her lips.

Placing her hands on Bryce's arms, Cassandra steadied herself against him as his kiss made her head spin with never before experienced desires. Unconsciously, she leaned into him, silently asking for more.

And Bryce willingly answered her.

Sliding his hands through her hair, along the curve of her neck, and around her back, he arched her into him as he deepened the kiss even further, plunging his tongue between her parted lips. Stunned, Cassandra could only hold on to Bryce as desire lashed through her at the carnal exchange. Her entire body began to tingle as Bryce stroked his hands along her spine.

Slowly, he lessened the intensity of the kiss, until finally he lifted his head. The burning light in his gaze made her heart race as she saw erotic promises within the flames. "Oh, my," she rasped, lifting a hand to press trembling fingers against her lips. "I hadn't realized a kiss could be so . . . wonderful."

"I believe we shall both gain unexpected pleasures from this marriage," Bryce murmured as he began to lower his head once more.

"Indeed," she agreed, feeling far more optimistic about her future than she had this morning. "Your decision to give me a good-night kiss was absolutely inspired."

His head jerked up abruptly. "*Good-night* kiss?" Bryce frowned slightly. "I'm far from ready to say good night."

Her heart lightened even further. "Then you'd like to talk? You're undoubtedly right again," she declared happily. "We *would* get to know each other more quickly if we exchanged midnight confidences."

Releasing her, Bryce stepped back, shaking his head. "I didn't mean that I'd like to chat by the fireplace with you, Cassandra. This *is* our wedding night, after all."

"True," she acknowledged, growing wary as Bryce's expression remained dark, "but since our agreement clearly states that we will not indulge in . . . intimacies for a minimum of six months, I'm afraid I don't understand your meaning."

"*Six months?*"

Cassandra flinched at Bryce's shout. "Please, my lord," she said. "There is no need to get upset."

"*No need to get upset?*" he repeated, not lowering his voice one bit. "You claim that I waived my husbandly rights for six months and expect me not to protest?"

"I'm not *claiming* anything other than the truth," Cassandra replied as she gave him a level stare. "You *did* read the agreement, didn't you?"

Thrusting his hand through his hair, Bryce began to pace the room. "All you asked for was fripperies and freedom to garb yourself as you saw fit." Stopping, he shook his finger at her. "There was no mention of this outrageous request."

She nodded slowly. "Number twenty-six."

"*Twenty-six?*" This bellow fairly shook the room. "Asking me to forgo seeking pleasure in my marriage bed for six months should have been your *first* request." Suddenly, he pierced her with his gaze. "But you *knew* I'd refuse you, didn't you? You purposely hid that little surprise within all of your foolish requests and hoped that I wouldn't read through all of those ridiculous provisions."

"I did nothing of the sort," she retorted, feeling a twinge of guilt as that was precisely what she had done.

Bryce scowled fiercely. "Not one day of marriage has passed and I discover you've betrayed me."

"Betrayed you?" She tossed back her head. "Hardly. If anything, *you* betrayed *me.*"

Crossing his arms over his chest, Bryce lifted an eyebrow. "Pray tell me precisely how you've reached that conclusion."

"You presented me with an offer for a marriage of convenience and I presented you with a list of my conditions in return. You accepted those provisions, so I accepted your offer." Pulling her wrap tighter around her, Cassandra met his cold gaze. "Now you have the gall to accuse me of betraying you when it's your own fault if you failed to read my requests thoroughly."

"You deliberately set out to deceive me," he ground out through clenched teeth.

"And what if I did?" she tossed back at him. "The only way you could have been fooled was if you were silly enough to sign a contract without reading it first."

His head snapped back as if she'd hit him. "Very well, madam. I shall leave you to your cold marriage bed and congratulate you on arranging for such an inauspicious start to our marriage."

"Thank you, my lord."

Her tart response earned a glare from Bryce before he walked from the room. The door snapped shut behind him with a finality that sounded like a lid shutting on a coffin.

Such a good tiding for their marriage.

The urge to call him back was strong. Why hadn't she tried to make him understand? If she'd told him about her first marriage, he might have understood.

Sinking onto the edge of her bed, Cassandra buried her face in her hands. But in order to make him understand, she'd have been forced to expose her darkest secrets. How could she have looked at her new husband and told him of her lack of experience in the marriage bed? Would he understand her embarrassment over the awkward groping she'd endured at Alfred's hands?

Dropping her hands into her lap, Cassandra realized that her request still made sense. Once Bryce recovered from his shock at learning she'd misled him, he would see that her desire to become acquainted, to overcome her fear of the marriage bed before becoming intimate was a solid decision. Still, his reaction seemed less than encouraging.

Poco leapt into her lap and began to rub his head against her. "You understand, don't you?" she murmured.

His loud purring soothed her heart. She couldn't forget all that had gone right tonight. She'd never known a kiss could be so sweet, so enticing, so wonderful. Lifting her hand, she touched her lips, trying to recapture the feelings Bryce had invoked. In all of her years of marriage, she'd never felt even a shimmer of desire, yet with one kiss, Bryce made her understand all of the hushed whispers that filled the ladies' salon.

"I'll tell you one thing, Poco," Cassandra began, looking down at her cat, "if Bryce's kisses are any indication, I just might not find my new marriage bed as distasteful as the last one."

His plate of kippers looked decidedly unappetizing. Setting down his fork in disgust, Bryce knew he wouldn't be eating anything on this foggy morning. He was in a foul mood . . . and the reason for his ill-humor had just stepped into the dining room.

"Good morning, Bryce," Cassandra said brightly, offering him an equally brilliant smile.

Bryce couldn't believe his eyes. Lord, was the woman mad? She tossed him from their wedding chamber and expected him to greet her with a smile and sunny welcome? His wife obviously suffered from delusions if that was the case.

He allowed his cool stare to answer for him.

Her smile wavered, but remained firmly fixed in place. "I see you're not in a talkative mood this morning," she said as she took a seat opposite him.

"I can't imagine why," he replied dryly.

Blushing, Cassandra leaned forward to gaze at him. "I understand you are still upset, but I'd hoped you might have come to see the wisdom of my request. After all, I have set aside my disappointment over your failure to read the contract."

"Bravo for you, madam." Bryce tossed his napkin onto the table. "Forgive me if I find it difficult to overlook the fact that my wife deceived me before we were even wed."

"As I pointed out last night, if you had only—" Cassandra broke off her protest. Taking a deep breath, she began again. "There is no point in arguing, my lord. We are wed and must find a way to live together peacefully."

"And just how do you propose we do that? Do you expect me to tuck my tail between my legs like a whipped dog and—*Good God!*—What in bloody hell is that thing?" Bryce finished with a roar as he caught sight of the ugly creature strolling into the dining room.

Cassandra stiffened at his outburst. Lifting her chin, she patted her knee and invited the cat onto her lap.

With crossed eyes, mottled color, one torn ear, and a pointed face, the animal was by far the ugliest Bryce had ever seen.

"This is Poco," Cassandra pronounced, "and he's my pet."

Bryce shook his head. He wasn't about to have that mongrel creature in his house. "Not any longer! That cat is not welcome in my home," he stated firmly.

"Don't you mean *our* home?" Cassandra replied coolly.

It was too much for Bryce. Who did this woman think she was, coming into his home, tricking him into forgoing the pleasures of marriage, and then trying to manipulate him into bending to her will? Placing both of his hands on the table, he said in measured tones, "As my wife, you will acquiesce to my requests without argument . . . and I am informing you that I do not want a mangy barn cat roaming about my house."

Gathering the cat closer to her, Cassandra glared

at him. "I'm afraid you voiced your displeasure too late, my lord, for you already agreed to allow Poco inside."

"I did nothing of the—" Abruptly, Bryce broke off with a sharp curse. "It's that damn agreement again, isn't it?"

A triumphant smile tilted up the corners of Cassandra's mouth. "Number forty-nine, to be precise."

Staring at her through a haze of fury, Bryce controlled the urge to shake his wife. Not here one day and all she'd managed to do was infuriate him! How could such a paragon of virtue wreak such havoc upon his life? Levering himself off his chair, he leaned toward his wife. "This is not how a *proper* wife should behave," he ground out. "Not at all!"

"Perhaps not," she agreed in clear tones, "but it is how *your* wife behaves."

Feeling his tenuous control on his anger slipping away, Bryce stalked from the room. Apparently, he hadn't learned anything from his first disastrous marriage, for once again he'd resigned himself to Hell.

As the sound of her husband's boots stomping against the floor faded, Cassandra released her pent-up breath and petted Poco, who curled up on her lap. It was dreadful to start the day with such unpleasantness.

"Quite the loving couple, I see."

Bracing herself, Cassandra looked at the young girl who strolled into the room. "Good morning," she said, ignoring the child's rudeness.

The girl propped her hands on her hips. "I hardly think this qualifies as a *good* morning," she scoffed.

Waving a hand toward the chairs, she bid the girl to sit. "If you're determined to be rude at least take a seat, for it's quite a strain on my neck to look up at you."

Flouncing over to the nearest chair, Elaina sat down and glared at Cassandra. "Just because I took a seat doesn't mean you have the right to order me around."

Cassandra shook her head. "Good Lord, don't you find it wearying to be so unpleasant? I vow between you and your uncle I haven't heard one cheery word all morning."

"What would you have me say? Welcome to my home? I look forward to having you order me about and try to act like my mother?" retorted Elaina with a sniff of derision.

"I have no desire to be your mother," Cassandra replied softly as understanding sank in. Elaina had just lost both of her parents, moved in with her irritable uncle, and been thrust into her first Season. Any *one* of those events would be enough to make a girl defensive, much less all three at once. "I would, however, very much like to be your friend."

Wariness and hope mingled in Elaina's gaze as she struggled to maintain her hostile expression. The look melted Cassandra. Casually, she poured herself a cup of tea. "I had planned on doing a little shopping this afternoon." She smiled at her niece. "Would you care to join me? It would be a lovely way to become acquainted."

As Elaina's gaze grew brighter, she forgot to look furious. "It might ease the boredom," she said finally with a shrug of her shoulder.

Cassandra blinked twice, before bursting out in laughter. "Yes, do be careful what you say or I might think you are looking forward to shopping with me."

Elaina's lips twitched.

Pressing a hand to her cheek, Cassandra exclaimed, "Oh, dear, you almost smiled. Goodness, whatever would I think then?"

Elaina's entire face transformed with her smile. Pleased with her success, Cassandra pushed back her chair and tucked Poco into one arm.

"Good God! What the devil is that thing?"

6

Under no circumstances should a lady express herself in a vulgar fashion.

Quoted from *A Lady's Guide to Proper Etiquette*,
written by Lady Cassandra Abbott

$\mathcal{A}$ hard knot tightened in the pit of his stomach as Bryce laid the marriage agreement on his desk. He'd been duped. Royally. To think he'd actually felt pity for Cassandra when he'd read the first few provisions made him even angrier now. Lord, but the woman was clever.

And she needed to be taught a lesson.

As he sat in his study, he heard a horrible yowling outside the door. It took him a moment to place the sound, but when he did, it darkened his mood even more.

The horrid caterwauling came from Cassandra's damn mongrel! Yet another one of her blasted provisions. He knew very well that if he wished to ignore the agreement he'd signed, Cassandra would have no legal recourse. If she tried to approach the House of Lords with a complaint that he took her to bed despite his promise not to, she would be made a laughingstock.

But it was his own damnable sense of honor that made him adhere to the provisions. Cassandra had already stolen his peace of mind; he'd be buggered before he allowed her to take his honor as well. No, he'd made this mess of his life and it was up to him to find a way out. Lord, he'd been played the fool . . . again.

Suddenly, he'd had enough. Slamming his hands down on his desk, Bryce vowed to take whatever measures necessary to make Cassandra settle into a proper wife. After all, if he'd pulled Francesca into hand, he would have undoubtedly saved both of them from heartache and tragedy. What utterly baffled him was the how-why-and-when the prim and proper Cassandra Abbott transformed into a cunning deceiver.

What was the old adage? Marry in haste, repent in leisure. Well, he might have done the first, but he had no intention of doing the latter. No, he would take control of his headstrong bride, twist her own game to his advantage, and let her know that he wouldn't be ordered about like her servant.

Hell, every time he kissed her, she'd responded with a sweetness that made him hunger for more. Yet he also felt the hesitancy in her embrace, almost as if she feared the intimacies of marriage. And, if that were the case, Bryce thought swiftly, then her demand to keep him from their wedding bed made sense as well.

Settling back in his chair, Bryce contemplated this new twist in the situation. Not only would he have to teach his wife who controlled this household, he would need to break through her inhibitions, to show her the heady sweetness of passion fulfilled, to help her blossom.

Indeed, he was beginning to eagerly anticipate the lessons.

Bryce turned the tiny piece of crafted leather over in his hands. Looking up at the falconer, he asked, "Are you certain this won't hurt the animal?"

Greeves shook his head. " 'Course not. Why, falcons been wearing masks like that for years and no harms come to 'em."

"That's certainly true," Bryce agreed, before signing his mark. "I appreciate your fine work."

"If ye've need of any more, I'd be happy ta help ye," Greeves said with a smile.

Thanking the falconer, Bryce stepped from the shop. If everything went as Bryce planned, he'd be enjoying the pleasures of his sedate wife and well-mannered niece in the comfort of his efficiently run home. The dream was an appealing one, Bryce thought with a sigh, knowing full well he was going home to a house frozen in chilled warfare.

For the past week, he'd pointedly ignored his wife as he'd arranged for her lesson. Now he was finally ready to put his plan into action.

With a whistle on his lips and a spring in his step, Bryce headed for home . . . eager to convince Cassandra of the error of her ways.

Wandering through the milliner's shop, Cassandra realized that while she wasn't precisely happy, she certainly wasn't unhappy with the current state of her marriage. "What do you think of this one?"

Elaina moved to stand beside Cassandra. "I don't care for the bow and the red is too garish."

With a laugh at Elaina's ever blunt manner, Cassandra picked up the hat and set it upon her head. "That is precisely what I like about it," she remarked with a smile.

Elaina's eyes widened as she leaned closer. "You know as well as I that Uncle Bryce would not approve," she advised softly.

The girl's concern touched Cassandra. "Oh, I'm quite certain of that," she said blithely, "but since he's avoided me ever since our wedding day, I rather doubt he'd even notice."

Frowning slightly, Elaina shook her head. "Doesn't his lack of attention upset you?"

"Good heavens, no," Cassandra responded with another laugh. "Why on earth would it bother me?"

"Because you are only newly wed and my uncle seems intent on ignoring you."

"Which suits me perfectly fine." Setting down the hat, Cassandra gave Elaina her full attention. "I am not a young girl to be wooed and courted, but rather a mature widow who well understands marriage." She worded her explanation carefully for she had no desire to set Elaina off marriage. "While your uncle's distance might seem somewhat callous to an innocent such as yourself, I assure you it is actually quite considerate. As newlyweds, we are naturally a bit wary of each other, so your uncle is very wise to allow us time to become better acquainted."

Elaina's brow smoothed. "So he's courting you *after* the wedding instead of before."

Feeling a twinge of guilt for deliberately misleading the girl, Cassandra glanced away, pretending to be distracted by a nearby hat. "Precisely," she replied after a moment. Though she hated to lie, Cassandra thought as she sneaked a peek at her niece, it was a necessary lie. Lord knew, the child was too young to realize that marriage was a burden women must bear rather than a romantic notion.

Still, the burden of this marriage wasn't nearly as great as her last one. Bryce was proving to be an acceptable husband, honoring his bond when he could just as easily break it.

And while she would have enjoyed experiencing another one of his kisses, she certainly had no desire for any further intimacies. Instead, she should merely content herself with her comfortable life. She now had financial security, the delightful, if somewhat shocking, company of her niece, and, for the most part, a worry-free existence.

Then why couldn't she stop thinking about Bryce? More troubled by that thought than she'd like to admit, Cassandra concentrated on the hats before her.

As soon as she arrived home, Cassandra headed up to her bedchamber to freshen her attire. Looking into the mirror, she began to smooth back the loose tendrils of hair. A movement to her right caught her eye and she glanced at Poco with a smile.

The smile froze upon her face as Cassandra turned to look at her precious cat. For a moment, she remained speechless, struggling just to catch her breath, but when she regained her voice, she used it. Loudly.

"Poco!"

Rushing forward, she scooped her cat off the bed and stared at Poco in shock. Or rather, she looked at the parts she could still see. A horrid leather mask covered the cat's entire face except for his eyes, ears, nose and mouth. Frantically, Cassandra tugged at the offending mask, but it remained snug upon her pet. Looking at the tiny lock holding the mask in place, Cassandra knew she wouldn't be able to remove the abhorrent thing without the key.

"Are you looking for this, perchance?"

Spinning around, Cassandra saw Bryce leaning against the doorjamb, wiggling a small key at her. "What sort of cruel jest is this?" she ground out.

"No jest, my lady wife." As Cassandra reached for the key, Bryce tucked it into his pocket. "Ah, ah, ah," he said with a grin. "Not so fast, darling."

"I want you to take this horrible mask off poor Poco this minute," she demanded as she took a step closer.

"You don't like your cat's attire?" He tilted his head to the side as he stared at Poco. "I think it's an improvement."

"You have no right to do this. This violates my provision."

"I beg to differ," Bryce began conversationally. "You see, I've had a chance to thoroughly review our little arrangement, and placing a mask upon this ugly creature of yours is perfectly acceptable according to your requests."

"That can't possibly be true."

"Ah, but it is." A triumphant smile tilted Bryce's mouth upward. "You see all you specified was that I allowed your cat to reside within my home. Nowhere does it state that I have to look at him." He crossed his arms. "The way I see it, this mask satisfies both of us."

"This is ludicrous." Taking another step forward, Cassandra pressed a finger against Bryce's chest. "I want this mask off, *now!*"

"I'd be more than happy to grant your request."

Bryce's capitulation was far too easy. "Naturally you wish for something in return," she said with a sigh.

"Ever the clever lady," he murmured with a smile that didn't reach his eyes. "As a matter of fact, I have made up my own list of provisions." Tugging a paper out of his coat pocket, he unfolded it before handing it over to Cassandra. "It's quite simple, really. You agree to one provision on my list and I grant your request."

Stunned, Cassandra accepted the proffered list, half expecting it to singe her hand. Dread filled her as she read the first request. "Bathe you?" she asked, unable to believe her eyes.

"Head to toe."

"Serve your meals to you for a fortnight."

"Breakfast in bed," he added, leaning forward to point at the specific item on the list.

Quickly Cassandra scanned over the rest of the ridiculous requests. "Grant you unlimited access to my bed!" she gasped.

"In order to secure an heir."

Crumpling the parchment in her hand, she thrust it back at him. "I will *not* agree to any of these demeaning requests."

"Very well, then." Bryce straightened from his post against the doorjamb and took a step back into his own room.

"Wait! What about Poco's mask?" Cassandra couldn't believe he would allow her poor cat to suffer.

"What about it?" he returned with a shrug. "I believe I made myself very clear, and since you refused to grant one of my requests, I have no intention of granting yours."

Looking down at her beloved pet, she knew her hand had been forced. "Very well," she ground out. "Number two."

Lifting his eyebrows, he turned his ear toward her. "Pardon me?"

She fought the urge to snarl at him. "I said I agreed to provision number two."

The smile of male satisfaction that spread across his face made her palm itch to slap him. "You shall serve me all my meals . . . including breakfast in bed."

"Yes, my lord blackmailer," she snapped, unable to listen to more of his crowing.

"I don't believe insults are part of my request."

"There is no specification that I must be pleasant while I serve you, grand pasha," she returned.

Bryce grinned at her. "I see I shall have to word my provisions more carefully in the future." Withdrawing the key from his pocket, Bryce swiftly unlocked the mask and removed it from Poco's head. "Damn, that is the ugliest animal I've ever seen."

But when Cassandra looked at Poco, all she saw was someone that loved her unconditionally. Rubbing her cheek against the matted-down fur on Poco's head, she tried to ignore Bryce.

"Just remember I am keeping this mask, so if you attempt to renege on your part of our agreement, I will be more than happy to refasten the mask."

"Bastard," she muttered softly against Poco's neck.

"Perhaps," he agreed with a wicked grin, "but I'm the bastard you'll be serving breakfast to tomorrow."

How on earth did servants do this? Cassandra wondered as she struggled to carry the heavy breakfast tray upstairs. Growing more disgruntled with every step, she finally made it to Bryce's door . . . and had no idea how to open it while holding the food-laden tray. She couldn't knock as she needed both hands to hold the tray, and she doubted if she could bend down and set the tray on the floor without dropping it.

At a loss, she kicked at the door.

"Ouch!" Rubbing her bruised toes against the back of one leg, Cassandra began to wobble, sending the plates dancing upon the tray. This was Bryce's fault.

"Bryce!" she called through the door. "I need your help opening the door."

"I believe the arrangement was for you to serve me breakfast in bed," he called back, his voice muffled.

"Blasted man," she muttered. "If I drop his breakfast, he'll have no one to blame but himself."

Propping the tray against one hip, she opened the door with her free hand. As she shifted the tray back around, she sent a sausage rolling off the plate and the milk sloshing out of the glass onto his eggs. She couldn't hold in her smile of satisfaction.

"Breakfast is served, Your Majesty," she said in droll tones.

Bryce chuckled within his bed curtains.

Setting the tray down upon the table, Cassandra headed for the windows and pushed aside the curtains to allow the sun to stream into the room. Then she made her way over to the large bed dominating the masculine room.

"Were you planning on lazing the day away?" she asked as she pushed aside the bed curtains. "Or were you simply waiting for me to serve . . ."

Her words trailed off as she caught sight of her husband's naked chest. Propped against his pillows, he was quite a sight to behold. A soft matting of hair covered the sleek curves of his chest, trailing downward to disappear beneath the covers. Having only ever seen her ancient husband's form before, Cassandra was quite literally speechless. She'd never realized just how beautiful a man could be.

"Does that ugly cat of yours have your tongue?"

Bryce's laughing remark snapped her out of her daze. Clearing her throat, she turned to retrieve the tray. "I assure you it would take far more than the sight of you to lose my tongue."

"Ohhhh," Bryce murmured, clearly amused. "Then you stared at me simply because you liked the way I looked?"

"Hardly," she retorted.

Hefting the tray into her arms, she carried his breakfast over to his bed, her arms trembling beneath the weight. As she leaned forward to place the tray across Bryce's lap, her knees hit the side of the bed, shifting her off-balance, and sending the plates sliding off the tray onto the blankets covering Bryce's lap.

For a moment, all she could do was stare in stunned silence.

"I take it breakfast is served."

Bryce's dry remark sent her into a fit of horrified laughter. Pressing a hand to her mouth, she watched as he picked up the plates and placed them back on the tray.

"Somehow this wasn't what I had in mind when I made my request," he said as he scooped up his ruined eggs and dropped them onto the tray as well.

"Again, my lord, you didn't specify how you were to receive your breakfast."

"Foolish me." Bryce plucked at the damp blankets. "Now if you don't wish to see even more of me, I suggest you leave so that I can—"

Heat flooded her face. "I . . . I . . ." Breaking off her stuttering, she fled without a backward glance.

His laughter chased her from the room.

"*Cassandra!*"

At her mother's call, the image of Bryce's naked chest she'd been savoring in her mind shattered. "Excuse me, Mother, I was lost in my thoughts." Lovely, enticing ones at that. Cassandra shook her head. All day she'd been preoccupied with thoughts of Bryce. When she'd seen him this morning, she'd felt an overwhelming urge to touch the sculpted planes of his chest, to run her fingers through the soft hair matting his masculine curves, to—

"Cassandra!"

Sheepishly, Cassandra smiled at her mother. "Sorry, Mother. I promise I shan't get lost in my thoughts again." Perhaps.

"I hope not." Settling back in her chair, Lady Darwood took a sip of her tea. "We really must focus on which party you should attend first as the new Duchess of Amberville."

"I've only been wed a week," Cassandra protested. "Surely that is too soon to resume my social schedule."

Her mother waved her hand. "Not at all. It would appear vulgar to spend any additional time alone with your husband. Besides—"

"Good afternoon, Cassandra. I wondered where you—" Elaina came skittering to a halt as soon as she caught sight of Cassandra's mother.

Rising to her feet, Cassandra grasped her niece's hand and pulled her toward them. "You remember my mother, Lady Darwood, don't you, Elaina?"

Like royalty, Cassandra's mother bowed her head slightly. "A pleasure to see you again," she murmured politely.

Elaina hesitated for a moment, before she finally said, "Thank you."

Her mother's eyebrows flew upward. "I believe the proper response is 'No, the pleasure is all mine.' "

Elaina tilted her head to the side. "Why? I believe my answer was just as polite."

Seeing her mother's eyes flare, Cassandra interrupted their exchange before it got out of hand. "Why don't we allow this matter to rest?"

Cassandra's mother set her teacup down with a clink. "Because this young lady—"

". . . is my niece and this is her home, so that, in essence, makes you her guest," Cassandra finished, knowing full well her mother's rigid adherence to the rules of etiquette would forbid her from arguing with her hostess.

As expected, her mother snapped her mouth shut.

Satisfied, Cassandra looked toward her niece. "Elaina, would you care for some tea?"

Wrinkling her nose, Elaina shook her head. "Do you have any chocolate?"

Cassandra smiled as she heard her mother choking back a reprimand. Instead of making a face, Elaina should have apologized for refusing the tea. But then her niece was not one to concern herself with the rules. "I'm afraid not," Cassandra replied finally.

"Oh." Elaina looked at the tray sitting on the table. "Then I'm going to ask Cook to fix me a cup."

Without so much as a by-your-leave, Elaina flounced out of the room.

"Dear heavens, Cassandra," exclaimed Lady Darwood the moment the door closed. "You must help that child."

Cassandra smiled at her mother. "If the truth be told, I find her honesty quite refreshing."

"Perhaps you do, but I assure you no one else in the ton will find her manners anything less than appalling." Concern darkened her mother's eyes.

"If you don't help that child, she will soon be shredded by sharp tongues."

Cassandra's teacup shook as she set it down. Dear Lord, her mother was right, she realized. Society was a harsh taskmaster, giving little room for those who were unique. While they might accept Elaina because of her family's status, they would never consider her one of them if she continually spoke her mind. No, the ton would present a very polite face to Elaina, then snicker behind her back.

"I shall speak with her," Cassandra said reluctantly, knowing that it was in Elaina's best interest.

A pleased smile softened her mother's features. "Now that we've agreed on what is best for your niece, we need to discuss the other matter."

"What other matter?"

A sigh escaped her mother. "I don't know what's come over you, Cassandra."

The problem was, neither did she. She'd never before been so intrigued with a gentleman as she seemed to be with her husband. It worried her that she couldn't thrust Bryce from her thoughts. No, she kept on seeing his clever gaze as he tricked her into—

"*Cassandra!*"

"Sorry," she mumbled, aware it wasn't the first time she'd had to apologize for allowing her thoughts to wander.

"Really, Cassandra, if you'd rather have me call upon you another time . . ."

"No, Mother," Cassandra said hurriedly. "I promise to give you my full attention."

Smoothing her skirts, Lady Darwood nodded.

"As I was saying, we must discuss at which event you should make your first appearance."

Cassandra stared at her mother. She'd become so engrossed in her vexing marriage that she'd almost forgotten there was a world outside her own home. "What do you suggest?"

"Well, Lady Marbury is having a costume ball next week and everyone I've spoken with plans to attend."

"I do so love costume balls," Cassandra admitted.

"I know you do, and since it might be the affair of the Season, I believe it will be the best forum to introduce you into society as Lady Amberville."

"I shall reply to Lady Marbury's invitation and let her know that we will be pleased to attend," Cassandra said in a distracted tone. At the thought of attending a ball, she was consumed by one question.

Would Bryce waltz with her again?

7

A lady should never appear too clever or intelligent lest she offend a gentleman.

Quoted from *A Lady's Guide to Proper Etiquette*,
written by Lady Cassandra Abbott

"What are you writing?"

Cassandra's hand jerked, sending ink spilling across the note. Caught off guard by her husband's nearness, she paused to glare at him before blotting the now ruined parchment. "I *was* writing a letter of acceptance to Lady Marbury."

Placing one hand upon the desk and the other on the back of her chair, Bryce leaned over her shoulder to look at the missive. "Hmmm."

She stiffened as he pressed himself against her back. "I fail to see what you're finding so interesting," she replied, hating the breathless quality to her voice.

Bryce turned his head until his lips brushed against her ear. "Ah, but you're not looking at it from my perspective." Slowly, he nuzzled his cheek against her hair. "The closer I get to you, the more you react, Cassandra. You're beginning to breathe faster, your cheeks are growing flush, you—"

"Sir!" Desperate to put distance between them, Cassandra lunged sideways out of the chair, landing in an undignified heap at his feet.

"That was impressive," Bryce said with a laugh. His gaze dropped to her exposed legs before holding out his hand. "Here, allow me to—"

Ignoring his proffered hand, Cassandra scrambled to her feet unassisted, swatting down her skirt in the process. "A gentleman would have turned his back, not looked at my limbs."

"Perhaps, but when I thought of how you cheerfully tossed my breakfast upon my lap this morning, I wasn't moved to exert myself. After all, that little treat was hardly befitting a lady," he pointed out.

For a moment, Cassandra could do nothing more than stand there staring at him with her mouth flapping open and closed. "That . . . that was an accident!" she finally managed.

"Then you could consider my eyes falling upon your glorious legs as an accident as well."

She propped her hands on her hips. "Hah!"

"Ah, the intellectual response."

She bit back an angry retort. Turning on her heel, she marched from the room, only to realize that Bryce was following her. "Leave me be," she hissed at him, keeping her voice low so as not to be overheard by the servants.

"No."

"No?" Cassandra couldn't believe her ears. "What do you mean by that?"

"I mean 'no, I won't leave you be,' " he informed her with a wicked gleam in his eyes. "In fact, I plan on shadowing your every move from now on."

"Have you gone mad?" she gasped.

"Mad?" Bryce rubbed at his jaw. "That is something to consider. After all, I was well and truly furious over your deception, so perhaps you are correct in your assessment. I am quite determined to give you a taste of your own medicine." He shrugged with one shoulder. "Regardless, the fact remains that the only way to be rid of me is to agree to another item on my list," he said with a flourish as he pulled the paper from his jacket pocket.

"I will never agree to another one of those ridiculous requests," she pronounced, enraged at him for believing he could manipulate her again.

"Very well," he agreed amicably as he folded the list and placed it back into his pocket. "Then we shall be spending quite a bit of time together." His expression sharpened and his eyes began to glitter with a dangerous light as he leaned into her until his face was mere inches from hers. "For I shall never stop bedeviling you until you've been taught a lesson."

His condescending tone raised her hackles. "And I suppose you're the one to teach me," she said dryly, acting unaffected by his closeness.

"I promise."

Cassandra's nerves were screaming by the time she shut the door to her bedchamber. True to his word, Bryce had hung upon her heels, listening to every conversation she'd had with Elaina and adding his own little asides whether he'd been included in the discussion or not.

Still, she would never give way to his devious plotting. When she'd asked for the provisions, she'd only been seeking time to become accustomed to him before engaging in intimacies. But his recent actions baffled her. It was almost as if he'd discovered her attraction toward him . . . and he was trying to seduce her.

Stunned, she sank onto her bed. That was it. Bryce was trying to seduce her into his bed. Instead of honoring her request, he was trying to find a way around it. Did he truly believe her to be so weak-willed that she couldn't withstand his attentions?

Determination to best her husband at his games filled her as she rang for her maid. If Bryce thought he could force her to bend to his will, he was seriously mistaken.

For more years than she cared to remember, she'd been forced to bow to her husband's demands, too afraid to naysay him, too aware of the horrid consequences that would befall her if she refused him. But those days were gone. Never again would she blindly follow the dictates of another . . . especially not her husband. Of that, she had no doubt.

After donning a nightgown, Cassandra dismissed her maid and sat at her vanity to brush her hair. Closing her eyes, she allowed the bristles to stroke her scalp, soothing her into a calmer state.

"You aren't in bed yet."

The brush fell from her hand with a clatter. *"What are you doing here?"* she gasped, staring at Bryce.

"Can't you guess?" Bryce asked as he stepped into the room and closed the door behind him. Taking a seat upon the settee near the fireplace, he made himself at home.

"Since you know perfectly well I will not agree to bed you, I can't even begin to guess as to the reason for your presence in my room."

Stretching his legs along the length of the settee, Bryce settled his long frame into the too short space as comfortably as possible. "It's part of this whole driving-you-mad-until-you-agree-to-another-item-on-my-list campaign."

She straightened her spine. "I'm made of sterner stuff than you can imagine, my lord."

"Since I once foolishly believed that you were made of prim and proper stuff, I suppose you could surprise me again." All the playfulness drained from his gaze. "You are certainly not the woman I thought I was marrying."

"Likewise, my lord." She lifted her chin, hurt by his quiet words. "I thought you were a sensible gentleman."

"I'm perfectly sensible," he protested with a frown.

"If that is so, then why are you spending the night upon my settee?" She blew out the candle on her bedside table, knowing she'd gotten the best of that exchange.

The fire sent a warm glow throughout the room, illuminating it enough so Cassandra could see the disgruntled expression upon her husband's face. Without removing her wrapper, she slipped between the covers, giving an exaggerated sigh of pleasure. "So comfortable," she said, pitching her voice just loud enough for him to hear.

"Keep tormenting me and I'll join you there, agreement or not."

Cassandra shut her mouth.

Rubbing at her eyes, Cassandra awoke slowly, feeling groggy and disoriented. She'd had a devil of a time falling asleep last night and it was all Bryce's fault. Every time she managed to relax, she'd hear him move or sigh . . . or breathe. She'd been painfully aware of his presence in her chamber. How was she expected to sleep with him so close?

Lifting her head just a bit, she glared at her husband, who lay sprawled upon the settee . . . and ended up staring at him in bemusement. He reclined against her settee like a great lion—lean, powerful, and fascinating. *Wonderful*, she thought as she pulled her gaze off Bryce, *now he'll be haunting my thoughts again*.

Sitting up, she rose from the bed and walked toward her dressing room.

"Are you off to fetch my breakfast?"

His sleep-colored question halted her in her tracks. Turning around slowly, she met her husband's half-open gaze. She smiled at him, allowing all of her triumphant feelings to show and taking great pleasure when his expression grew wary. "Not this morning."

He lifted a brow. "Reneging on your end of the agreement?"

"Not at all," she remarked brightly. "I agreed to bring you breakfast in bed for a fortnight. And that, my lord, is *not* a bed." Pausing, she pointed at her settee. "You chose not to sleep in your own bed, and, as a result, you freed me from my obligation."

His glare promised retribution, but she was far too pleased with her victory to care. Cassandra hummed softly as she made her way into her dressing room, pleasantly aware of Bryce fuming behind her.

The clever minx.

As Bryce watched his wife disappear behind the door, he felt an odd mixture of annoyance and admiration. He would have to look over his list to ensure all the wording was exactly how it should be in order to avoid giving Cassandra room to wiggle out of the agreement. Not in the bed, indeed.

His body groaned in protest as he forced himself into a sitting position. Here he'd spent a dreadfully uncomfortable night cramped upon this miserable settee and he wasn't even going to get his breakfast served. Still, he wasn't going to complain out loud, for his plan had been an undeniable success.

Even with her smug expression, Cassandra had appeared exhausted. Hell, he'd heard her tossing and turning half the night. Small steps, he assured himself, each one bringing him closer to reining in his obstinate wife. Once he'd seduced her, helped her overcome her fear, he was confident it would be easy to mold her back into the woman she once was.

His neck cracked as he rose and headed for his own room. After all, he had to dress quickly if he was going to continue his plan to trail after his wife.

* * *

There was a spring in Cassandra's step as she made her way into the dining room. "Good morning, Elaina," she said brightly.

Craning her neck, Elaina peered around Cassandra. "Where is Uncle Bryce?"

"I'm not quite certain." Sitting down, Cassandra smiled her thanks at the servant who brought her tea.

Elaina's expression lit with curiosity. "Then he no longer plans to follow you?"

"Of course I do," Bryce announced as he strode into the room.

A frown darkened Elaina's features. "Naturally. I would expect nothing less from *you*," she said in a frosty tone.

"Elaina!" Cassandra exclaimed sharply. "You may not speak to your uncle in such an appalling manner."

Tossing back her head, Elaina scowled at Cassandra. "Why not?"

Heat flooded Cassandra's cheeks. "Because Lord Amberville is—"

Bryce laid a hand upon her shoulder, cutting off her reprimand. "It's all right," he said quietly, not taking his gaze off Elaina.

Shaking her head fiercely, Cassandra looked up at her husband. "No, it is not, my lord."

His fingers tightened upon her shoulder as he finally shifted his gaze onto her. "Yes, it is," he stated in a tone that brooked no argument. "For now."

Something inside of Cassandra softened as understanding flooded her. "Though you might understand and empathize with her reasons, that does not justify Elaina's blatant rudeness. She should not be allowed to speak to—"

"Will you both please stop discussing me as if I weren't here?" Elaina cut in. "And you tell me *I'm* the one lacking manners?"

"Elaina," Cassandra sighed in frustration. "Please stop being so disrespectful to your uncle."

Giving Cassandra a sulky look, Elaina settled back in her chair, crossed her arms, and sent her uncle a nasty glare. At least she was blessedly silent, Cassandra thought as she slid out of her chair. "Excuse us, my lord, but Elaina and I have an appointment to see the modiste."

Bryce flicked a glance at Elaina and nodded once. "Very well."

"Surely you don't mean to accompany us?" Cassandra gasped.

Elaina groaned loudly. "Cassandra, tell him he can't come."

"I have every intention of accompanying you," Bryce insisted, his frustration at Elaina slipping into his voice.

Leaning in closer to keep Elaina from overhearing her protest, Cassandra whispered fiercely, "Come now, my lord. Surely you don't intend to carry this private battle of ours into the public arena."

His gaze intensified. "I most certainly do . . . unless you'd like to choose another item on my revised list."

Distracted by his words, she frowned at him. "You can't revise your list."

"Since it's my game, darling, I can do anything I please . . . even accompany you and my charming niece to be fitted for gowns," Bryce finished on a less-than-pleased note.

Glancing at Elaina's annoyed expression, then at Bryce's set features, Cassandra groaned at the horrid day stretching out before her.

Just lovely.

"I like this bit of lace," Bryce offered, fingering a finely woven piece.

Elaina snorted rudely. "You say that as if someone here values your opinion."

Closing her eyes, Cassandra prayed for the afternoon to be over. Elaina's appalling remarks to Bryce had gotten worse as the day wore on. "Elaina, if you have nothing nice to say, don't say anything at all."

"If she does that, then she'd never speak to anyone," Bryce muttered under his breath.

"I heard that!" Elaina tossed down the fabric she'd been considering.

"Good." His eyes narrowed as he glared at Elaina. "I well understand how unhappy you are at the moment, Elaina, which is why I am willing to overlook your blatant rudeness. But you need to understand that I have my limits . . . and you are fast approaching the end of my patience."

Thrusting her chin out, Elaina met Bryce's anger with her own. "Is that supposed to frighten me?"

Bryce groaned in exasperation.

"Enough!" Cassandra pressed her hands onto her temples, rubbing the tips of her fingers against the throbbing points. "Lord, I can't take much more of this."

"You?" exclaimed Elaina. "You aren't the one who—"

Reaching out, Cassandra placed her fingers against her niece's lips. "Your behavior is making my head pound," Cassandra whispered fiercely. Removing her hand from Elaina's mouth, Cassandra turned her attention to Bryce. "And as for you, sir, you are the adult in this situation, so you should rise above this endless bickering."

"She would provoke God himself into—"

A strangled sound reverberated from Cassandra's throat. "I'll agree to a foolish item on your list if it will make you leave."

His eyes flared an instant before he clasped her hand and tugged her into the empty back room. The moment they were alone, he turned her around to face him. Withdrawing the list from his pocket, he held it out to her. "Which one?"

She gave him a dark look. "I wonder if you continued to argue with your niece just to aggravate me enough to agree to one of these silly provisions."

A side of his mouth quirked upward. "That is always a possibility."

"If that is the case, then you are even more shameless than I imagined."

His expression sobered. "Do you honestly believe I would do something like that to my niece?"

Looking into his eyes, Cassandra saw the truth. For some reason, Elaina seemed to have an unreasonable anger toward Bryce. Their arguments had all been started by Elaina and, if anything, Bryce had shown unbelievable restraint in his attitude toward the girl. "No," she finally admitted, "but I do believe you're not above taking advantage of the situation."

"I never claimed to be a saint."

Glaring at him, she snapped the paper from his hand. The choices on his list left much to be desired . . . especially in their newly revised form. "I suppose the best one left is bathing you," she grumbled.

"Ah, ah, that tone won't be tolerated," Bryce corrected her with a devilish smile.

"Yes, I see that." She shook her head. "It says here that I must 'have a pleasant demeanor, converse politely, use hot water, refrain from dunking your head underwater, scrub in a light, but firm touch, and in all other ways, bathe you as I would myself.' " She lifted her eyebrow. "You seem to have given this revised list considerable thought."

"After the way you wriggled out of serving breakfast to me this morning, I thought it wisest to be perfectly clear in my requests."

Cassandra really couldn't blame the man. After all, she just might have been tempted to dunk him in the bath water.

"I shall arrange to have the tub brought to my chambers this evening."

Her gaze flew to his face. "This evening?"

"Naturally. Why should we delay such a pleasurable event?" Retrieving his blasted list, he tucked it back into his pocket. "I hope you realize that my provisions are now down to eight."

Not only did she realize that fact, but she also knew the remaining items were very intimate in nature. "I don't concern myself over that minor fact, my lord, since I shall not be forced to agree to another one."

The challenge created a gleam in Bryce's eyes. Lifting one hand, he trailed the tips of his fingers along her jawline. "I do believe that is what you said last time," he remarked with a laugh, before turning on his heel and striding from the room.

Cassandra tossed a spool of thread at his retreating back. "Infuriating man," she mumbled. As soon as Bryce was gone, she sank down into a nearby chair. Lord, how was she supposed to bathe him, to run her hands over his body, to see his flesh glistening with water, and still keep hold of her sensibilities. The mere sight of his chest and legs captured her thoughts. How would she ever be able to think of anything other than him after she'd run her hands over his body?

Still, she had to act unaffected. It wouldn't do to let him believe he had the upper hand. She could, of course, simply refuse to bathe him, but her own sense of honor made her discard that course of action. If Bryce were honorable enough to respect her provisions, then she could do no less in return.

Their marriage had become a battle of wits . . . and she did not intend to lose the war.

8

A lady submits without complaint to intimate relations
with her husband.

Quoted from *A Lady's Guide to Proper Etiquette*,
written by Lady Cassandra Abbott

*I*t was time.

Cassandra began to pace across her bedchamber. She'd had all afternoon to think of this moment, to grow more nervous as the minutes slowly ticked by. As soon as she'd emerged from the back room at the modiste's shop, Elaina had announced that she wanted to return home. Frazzled, Cassandra had readily agreed, nor had she protested when Elaina announced she needed time alone when they'd arrived back at the townhouse.

Her fingers ached, causing Cassandra to look down at her hands. Why, she was wringing her hands. Immediately, she dropped her hands to her sides, stunned that she'd been doing it at all. She wasn't the wring-her-hands type. Bryce had her completely turned around.

Taking a deep breath, Cassandra made herself focus on the upcoming bathing ordeal. And it was far too easy to imagine him sitting back like a spoiled prince, awaiting his bath. Still, according to the provision, she was limited in ways she could extract her revenge. After all, she'd promised to bathe him as she would herself.

As she would herself.

A slow grin formed upon her face as she devised the perfect plan.

Bryce hurried the servants out of his chamber as soon as the tub was brimming with steaming water. He barely resisted the urge to rub his hands together in anticipation as he swiftly stripped off his clothes. Reaching for his robe, Bryce hesitated, his hand hovering over the garment. Slowly, he drew back and reached for a towel instead.

Wrapping it around his waist, Bryce settled against the window seat and waited for his wife. He knew full well that despite her annoyance at having her hand forced, she would indeed arrive to bathe him. After Francesca's faithlessness, it pleased him to realize that Cassandra would keep her word.

He also took reassurance from that fact, believing that once he helped Cassandra overcome her fear of the marriage bed, they could settle into a proper marriage. For the moment, he didn't mind this little game they were playing, for he was certainly going to reap the benefits. He felt overheated just thinking of Cassandra's hands running over his body, her fingers tangled in his hair.

A soft knock on the door adjoining their rooms brought Bryce from his reverie. "Come in."

Still clothed in her high-necked gown, Cassandra stepped into his bedroom. "Good evening, Bryce. I've come to . . ."

He watched with interest as her eyes widened, her gaze slid over his entire body like a caress, and a blush stained her cheeks. Finally, she lifted her gaze to his and he smiled over the expression in their blue depths.

"Something the matter?" he asked with a chuckle, knowing full well what was disturbing his pretty wife.

"No," she returned. "I was merely taken aback by your lack of modesty."

The squeak in her voice belied her words. "Liar," he murmured softly.

Her flush intensified. "Still behaving like a gentleman, I see," she returned, her voice a bit steadier. Snapping her gaze away from him, Cassandra began to roll up her sleeves. "Shall we get this over with?"

"Ah, ah, ah," he said, wiggling his finger at her. "Remember the specifics of my provision."

She looked like she wanted to strangle him. "My apologies," she replied through clenched teeth. "I shall endeavor to be polite."

Rising from the window seat, Bryce walked toward her, smiling as he saw wariness flare in her eyes. He came to a halt mere inches from her. Her alluring scent called to his senses and he inhaled deeply. "That's more like it," he whispered finally.

Stepping toward the tub, he allowed the towel to drop from his body . . . and smiled as he heard

Cassandra's gasp as she spun away from him. After lowering himself into the steaming water, he glanced at his wife's rigid back. "I'm ready," he called cheerfully.

Stiffly, she dropped to her knees beside the tub. "Close your eyes," she instructed moments before she dumped water over his head.

Leaning forward, Bryce nearly groaned as Cassandra sunk her fingers into his hair, scrubbing lightly against his scalp. How he would love to have those nails scrape down his neck, along his shoulders, and . . .

His thoughts were interrupted by an alarming scent. "What the devil!" he exclaimed, his eyes flying open in shock. "This soap smells like *roses*," he roared.

Her eyes widened innocently, but she couldn't hide the gleam of satisfaction in their depths. "Precisely, my lord," she murmured.

"This is not part of our agreement," Bryce replied as he wiped the soap from his eyes.

"I beg to differ." Cassandra settled back on her heels. "You specifically said that I should bathe you as I would myself. Well, this is the soap I use."

Bryce rolled his eyes. The blasted woman was far too clever for her own good. Another stream of suds slid down his forehead and into his eyes. "Bloody hell," he grumbled, washing off the offending soap with a splash of water. "That stings."

"Hmmmm," Cassandra murmured as she resumed her scrubbing of his scalp. "Soap in the eyes often does."

"I'm glad you find this all so amusing." Bryce knew his reply didn't have much heat; her fingers were working magic on him. For a few minutes, he luxuriated in the feel of her fingers in his hair, ignoring the stinging in his eyes.

He almost moaned when she took away her hands. "I'm going to rinse," she warned him.

An instant later, warm water splashed over his head, sending suds cascading down over his shoulders and back into the water. The scent of roses filled the air, reminding him that he was meeting friends at White's this evening. Now he would show up smelling like a lady's garden.

Still, if having her scrub him with her rose soap was the price he had to pay, he considered it a fair bargain.

Leaning back against the tub, Bryce watched Cassandra through half-closed eyes as she ran the sudsy washcloth along his shoulders, then down his right arm. Lifting his hand, she dipped the cloth in between his fingers, each stroke making his blood race a bit faster.

"You're flushed," he whispered as she moved the washcloth along his chest, pausing ever so slightly upon his masculine nipples.

"The water is warm," she replied by way of explanation, studiously keeping her gaze upon her hand.

The devil tapped him on the shoulder and Bryce didn't bother to fight it. With a flick of his hand, he sent water spraying onto the bodice of her gown, the wetness soaking through the material, molding it against her skin.

"Bryce!" She plucked at the material, but the gown clung stubbornly to her.

"*Finally* you say my name," he remarked with a grin. "If that's all it takes, I'll be certain to keep water at hand whenever I'm around you."

Her eyes twinkled with ill-concealed humor. "You are a troublesome man."

"True, but at least I'm clean now." Holding out his arm, he invited her to see for herself.

The washcloth splashed into the water. "I believe I've finished—"

"But you forgot my legs," he said, lifting his right leg onto the edge of the tub.

This time it was her turn to roll her eyes. Without another word, she retrieved her cloth and hurriedly scrubbed down his leg and along his foot. Obligingly, he offered her his left one, and she repeated her ministrations.

As soon as she finished that leg, she tossed the cloth back into the water with a splash. "Finished," she pronounced, relief coloring her voice. Rising to her feet, she headed toward the door. He waited until her hand rested on the knob before calling out to her.

"Aren't you going to wash my back?"

Without a hitch in her gait, she headed back toward him, picked up the cloth, pushed him forward and swiped down his back three times. "Don't even *think* about asking for any other areas," she warned as she reached over his shoulder and threw the cloth down into the water again.

Before she had a chance to pull back, he clasped her hand and tugged it down to his mouth. Capturing her gaze with his, he pressed a soft kiss onto the back of her fingertips, then turned her hand over and gave her a moistened kiss upon her palm. He saw the pulse beating in her slender wrist and couldn't resist kissing her there as well.

Her lips parted as she watched him caress her. Drawing her index finger into his mouth, he swirled his tongue around her flesh. Slowly, he pulled her finger free so he could turn his attention onto her palm once again.

Pressing one last lingering kiss into the damp flesh, he moved onto the pad at the base of her thumb and gently bit the tender mound, before lifting his head to smile up at her. "I thank you for your tender touch," he whispered in a low, desire-colored voice.

"I . . . I . . ." she stuttered before abruptly breaking off her reply. With a sharp tug, she freed her hand and headed toward the door as if the devil himself were after her.

Bryce chuckled at her speedy exit. "Leaving so soon? What about drying me off?"

"There was no mention of drying in your provision," she retorted over her shoulder an instant before she shut the door behind her.

Bryce knew he was grinning like a fool, but he couldn't care less. He'd bothered his lovely wife, all right. One glance at her taut nipples beneath the wet gown had told him all he needed to know.

Yes, his plan was progressing nicely. Before long, she would be right where he wanted her—in his bed and behaving like a proper wife.

* * *

Peeling the sodden dress off her body was difficult, but Cassandra was determined to do it on her own, even if she ripped the darn thing. She had no desire to let a maid see her in such a state of agitation. All because of . . . all because of . . .

. . . her breath-stealing, mouth-watering, heart-stopping husband.

Finally free of the miserable dress, Cassandra sank down onto the edge of her bed. Touching Bryce had made her pulse pound and she'd wanted to explore more of his body . . . especially the part she'd only dared glimpse at through the water. When he'd kissed her hand, she'd almost melted at his feet. Lord, how she'd wanted to feel that mouth upon hers again.

So, why was she fighting herself, her desires? Why not waltz into his bedchamber and announce she was ready to explore the intimacies of marriage?

Because then he would win in this horrid little game they'd begun.

Then he would believe all he needed to do was back her into a corner, badger her, break her down, and she'd become putty in his hands. No, thank you. She'd been less than a mere shadow in her first marriage; she wouldn't accept that in her second. If she gave in to her desires, Bryce would never respect her as his partner, as his equal.

And that wasn't what she wanted at all.

She knew she needed to stay her course, to outwit him at every turn until she earned his respect. Then and only then could she lower her guard and allow herself to indulge in the passion he aroused in her.

Her only problem lay in resisting her impossibly appealing husband.

Bryce found himself whistling as he made his way into White's. Handing his cloak to the doorman, he headed toward the chair where Jonathan sat reading the evening's news.

"Good evening, Dunham," Bryce remarked cheerfully as he took the seat opposite his friend.

"You're in a chipper mood this—" Jonathan broke off his greeting and began to sniff at the air. "I say, do you smell roses?"

Bryce shook his head firmly. "No."

"I swear I smell—"

"*I do not smell roses,*" Bryce ground out. "Can we please discuss something else, something of interest perhaps?"

A slow smile spread across Jonathan's face. "Ahhh, I see," he murmured softly.

"You see *what* precisely?"

"You must have finally decided to indulge yourself with a ladylove . . . one who prefers to bathe with rose-scented soap."

Gesturing for a brandy, Bryce waited for a moment before admitting, "Actually, it's my wife who prefers the scent."

"Really?" Jonathan rolled the word around on his tongue, savoring it. "My, my, things have certainly changed from your days with Francesca."

"Indeed," Bryce murmured, waiting for the pain and anger he felt whenever he thought of Francesca. Oddly enough, it didn't come. Perhaps time *did* heal all wounds. Luckily, he would never have to go through that pain again . . . not with Cassandra. She might be infuriating, headstrong, and willful, but he could never imagine her being unfaithful.

"I shall have to get to know this paragon of virtue you married," Jonathan said, his gaze bright.

Bryce went still. Perhaps he wasn't completely over Francesca's betrayals; the moment his friend expressed interest in Cassandra, Bryce felt himself go on guard. Utterly ridiculous. "My Cassandra is indeed an honorable woman," he said evenly, keeping his ongoing one-upmanship with his wife to himself. That bit of information he preferred not to share.

Jonathan's expression sobered. "I'm happy for you, my friend. You went through Hell, so you deserve your share of contentment."

And Jonathan only knew of a handful of Francesca's numerous betrayals. Again, that was information Bryce kept to himself. It was bad enough Jonathan, no, all of society, knew of Francesca's infidelities with members of the ton; there was no need to add to that humiliation by discussing her numerous trysts with servants, journeymen, and merchants. "Thank you," he murmured.

Jonathan's gaze flickered behind Bryce. "Speaking of Francesca, brace yourself, for here comes her brother."

Clive Milford, Earl of Kingwood. The man who had delighted in taunting Bryce about his lacking as a man, the man who had gone to great lengths to expose Bryce's failure as a husband . . . the man who still blamed Bryce for Francesca's death.

Stiffening, Bryce rose to his feet, unwilling to give Clive any sort of advantage over him. As his ex brother-in-law came to a halt before him, Bryce fired the first shot. "Can I help you with something, Kingwood?"

"I heard you replaced my sister already."

"Already?" Bryce repeated incredulously.

Jonathan stood as well. "It's been years, man."

"Not long enough for me to forget how you mistreated her," Kingwood ground out, pointing a finger at Bryce.

Looking at Clive, Bryce felt transported back to the years when Francesca had glared at him in such a manner. A shiver shook him. "I have no wish to argue with you," he said coolly. No, he'd had more than enough arguments with both Clive and his sister to last him a lifetime. "Good night, sir." Turning away from Clive, Bryce sat back down and sipped at his brandy.

Two swift steps brought Clive around to face him. "You won't find it so easy to dismiss me when I make you pay for what you did to my sister."

Bryce didn't even spare Clive a glance.

Reaching out his hand, Jonathan glanced around the room pointedly. "You're making quite a scene, Kingwood."

Containing his fury, Clive straightened and tugged down at his jacket. "You *will* pay, Amberville," he repeated before striding away.

Whistling under his breath, Jonathan took his seat again. "You have an enemy there, old boy."

"He blames me for making his sister so miserably

unhappy that she began to have affairs. He believes it is my fault that she was on her lover's boat on the day it sank."

"Rubbish," scoffed Jonathan. "You've told me about Kingwood's foolish misconceptions, but I found it hard to fathom the man truly believed you were responsible for her death."

"Well, it's true. And, amazingly enough, Kingwood isn't the only one who blames me for Francesca's death." Bryce nodded toward the right side of the room. "Do you see Evan Stanford over there?"

"The Marquess of Dranwyck?"

"One and the same," Bryce agreed. "He was another of Francesca's lovers and he too blames me for her death." Lifting his glass, Bryce took another sip of his brandy. "Here the faithless woman dies while with one lover and another lover somehow blames me. There is a certain irony to that, isn't there?"

"You aren't exactly lacking in mortal enemies, are you?" Jonathan remarked with a shake of his head.

"My darling Francesca's legacy to me," Bryce replied, tipping his glass forward in a salute.

Leaning forward, Jonathan's expression became grave. "You don't really think they'd try to exact revenge, do you?"

Bryce shrugged the question off. "If they were ever going to act on their threats, they would have done so years ago."

Jonathan considered that for a moment. "I suppose you're right."

"Of course I am. Besides, I'm far too busy with

my wife and niece to spend even a moment's thought on them."

"True enough," Jonathan concurred with a smile. Lifting his glass, he said, "Here's to ladies and their rose-scented soap."

Grinning, Bryce lifted his glass as well. "Amen."

9

Respect to all peers is given without hesitation.

Quoted from *A Lady's Guide to Proper Etiquette*,
written by Lady Cassandra Abbott

Cassandra found it much easier to hold the heavy breakfast tray and open Bryce's door this morning. Walking into his room, she set the tray down on the table and went to pull back the window curtains as well as his bed curtains.

Bryce's smile reminded her of Poco's after he'd gotten a particularly fine treat. Cassandra knew her husband was thinking about the bath last night. Knowing Bryce, she realized he was undoubtedly aware of how he'd affected her, a fact that could prove dangerous to her well-being.

"Good morning, my lord," she murmured politely as she went to retrieve the tray.

"Back to my lord, eh?" He looked pointedly around the room. "Where is a bath when you need it?"

Her lips twitched, but she refused to give him the satisfaction of a smile. "Your breakfast, my lord," she said formally as she leaned over to place it upon his lap.

Having learned his lesson from the other morning, Bryce quickly sat up and guided the tray down over him. "Smells delicious."

"I shall pass along your compliments to Cook," she said, before excusing herself.

"Wait."

Bryce's call halted her steps. Glancing over her shoulder, she gave him an inquiring look. "Yes, my lord?"

"I thought you might like to join me."

Cassandra lifted a brow. "That is not part of—"

"Forget the bloody provisions," he interrupted sharply, slashing his hand through the air. "I am asking if you would like to partake of this breakfast with me."

Part of her wanted to agree, to call a truce and enjoy his company, but the other half wondered if this was simply another tactic in his game. "The one I served you in bed?" she asked briskly, before shaking her head. "No, thank you, my lord."

He remained silent as she walked from the room, but Cassandra could almost feel his brooding. As soon as she closed the door behind her, she turned and pressed her ear to the wood. A few moments later, she heard what she was waiting for.

"Cassandra!"

Smiling as she heard Bryce begin to cough, Cassandra turned and headed down the hallway. Apparently, the large dose of pepper she'd added to his breakfast didn't appeal to him.

He'd never specified she couldn't spice things up.

Cassandra found Elaina in the library where she was curled up with a book. "There you are."

Glancing up, Elaina smiled in welcome. "Were you looking for me?"

"Yes," Cassandra replied, taking a seat across from her niece. "I wanted to talk to you about what happened yesterday."

"Yesterday?"

"When you were so unpleasant to your uncle," Cassandra clarified.

Immediately Elaina's expression shifted. "I don't wish to discuss that."

Cassandra remained undaunted. "That is unfortunate, for I am determined to understand why you are so angry with Bryce."

Slamming her book closed, Elaina glared at Cassandra. "He's always telling me where I can go, who I can see, how long I can remain out for the evening. My uncle believes he can order me about like I was his servant."

"While not his servant, you *are* his ward," Cassandra pointed out, purposely keeping her tone level. "And as such, he *does* have the right to supervise your actions."

Elaina crossed her arms. "Even so, he doesn't have to be so unreasonable."

"I'm quite certain that if you spoke to him calmly and rationally he would listen." And, oddly enough, Cassandra truly believed that. After all,

Bryce had honored his promise and abided by her provisions, despite his anger over them. He tried to find a way around them, to force her into accepting his own provisions, but he hadn't broken his bond even though they both knew she would have no recourse if he had chosen to do so. "Your uncle is an honorable man."

"Overbearing is more like it," grumbled Elaina.

"That is quite enough." Cassandra leveled a stern look at her niece. "You are ten and six now, Elaina, a young lady. It is time that you begin to act in accordance with your age. If your uncle seems a bit rigid in his rules, I am quite certain it is only because he is doing what he feels is in your best interest." Leaning forward, she placed a hand upon Elaina's folded arms. "Behaving like a child every time you see him certainly doesn't make him believe that you are ready to take responsibility for your own actions. Next time you see your uncle, try to be pleasant. I'm positive Bryce would be far more willing to listen to your complaints if you were nicer to him."

Though Elaina remained silent, Cassandra could tell she was considering the advice.

Settling back in her chair, Cassandra decided she'd said enough on the topic. "I'm going to shop for some jewelry with my mother. You're welcome to come along if you'd like."

Elaina grimaced. "I'd rather be tarred and feathered than spend time with your mother."

Cassandra fought back a grin at the girl's irreverence. "Come now, Elaina. You must learn to temper your responses."

Distress flickered within Elaina's eyes before she

masked the emotion. "You are finding quite a few faults with me today. First I need to behave differently with my uncle, now you wish I weren't so honest. My goodness, how ever did I survive without you around to tell me what I'm doing wrong?"

Cassandra shifted onto the settee next to Elaina and placed her arm around the girl's shoulders. "I admire so many things about you, Elaina. I'm only trying to guide you, to help you adjust to this new world you've entered."

Elaina's expression softened. "I still haven't gotten used to all the rules of polite society," she admitted.

"And you must miss your parents still." Cassandra's heart melted at the sadness that filled Elaina's gaze. Leaning closer, Cassandra tried to bring a smile back onto the young girl's face. "I'm sorry you won't be joining me today, but I well understand. Truth be told, there are times when my mother can be so unyielding that I'd rather face a firing squad than her barrage of questions."

Elaina's laughter was her reward.

"You know, Cassandra, I've been thinking."

Oh, Lord. Where was a firing squad when you needed it? Forcing a smile onto her face, Cassandra looked at her mother. "About?"

"The Marbury affair." Cassandra's mother picked up a diamond brooch. "What do you think of this one?"

"I think that for someone who was two steps away from debtor's gaol a few days ago it is far too extravagant," Cassandra whispered. "Why don't you look at those more reasonably priced items over there?"

With a regretful sigh, Lady Darwood set the brooch back down in the velvet box. "As I was saying, I've given the Marbury affair quite a bit of thought and believe you should have your new husband accompany you."

Cassandra blinked twice. "Why? Few husbands accompany their wives."

"True, but, in this case, as a newlywed, it might be best if Lord Amberville accompany you. That way you would be introduced as a married couple for the first time in public."

"I fail to see why you believe that is important," Cassandra remarked, giving up all pretense of looking at the jewelry.

"Because of your marriage to Linley," Lady Darwood said. "You must admit that your previous marriage was not what people consider normal. You all but fell off the face of the earth after you wed Linley. Everyone is still talking about it."

"About *what?*" Cassandra shook her head, not understanding the reason behind her mother's concern.

"About your disappearance from polite society. They are speculating whether or not your marriage to Amberville will be any different. After all, you must remember that until recently, when he inherited the title, Amberville himself had withdrawn from society."

All the blood drained from Cassandra's face.

"Which is why I suggest you arrange for Amberville to be at your side when you arrive at Marbury's ball tonight. In one stroke, you will squelch all the nasty rumors."

Her mother's argument made sense, Cassandra realized, but there was just one problem.

She didn't know how receptive her husband would be to granting this request . . . especially if he hadn't yet recovered from this morning's breakfast.

Cassandra knocked softly on Bryce's study door. "Enter."

At his muffled command, she took a deep breath and stepped into the room with a smile. "Good evening, Bryce."

"So it's Bryce again," he remarked, leaning back in his chair. "You must need something."

She felt her cheeks heat. Praying she didn't look too guilty, she wandered farther into her husband's private sanctuary. "Why do you say that?"

"Because you only refer to me by my Christian name when you're flustered or you want something," he pointed out logically, "and since you appear unruffled, I simply assumed it was the latter."

Glancing down, she realized she was wringing her hands again. Snatching them behind her back, she took a calming breath. "As circumstances would have it, I did indeed come to make a request."

He folded his hands over his midsection. "I do so love your requests . . . for then you grant one of mine."

She ignored that comment. "It's more of a favor, actually. I would appreciate it very much if you would escort Elaina and me to Marbury's ball this evening." When Bryce failed to respond, Cassandra plunged onward. "As this is our first event as a married couple, I would feel more comfortable being introduced as the Duchess of Amberville with you by my side."

"Of course," he replied in a magnanimous tone. "I'd be more than happy to escort you tonight." Reaching into his pocket, he withdrew his list. "Now which item will you chose in return."

Cassandra drew back, wounded. "This isn't part of your foolish games, Bryce. This was a favor I requested of you as my husband, since I'm feeling apprehensive about my first outing as your wife." She shook her head fiercely. "However, since you seem determined to reduce every moment of our marriage into some sort of bartering exchange, I withdraw my request." Lifting her chin, she continued, "Your company isn't worth the price."

Vibrating with anger, she turned on her heel and marched from the room.

Hours later, fully dressed and ready to depart for the ball, Cassandra remained furious at her husband. "I'm afraid I've made a dreadful mistake, Poco," she said to her cat as he lounged in front of the fire. "I thought him reasonable. I believed he was honorable." She paced across her room. "But tonight I learned he was neither of these things. He's a swine. No, he's lower than a swine. He's . . . he's . . ." She heaved an exasperated sigh. "I can't think of anything bad enough to call him, but give me time. I'm certain I'll be able to think of something."

She broke off her ranting when she heard a soft knocking on her bedchamber door. "Cassandra?"

"Coming, Elaina," she called, masking her annoyance with Bryce. The situation between Bryce and Elaina was precarious enough without the girl learning of this latest problem. Reaching down to give Poco a farewell stroke, Cassandra whispered, "I'll let you know when I've thought of a fitting name for Bryce."

Poco swished his tail against the fireplace tiles in response.

Brushing down her skirts, Cassandra walked to the door, opened it, and greeted her niece with a warm smile. "Why, Elaina, you look breathtaking."

"As do you," Elaina returned, stepping back to allow Cassandra to exit her room.

Placing her hand on the balustrade, Cassandra headed down the stairs. "I'm eager to see who—" She broke off her comments and stumbled to a halt on the third step when she caught sight of Bryce standing at the base of the staircase in all his finery.

Lifting his hand, he met her gaze. "I've been a boor," he said simply. "Forgive me."

And with that quiet admission, her anger drained away, leaving her breathless. "Blast you, Bryce Keene," she returned with a helpless shake of her head. "Just when I decide you have no redeeming qualities, you go and do something like this."

A side of his mouth quirked upward, enhancing his bedeviling fine features. "Poorly done of me, I know, but every now and then one of my finer qualities raises its ugly head. The thought of you attending this affair without my escort was intolerable."

"Intolerable, you say," she murmured as she resumed her descent.

"Completely."

She came to a stop next to his outstretched hand. Looking down at the peace offering, she lifted her gaze to stare into his eyes. "You hurt me," she whispered softly enough that Elaina couldn't overhear her.

Bryce's expression sobered. "I know. I'm sorry."

His apology rang with sincerity. Nodding once, she felt the knot in her stomach ease. "You won't do it again?"

"Never."

Cassandra accepted his hand.

10

Above all, a lady never makes a spectacle of herself.

Quoted from *A Lady's Guide to Proper Etiquette,*
written by Lady Cassandra Abbott

"The Duke and Duchess of Amberville and Lady
Elaina Keene."

Heads turned at the introduction by Lord Marbury's butler. The avid speculation of the crowd
made Cassandra doubly glad for Bryce's firm clasp
upon her elbow. Bryce glanced at her with an
amused smile as if he knew precisely what she was
thinking. The warmth that had filled her when
she'd accepted his hand intensified.

Elaina clasped Bryce's other arm as he guided
them across the room. "Cassandra, you remember
my friend, Jonathan Conner, Earl of Dunham?"

"Of course." Dipping into a curtsey, Cassandra
held out her hand. "It is a pleasure to renew your
acquaintance, Lord Dunham," she murmured as he
bent over her gloved hand.

"The pleasure is all mine."

Curving his hand around Elaina's elbow, Bryce

nodded toward her. "I'm not certain if you've had the pleasure of meeting my niece, Lady Elaina Keene, at the wedding."

"No, you've been most neglectful in your duties," Jonathan chided Bryce.

Elaina tilted her head to the side. "Aren't you going to bow over my hand as well?"

While Bryce groaned, Cassandra coughed lightly to cover her laugh.

Obviously amused, Jonathan smiled at Elaina. "Forgive me, my lady," he murmured, accepting her outstretched hand and bowing over it. "I meant no offense."

"It's quite all right," Elaina said after Jonathan straightened.

"I am most relieved to hear that," he replied, his smile deepening into a grin. Turning toward Cassandra, he asked, "Might I have the honor of this dance?"

Automatically, Cassandra glanced at Bryce for his permission. With a pleased expression, he nodded in response. Tucking her hand into Jonathan's, she followed him onto the dance floor where the quartet struck up a quadrille.

As she whirled around on Jonathan's arm, Cassandra caught her husband's gaze. The intimate light in his eyes made her blush, an action he didn't appear to miss as he began to smile broadly. How would she ever resist the man? Cassandra wondered not for the first time.

"Bryce speaks quite highly of you."

Drawing her attention from her husband, Cassandra refocused on her dance partner with his all too sharp gaze. "I should hope so," she murmured.

Jonathan glanced over at Bryce. "You make my friend happy."

Was Jonathan mad? She made Bryce feel many things—anger, frustration, even regret—but happy? She didn't think so. Still, the details of her marriage were far too intimate to be bandied about a ballroom. "Thank you," she murmured finally.

He spun her around. "You will also be a steadying influence on his niece."

"Elaina?" His remark surprised her. "I thought you'd never met her before this evening."

"While that is true, I have certainly heard of her."

Cassandra shook her head. "I don't pay much heed to idle gossip."

"Not gossip, Lady Amberville, but the truth as told to me by your husband," Jonathan corrected quietly.

"I appreciate your concern, my lord, but I would prefer not to discuss private family matters."

"Most commendable," Jonathan returned, before changing the subject.

As Lord Dunham began to regale her with tales of his latest trip to the Scottish Highlands, Cassandra mulled over how she was going to deal with her niece.

Bryce didn't release his hold upon her as he escorted her off the dance floor, the small action making Cassandra's heart leap. "We've danced together twice this evening," she murmured, slanting a look up at him. "People will begin to talk."

His smile had a decidedly rakish tilt. "We're

newly wed, Cassandra. If I am too attentive to you this evening, people will merely speculate that I am very pleased with my bride."

The giddiness inside of her faded. "Then they would be incorrect in their assumptions."

"Oh, I don't know about that," Bryce replied quickly. "If I consider that my new bride has bathed me, fed me, and never made me suffer boredom, then I'd have to say the ton would be correct in their assessment."

Cassandra grew more sober at each item he listed. "None of those things were done willingly," she admitted softly.

"Ah, but that is just the point, my dear," he returned swiftly. "You didn't have to honor your promises made in our little games, yet you did." Picking up her hand, he pressed a soft kiss upon her fingers. "And that, my beautiful Cassandra, pleases me very much."

Her breath caught in her throat. "Bryce," she whispered longingly. "I am—" She broke off her admission, uncertain how to phrase the odd emotions growing inside of her.

Bryce opened his mouth as if to respond, but shut it again as his gaze shifted over her shoulder. "Good evening, sir," Bryce said as he released her hand.

Spinning around, Cassandra faced her father. "Papa!" she exclaimed, rising up onto her tiptoes to press a kiss upon his cheek. "How wonderful to see you."

Her father's eyes twinkled. "You look well, Cassandra. I hope I didn't interrupt anything."

"Not at all," Bryce assured her papa before she

could respond. "Now if you'll excuse me, Cassandra, I shall go fetch you some refreshment while you visit with your father."

Bryce's thoughtfulness warmed her. "Thank you," she murmured softly. "I am fairly parched."

Bowing to her, Bryce straightened and headed toward the drawing room. Watching him go, Cassandra felt one thought pounding through her. She could easily fall in love with this Bryce.

"This marriage seems to suit you, poppet."

She started at her father's observation. "What makes you say that?"

Papa grinned broadly. "You're making little effort to hide your affection for Amberville, Cassandra. Everyone has noticed his unwavering attentions."

Doubt pricked at her bubble of happiness. Was Bryce perhaps being so charming to her simply to impress society? But she dismissed that notion in an instant. No, the man who greeted her at the bottom of the stairs this evening had no ulterior motive.

Nodding, Cassandra agreed with her father. "I do believe you're right, Papa. This marriage does suit me," she admitted softly.

Papa hugged her close for a quick moment, then released her before anyone even noticed the embrace. "I'm so relieved." Looking away, Papa murmured, "I deeply regret the mistake I made with Linley."

A gasp broke from Cassandra at her father's admission. Never once had Papa admitted that he'd made a mistake in his choice of her first husband.

"I never would have agreed to the suit if I had known that he—"

"I know, Papa," Cassandra said, laying a hand on her father's arm.

Sighing, her father patted her hand. "And I'm sorry that you were forced to remarry because of my mess. So, it relieves me no end to see you happily married this time."

Happily married.

Cassandra turned the phrase over in her mind. She'd hardly consider herself happily married, but a few more magical evenings like this one would certainly change her opinion. She didn't know what had happened to change Bryce's attitude toward her, but she wasn't going to question her good fortune.

Instead, she would simply enjoy the beautiful evening.

"You've a fine husband, Cassandra."

She smiled at her father. "I believe you're right, Papa."

Hoping he'd given his wife enough private time with her father, Bryce headed back into the ballroom with a glass of punch. He stumbled as he caught sight of his smiling wife. Excitement began to sizzle along his veins and, for a moment, the intense emotion alarmed him.

But, in an instant, he dismissed the feeling. After all, it was only natural that he be excited to return to his wife, especially since he'd finally managed to get her to see reason. When she'd stormed from his study this afternoon, Bryce had been tempted to call her back, but he'd managed to refrain. He hadn't yet sorted out what her reaction had meant.

She'd asked him to accompany her, then grown

angry and stormed from the room when he'd mentioned his list. It was only upon careful reflection that he'd realized that she hadn't tried to trick him this time, nor had she believed she could charm him into granting her request. By her telling actions, Bryce now knew he'd won a major victory in their ongoing battle. Finally, Cassandra was well aware that she couldn't force . . . or charm him into doing anything he didn't want to do.

And that had left him free to grant her request.

He'd never forget her expression when she'd first seen him waiting for her at the bottom of the stairs. As he watched his wife converse with her father, Bryce felt his chest tighten. Lord, but she was beautiful.

Pushing aside the fanciful thought, Bryce strode forward. "My dear," he murmured, offering her the glass of punch.

When Cassandra turned her pleased gaze upon him, he almost grinned like a fool. "Thank you, Bryce," she said.

Unable to stop himself, he reached out and laid a hand lightly upon the small of her back. "My pleasure."

It took considerable effort to turn back to his father-in-law. "So, my lord, how are—"

"Everything's fine," Lord Darwood replied briskly. "And I'm quite certain that you would prefer to dance with my daughter than have a conversation with an old dodger like me."

"Not at—"

But Lord Darwood cut off his protest. "Pish-posh," he retorted as he snatched the half-empty punch glass out of Cassandra's hand. "Now, why don't I take this and you waltz with my daughter?"

Bryce couldn't hold in a laugh. "Why don't I indeed?"

And with that, he tightened his hold upon Cassandra's waist and swung her into his arms.

"Thank you, Papa," Cassandra called over her shoulder as she clasped Bryce's hand.

As Bryce waltzed Cassandra around the room, he pressed her closely against him. He bit back a sigh of satisfaction at finally having her in his arms again. "Cassandra . . ." he began softly, "This evening has been—*Oof!*"

The breath was knocked out of him as a couple banged into his back.

"What the devil," he muttered, frowning after the wild couple whirling madly around the dance floor. Some people had no respect for others. Why, just look at them careening around the floor, completely out of control. They were waltzing so vigorously the lady's blue skirts were kicking up to show flashes of leg.

Blue skirts.

Dread hit the pit of his stomach as Bryce raised his gaze to look into the smiling face of his niece. Elaina. He should have known. "Good God!" he muttered grimly.

Glancing down at Cassandra, Bryce noted her paleness. "You already knew it was Elaina, didn't you?"

"I saw her face when they knocked into you," Cassandra admitted.

"That girl is determined to ruin herself." Steeling himself, Bryce began to waltz toward Elaina and her companion, Lord Conover. As soon as he was close enough, he clasped a firm hand upon Conover's shoulder, guiding them to the edge of the dance floor, and bringing the dance to an end. "Damn it, man, have you no sense?" Bryce ground out in a low voice, not bothering to hide his anger.

Forcing a smile onto his face, Bryce offered an arm to his wife and niece. He pitched his voice loudly enough for everyone around them to hear. "Now, if you'll excuse us, we must be off."

Without pausing, Bryce grasped Cassandra's elbow and practically tugged her toward the entrance, where they collected their cloaks. After ordering their carriage brought around, he fell silent. Watching Bryce, Cassandra knew full well that this situation was far from over. Like a storm brewing, she could feel the emotions swirling inside of him.

When the carriage arrived, he hurried them out of Marbury's townhouse. Inside the quiet confines of the carriage, Cassandra tried to broach the matter. "Bryce—"

"Not another word."

Alarmed, Cassandra fell silent. Bryce's voice had been so raw, so furious, he hadn't even sounded like himself.

Elaina shifted on her seat. "What is wrong with—"

As Bryce leaned forward, a ray of moonlight caught his face, illuminating his savage expression. "You behave in an appallingly outrageous manner and then you wonder what is wrong with *me?*

Bloody Hell, Elaina, have you no sense of decorum?"

"I was merely dancing," she returned in a mutinous tone.

"You aren't even aware of how scandalous your behavior was, are you?" Bryce closed his eyes for a moment. "God help me."

Before Elaina could reply, the carriage rocked to a stop. Bryce leapt out, then reached inside for them. Cassandra tripped as she exited the carriage, but Bryce simply clasped her elbow and all but pulled her up the front steps. When they entered the foyer, he glared down at Elaina. "Go to your room."

Elaina stood her ground. "You can't tell me—"

Bryce's entire frame began to shake with barely restrained fury. "If you don't go to your room this instant, I will drag you up there myself and lock you in for a week."

Sending a hate-filled glare at her uncle, Elaina rushed up the stairs. Bryce waited until she cleared the top landing before he tugged Cassandra behind him into his study. With a twist of his arm, he sent her spinning into the room as he clicked the lock.

Cassandra watched silently as Bryce leaned his forehead against the door. For a moment, he remained motionless until finally he turned to face her.

11

A husband becomes a lady's lord and master.

Quoted from *A Lady's Guide to Proper Etiquette*,
written by Lady Cassandra Abbott

"Why haven't you begun to guide Elaina?" His steps were measured as he moved closer.

"I've spent time with her and—"

Bryce held up his hand. "That's not what I mean, Cassandra, and you know it," he interrupted. His shoulders sagged forward as he sank into a chair.

The defeated air about Bryce alarmed Cassandra far more than his anger.

"I love my niece," he admitted quietly, leaning forward to rest his elbows upon his knees. "And it kills me to see her destroy her future bit by bit, foolish act by foolish act."

"Bryce," Cassandra murmured, sinking down onto her knees before him.

His eyes glittered with a volatile mixture of frustration, grief, and love. "I need your help, Cassandra. Please."

Bryce needed her. She melted at his entreaty.

"Of course, Bryce," she murmured, reaching out to place a hand upon his. "I'll speak with Elaina in the morning."

A shudder ran through Bryce. "Thank you."

His soft whisper touched her deeply. "You're welcome."

Pausing in the foyer to tug on his gloves, Bryce heard Cassandra's voice wafting out of the ladies' salon.

". . . the importance of behaving in a manner . . ."

He smiled as he strode from the house. If his wife was finally taking his wild niece in hand, then the upheaval of last night had at least produced some positive results. While he was still uncomfortable with having exposed his emotions to Cassandra, he couldn't complain about the outcome.

Another benefit of his confrontation with Cassandra had been his unspoiled breakfast. Instead of having his food land upon his lap or scorch his tongue, Bryce had enjoyed a delicious breakfast, served with a smile and a pleasant greeting.

His wife was finally coming around and acting in a manner befitting the Duchess of Amberville.

With his smile firmly in place, Bryce entered White's. The lightness in his step dimmed a bit when he noticed all eyes upon him. When he reached Jonathan, Bryce took a seat, thankful that the leather back of his chair protected him from some of the stares. "What the devil is everyone looking at?"

Jonathan's eyes glittered with a teasing light. "Perhaps they're all merely envious of you."

"*Me?*" Bryce thought of the previous evening's

debacle and couldn't fathom why anyone would envy him. "Why?"

"I believe all of the gentlemen present, myself included, are envious of the obvious affection your wife holds for you."

Warm memories of holding Cassandra in his arms flickered through Bryce. "As well they should be," he returned with a laugh.

Leaning forward, Jonathan dropped his teasing manner. "I mentioned to your wife that Elaina's behavior was somewhat . . . wild." He clasped his hands together. "However, she didn't wish to hear any details. Instead she informed me that she had no desire to discuss private family matters."

Cassandra's loyalty pleased Bryce. "Good for her," he returned. "She was quite correct in not wishing to gossip about her niece in such a public setting . . . and with someone she'd only met twice."

Jonathan chuckled softly as he leaned back in his chair. "All that wisdom . . . and she gives rose-scented baths as well."

". . . I've already explained this to you, Elaina. If you show an excessive amount of your limbs, then you give the impression that you are of loose morals," Cassandra said, utterly exasperated at the girl's continued refusal to accept guidance.

"How does seeing my legs make—"

"Your *limbs*," Cassandra corrected automatically. "A lady never refers to her lower extremities as legs."

Elaina's brows drew together. "Why on earth not?"

"Because it is considered vulgar." Rising, Cassandra walked over to the sideboard and poured herself another fortifying glass of sherry. Detouring toward the desk in her salon, she retrieved a copy of her book. "Perhaps you should read this," she instructed as she handed it to Elaina.

"A Lady's Guide to Proper Etiquette." Glancing up from the title, Elaina asked, "What is this?"

"Precisely what it appears to be—a book I wrote on the rules of polite society." Cassandra took her seat again. "If you read it, I'm certain you will find it most edifying."

Curiosity colored Elaina's expression as she flipped open the book to a page in the middle. *"A lady never stirs her tea too vigorously and she never taps her spoon on the side of her cup more than twice."* Elaina burst into laughter. "Surely this is a jest."

"Not at all," Cassandra protested. "Any more taps and you will be considered ill-mannered."

"While I commend you for writing a book, surely there were far more interesting topics to cover." Elaina grinned as she continued to peruse the book. "I know you believe it is important to follow proper etiquette, Cassandra, but when has obeying all the rules ever made anyone happy?"

Elaina's simple question reminded Cassandra of how she'd wondered that very same thing.

"Many of the matrons are sticklers for the rules, but they are the most miserable old crows I've ever met. Does adhering to the dictates of a pampered society make them any happier?" Elaina shut the book and handed it back to Cassandra. "I don't believe there is anything in here that will make my life any easier."

Cassandra's fingers closed around the book. "I wish you would reconsider and just read it through once."

"Nothing in that book will help me fit into society any better," Elaina said firmly as she shook her head. "I'm too outspoken, too free with my emotions. So, if I will never be completely accepted by the condescending ton, then why should I even attempt to follow their ridiculous, endless rules?"

Hearing the pain in Elaina's remarks, Cassandra leaned forward to place her hand upon Elaina's knee. "You are Lady Elaina Keene, the daughter of the twelfth Duke of Amberville. With your title and wealth alone, you would be accepted." She smiled gently at her niece whose gaze suddenly appeared older than her years. "Besides, you are witty, vivacious, and immensely entertaining."

Blinking tears, Elaina rose abruptly, breaking Cassandra's hold upon her. "Then let the ton come to appreciate me for those things, for who I am . . . instead of trying to make me fit their perfect mold like you do."

An instant later, Cassandra was alone in her salon. *Fit their perfect mold.* As a young girl, that was precisely what she had done, believing like so many others that her adherence to the rules would guarantee her a perfect life. Instead, she'd ended up in a painful marriage, been left with no money for all her years of suffering, and finally forced to barter herself in order to live.

Yet with Bryce, she *hadn't* followed all the rules.

She was headstrong, argumentative, and unyielding . . . and she'd never been happier. Instead of following the rules, she was following her heart. Startled by the radical concept, Cassandra looked down at the book in her hand. Had she been completely and utterly wrong in her ideas all these years?

Setting down her glass, she hurried from the room and up the stairs to her chamber. She locked the door behind her before taking a seat near the window. An instant later, Poco jumped up onto her lap. Absentmindedly, she stroked the cat as she opened her book and began to read.

The last rays of sunshine slipped into her room as Cassandra closed her book. She sat there, unable to move, as a multitude of questions, rebellious questions, swirled around in her mind. She now knew that so many of the things she'd once believed were just plain false.

Bryce was not her lord and master. Where would the sin be in calling upon someone before the noon repast? How would her life be affected if she mistakenly addressed an earl before a duke? So many foolish rules to abide by. She'd once believed that straying from the course of proper etiquette would lead to chaos and disaster. Well, she'd followed the straight and narrow, yet landed in the midst of chaos and disaster nonetheless.

Setting down the book, Cassandra gently lifted Poco off her lap and walked to Elaina's room. Tapping lightly on the door, Cassandra called, "Elaina? Are you in there?"

"Come in."

At her niece's bidding, Cassandra stepped into the pretty room. "I wish to discuss something with you."

Placing her brush on the table, Elaina sat down upon the stool. "If this is another lecture on how I need to—"

"No, that's just it," Cassandra said, unable to hold in her excitement. "I can't possibly lecture you on how you should live your life." Her lips twisted as bitter memories flooded her. "I haven't exactly done perfectly with mine."

Elaina's brows drew together.

"Still, there are certain things that I know are important, like treating people with respect and being honorable to others as well as yourself and being of sound morals." Cassandra sank down on the bed. "What I believe we need to do at this point, Elaina, is to create our own rules . . . within limits."

Disappointment colored Elaina's gaze. "I should have known you'd tag on qualifications."

"You have to," Cassandra insisted. "While we have the right to live as we see fit, it is reprehensible to do so at a cost to others." Leaning back on her hands, Cassandra made her point. "For instance, last night when you danced and created a scene, your uncle was very upset . . . for you," she hurried to clarify. "He loves you very much and is concerned that you will destroy any chance for future happiness."

"That's not the reason behind his anger," Elaina said bitterly. "He's afraid I'll embarrass him."

Cassandra shook her head. "That's not true. He only wants what is best for you."

Thrusting to her feet, Elaina began to pace across her room. "He wants what is best for *him.*"

A protest rose to her lips, but Cassandra bit it back when she noted the stubborn tilt to Elaina's chin. "I could tell you of your uncle's affection, but you'd never believe me, would you?"

Elaina's silence spoke volumes.

"I didn't think so," Cassandra replied with a sigh. "Luckily for both of you, time is your ally." She smiled softly as she placed a hand upon Elaina's cheek. "But for now, we'll focus on creating rules that satisfy both you and your uncle."

After a moment's hesitation, Elaina reached out to hug Cassandra. "Thank you for understanding," she whispered.

Savoring the moment, Cassandra squeezed Elaina tight, but immediately dropped her arms when she felt her niece pull away. "I hope you realize that I will still be giving you advice, Elaina. I've made many mistakes in my life and I have no intention of standing by and watching silently if I see you heading for trouble. There is no sense in us both making the same mistakes."

Elaina's eyes sparkled as she shook her head. "Absolutely not. I'm more than willing to make my own."

Still laughing as she left Elaina's room, Cassandra returned to her own chamber, feeling as if she'd just made the right decision.

Suddenly, a sound from Bryce's room captured her attention. If she was setting her life to rights, there was one thing she truly needed to address. Her marriage. Cassandra stepped briskly to

Bryce's door before she had a chance to think twice.

Taking a bracing breath, she rapped sharply on the door.

Bryce's head snapped around at the sound. "Cassandra?" he called out tentatively.

"Might I speak with you for a moment?"

His hand paused upon his loosened cravat for the briefest moment before he strode to the door and opened it wide. "Of course. Please, do come in."

Two steps into his room, her gaze dropped to his unfastened waistcoat and his untied cravat. "I've interrupted your ablutions," she said, immediately turning around to return to her chamber.

"Not at all," he returned, closing the door before she could make her escape. This was the first time she'd come willingly into his bedchamber. He wasn't about to let her flee quite so quickly. "I was merely making myself more comfortable."

Cassandra laughed nervously. "There is something to be said for comfort."

Her inane reply made Bryce wonder what his wife was about. "To what do I owe the pleasure of your visit?" he asked, deciding to cut through the layers of polite remarks and replies.

"I wished to speak to you about our marriage."

That statement put him instantly on guard. Wading his way through the treacherous waters of a woman's mind, Bryce worded his reply carefully. "I believe we are getting on quite well."

"*Quite well?*" Cassandra exclaimed, her hands pressing against her stomach.

Apparently he hadn't worded his reply carefully *enough*. This time, he wisely chose to remain silent, waiting for Cassandra to make her point.

"Oh, dear," she muttered, fiddling with a ribbon on her bodice. "I'd rather hoped you felt the same as I do about the state of our marriage."

With that, he gave up. "To be perfectly honest, Cassandra, I have no bloody idea how you feel about our marriage. If you'd care to tell me, then I'd be more than happy to let you know if I feel the same way or not."

Expecting anger, he was stunned to see a huge grin split her face. "I must tell you, Bryce, I admire the way you speak your mind."

She did? Lord, Francesca used to become enraged whenever he spoke bluntly, telling him he had no refinement. But what else could she expect from a lowly, second son, Francesca had sneered. Thrusting away thoughts of his first wife, Bryce concentrated on Cassandra. "I'm relieved to hear that," he said truthfully, "for I fear I shall always be blunt."

Her smile reached her eyes. "I don't mind at all." Glancing away, she took a deep breath. "As to our marriage, I wish to start again."

Confused, he shook his head. "You want to exchange our vows again?"

"No, I would like it if we put aside our games, if we spent time together and got to know each other before . . . before . . ."

He hazarded a guess. "We become intimate?"

"Exactly," she said, relief deepening her voice.

Warmth spread inside his chest. "You want me to court you," he murmured, a side of his mouth quirking upward. It amused him to realize that a few short weeks ago he had only wanted a marriage of convenience. But last night as he'd lain awake in bed, he'd realized he wanted more.

He wanted her to love him.

Indeed, with her rare blend of honesty and loyalty, she was an ideal wife, one he could trust implicitly. If she fell in love with him, it would undoubtedly make her happier and he would hold her feelings in safekeeping.

"What do you think of the idea?"

Reaching out his hand, he lifted the tips of her fingers to his mouth, never allowing his gaze to falter from hers. A pretty blush stained her cheeks, telling him far more of her feelings than her words ever could. Pressing a tender kiss upon her fingers, he slowly lowered her hand, sliding his fingers across her palm to clasp their hands together.

"What do I think of your idea?" he repeated softly. "Why, my sweet wife, I think it is positively inspired."

12

A lady should never draw undue attention upon herself.

Quoted from *A Lady's Guide to Proper Etiquette*,
written by Lady Cassandra Abbott

"Did they have to play the waltz?" groaned Bryce as he watched Lord Ansley escort Elaina onto the dance floor.

Cassandra laughed up at her husband. "Don't worry, Bryce. I doubt if we'll have a repeat of three nights ago."

Glancing around the Howards' ballroom, Bryce muttered, "I pray you're right, Cassandra. If you'll notice, those matrons over near the fireplace are keeping their gazes trained upon Elaina, just waiting for her to stumble."

Since she'd been working with Elaina on modifying her behavior, Cassandra remained confident that her niece would weather the affair splendidly. "You need to trust me, Bryce."

"I do, but—"

She pressed two fingers against his lips. "No buts. Now why don't you fetch me some punch."

Bryce kissed the tips of her fingers, making Cassandra shiver. "Why don't I?"

The sensual light in Bryce's eyes intensified the warmth spreading through her. "I'll be back in a moment."

"I'll be right here."

A corner of his mouth tilted upward. "Then I'll hurry."

Laughing at his return, Cassandra watched him cross the room. For three glorious days, Bryce had been so charmingly attentive toward her . . . and she found herself slipping quietly into love with him. *What a glorious feeling indeed*, she thought with a happy smile.

"Amberville seems quite taken with you."

Her hand flew to her chest as she turned around. "Goodness, my lord, you startled me."

"My apologies," the gentleman murmured, dipping into a deep bow. "That was not my intention."

As he straightened, Cassandra felt her stomach tighten and didn't understand the reason behind the feeling. Being approached by a stranger shouldn't make her feel so apprehensive. "Have we met?" she asked warily.

"I don't believe we've had the pleasure," he murmured, one side of his finely shaped mouth drawing upward. "Clive Milford, Earl of Kingwood, at your service, Lady Amberville."

For some reason that name struck a chord within her, but she couldn't remember where she'd heard it before. "An honor," she returned politely.

His brilliant blue eyes lit with amusement. "Simply an honor and not a pleasure?"

She found his familiar manner very off-putting. "Do you know my husband?" she asked, instead of responding to his question.

"Quite well," Lord Kingwood replied, the light in his eyes cooling as he tossed back his thick, dark hair. "And I would like to know you even better."

"*Sir!*" gasped Cassandra. Frowning at the odious man, she flicked open her fan. "Your comments are most unwelcome."

"Please, my lady," he said cajolingly, holding out his hand. "I meant no disrespect. I am simply over-whelmed with your grace and beauty that it moves me to boldness."

"What a pity," she replied coldly.

Lord Kingwood's laugh slid down her like a piece of ice. "You are very witty, Lady Amberville. I do so enjoy humor in a woman."

Drawing herself up, Cassandra glared at the odious earl. "Excuse me, sir, but I believe it is past time I rejoin my husband."

Immediately Lord Kingwood's hand snaked out and clasped her wrist, holding her in place. "But I am so enjoying our conversation," he said in a low voice.

"Release her."

Both she and Lord Kingwood turned to the side and came face-to-face with a young gentleman. "Go away, you toad," snapped Lord Kingwood.

The young man flushed up to the brown roots of his hair and his Adam's apple bobbed a few times, but he remained standing firm. "I cannot do that, sir, for it is apparent to me that the lady wishes to be free of your company."

Admiration for the youth's gallant actions filled

her. "You're correct, my lord, as I am finished conversing with Lord Kingwood," she assured the younger man as she took advantage of Lord Kingwood's distracted state to tug her hand free. "In fact, the earl was just leaving."

For a moment, she thought Lord Kingwood would argue when she saw his expression darken, but after a quick glare at the young gentleman, Lord Kingwood turned on his heel and slipped through the crowd.

She released the breath she hadn't even been aware of holding. "I thank you for your assistance," Cassandra said sincerely as she turned to smile at her savior.

He reddened further. "Always glad to be of service," he returned, before executing a jerky bow. "Andrew Polk, Viscount of Trinslow."

"Lady Amberville." Reaching into her reticule, she retrieved a card. "I would be pleased if you would call upon me so I might thank you again over tea."

Why, the poor boy's hand shook as he accepted her card. "I would be honored," he said, tucking the card into the pocket of his dreadfully rumpled waistcoat. Clearing his throat, he bowed again, before stammering, "M-m-might I have the pleasure of this dance?"

Touched by his youthful nervousness, she accepted gracefully. "I would be delighted," she replied, tucking her hand into his arm.

As Lord Trinslow led her onto the dance floor, Cassandra saw Bryce return with her punch. Lifting the glass, he grinned before taking a sip of the very drink he'd fetched for her. Smiling, she shook her head at him, then stepped into the dance.

Apparently Lord Trinslow had noticed Bryce's presence as well for he said, "After this dance, I shall return you to Lord Amberville's safekeeping and inform him of the insult you received from Lord Kingwood."

The minute Lord Trinslow informed her of his plans, Cassandra felt her heart tighten. All evening, Bryce had been in a playful mood. It was only natural that he act his charming best, Cassandra thought, because he was truly courting her. She felt a little giddy from the mere thought alone. Perhaps he would even kiss her again, she prayed, the thought sending a shiver of anticipation along her spine.

But she knew the moment he heard of Lord Kingwood's advances, his anger would overshadow his desire to tease her, to seduce her. And for this night, this one night, she wanted nothing to mar her pleasure. Selfish or not, she would hold off on informing Bryce about Lord Kingwood until the morning.

Smiling at Lord Trinslow, Cassandra walked beneath his arm in the flow of the dance. "I do so appreciate your offer to inform my husband of Lord Kingwood's insults, but I would ask you to allow me to tell Lord Amberville."

"But surely you would prefer if I informed him and assured him that you defended your honor admirably," Lord Trinslow protested.

"I assure you, my lord, that my husband knows quite well that I would never do anything to cast aspersions upon the Amberville line." Cassandra could only pray that was true. "So I am asking you, as the Duchess of Amberville, to allow me to inform my husband of the insult."

Cassandra knew full well that the young lord could not refuse her request. "If that is your wish," he finally murmured.

Relief flooded Cassandra. She would have her night of magic after all. "You are a true gentleman, Lord Trinslow," she said softly, "and I shall look forward to your visit."

Still flushed by the time the music ended, the young gentleman returned Cassandra to the place she wanted to be.

At her husband's side.

"Are you certain Elaina will be fine?" Bryce asked as he escorted Cassandra up the stairs to their bedchambers.

"Most definitely." Cassandra slanted a glance at her husband. "My parents agreed to escort her home after the ball. She will be perfectly fine in their care."

Twisting the knob, Bryce swung open the door to Cassandra's bedchamber. "I had a lovely time this evening," he said softly as she paused in the open doorway.

"As did I." Leaning forward, she pressed a kiss against his cheek. "Good night, Bryce."

Cassandra stepped into her room and closed the door behind her. Standing in the hall, Bryce was well aware that he must appear the idiot, but he didn't care. His wife had not only willingly spent time in his company, but she initiated a demonstration of affection. Yes, his plans were progressing nicely.

Whistling softly, he took two steps to his own door. He tried to twist the knob, but it wouldn't move. Rattling it a second time, Bryce finally realized that it was locked. Thrusting a hand through his hair, he returned to Cassandra's door and rapped on it with two knuckles.

When she opened the door, Bryce fell speechless at the sight of her long, lustrous hair falling over her shoulder, across one breast, and ending at her waist. In all his life, he'd never seen anything quite as alluring. Like a Lorelei bidding him closer, Bryce couldn't resist touching the chestnut mass. Lifting her hair, he gently stroked along the shimmering length, feeling the warmth of her body through the silky strands. "You are so beautiful," he rasped, finally lifting his gaze to meet her bemused one.

"Thank you, Bryce."

Her words broke the spell he'd fallen under. Through sheer strength of will, he pulled his hand away from her. "I'm sorry to bother you—" he began, only to have her cut him off.

"It's no bother."

The breathless quality to her voice pleased him. Regaining his balance, he smiled at his wife. "I'm relieved to hear that, for I must ask your indulgence." He pointed to his door down the hall. "I've locked myself out of my room and was wondering if I might go to my chamber through the connecting door in your room."

"Of course," she murmured, stepping back to allow him entrance.

Bryce felt as if he'd intruded into a feminine sanctuary. Candles burned on the dressing table and on the bedside table while a fire crackled cheerfully in the hearth. Cassandra's cat lifted his head from his perch near the blaze and oddly enough, Bryce didn't think the animal looked as homely as before. Perhaps the damn thing was growing on him.

"This door is unlocked."

Cassandra's voice caught his attention and he turned to face her. She'd opened the connecting door and stood against the frame with her hand on the knob.

"So now it's *your* turn to open the door?" he said, reminded of her responses to his polite gesture of moments ago.

Strolling forward, he tapped one finger against his chin. "What did you do next?" he mused. "Ah, yes, then you bid me good evening." Coming to a halt before her, Bryce smiled gently. "Good night, Cassandra."

Reaching out, he fanned her hair between his fingers. "Foolish me, I skipped over when you kissed me good night." He captured her gaze with his. "I wouldn't wish to be any less courteous than you, my dear wife."

"No, you wouldn't want that," she whispered in reply.

Taking her response for the invitation it was, Bryce slowly leaned forward, lifting his hand to bury it in the wealth of hair at the nape of her neck to hold her steady. He brushed his lips against hers, once, twice, until he could stand the torment no longer. With a groan, he deepened the kiss, tasting her, needing her.

When he felt her hands sliding up his arms to curl around his neck, Bryce murmured his pleasure into her mouth and pressed against her. Tilting her head back, he sent his tongue delving into her warmth. Desire pulsed through him as he sensed the passion building within her. Sliding his hand downward, he cupped the soft mound of her bosom.

Cassandra started beneath the touch, but an instant later, she arched into him with a soft moan. The breathless murmur urged him onward. Breaking off their kiss, Bryce began to press his mouth against her neck, tasting her, working his way down until he nibbled upon the curve of her breasts peeking out of her dress. Lifting her breast upward, he sampled the offering, sucking the soft skin into his mouth and laving it with his tongue.

"Oh, Bryce," Cassandra gasped, her fingers curling into his neck.

Passion thundered through him as Bryce lifted his head and captured her moan with his mouth. Indulging in his need for this woman, he kissed her over and over again until his manhood pounded for release. Realizing he was on the brink, Bryce tore his mouth away from hers.

His breath sawed out of his chest as he stared down at his wife. *His wife*. Satisfaction roared through him at the thought. Cupping her head with both his hands, Bryce tipped her head back as he swayed against her, enticing her. Unable to resist, he bent down and claimed her lips once more in a fierce kiss.

Pulling back, he gazed down at her. "Now *that* was a good-night kiss," he rasped.

Cassandra's hands slid down his chest before they dropped to her sides. She gave him a passion-softened smile. "I do so enjoy your kisses."

Her quiet admission made Bryce want to pull her back into his arms, to claim that pouty mouth for his own, to kiss his way down her entire body and then work his way back up again. He shook with the effort to hold back his desire.

He'd promised to court Cassandra, not bed her. After a few more nights of love play, she'd declare her love for him, and then and only then would he satisfy the raw desire pulsating through him.

Clenching his teeth, Bryce walked into his room.

"Good night, Bryce," Cassandra whispered before shutting the door between them.

Standing there, aching with unfulfilled desire, Bryce wondered if his new plan for marital comfort would slowly drive him mad.

The next morning, Cassandra still felt as giddy as the night before. After she'd closed the door behind Bryce, she'd whirled around her room, feeling like a young girl again. No, Cassandra realized, she'd *never* felt like this before.

At the beginning of her first Season, her parents betrothed her to Lord Linley, so she'd never experienced the thrill of gentlemen callers. And, Lord knew, she'd never, ever experienced anything like Bryce's kisses. Just the memory of them set her all atingle.

When Bryce had first touched her breast, she'd stiffened, afraid that he would grope and squeeze her painfully like Linley used to do. But instead he'd cupped her gently, lifted her breast to his mouth, and worshiped her flesh. Growing flushed, Cassandra put those thoughts from her mind. They were far too intimate to dwell upon.

Levering Bryce's breakfast tray on her hip, she knocked once, then pushed open his door. Automatically, she set the tray on the table and went to draw back the curtains.

"Thank you," Bryce mumbled from behind his bed curtains.

Walking over to the bed, Cassandra pulled the curtains back. "You're quite welcome."

"Cassandra?" Bryce murmured sleepily as he levered himself up onto one elbow. "Why on earth are you serving my breakfast?"

Confused, she shook her head. "What do you mean? I've served you breakfast in bed before."

He pushed into a sitting position. "I know, but not for a few days, not since we agreed to end the games."

Understanding brought a smile. "Perhaps I felt like doing it this morning," she said softly.

As she turned to retrieve his breakfast, he caught hold of her hand and lifted it to his mouth. Keeping his gaze fixed upon her, he pressed a slow, intimate kiss into the palm of her hand. "Then I appreciate your effort."

Heat flooded her as the enticing memories from last night filled her. "Bryce," she whispered achingly.

His eyes darkening, Bryce tugged on her hand, pulling her toward him. Just as abruptly as he'd grabbed hold of her hand, he released it, sending her stumbling backward.

Straightening, concern filled his eyes. "Are you all right?"

"Yes, of course."

He must have heard the twinge of confusion in her voice, for he explained his odd actions. "I'm sorry, Cassandra. I forgot myself for a moment and almost pulled you onto my bed." He gave her an intense stare. "If I had, I don't know if I could have stopped myself from—"

She jerked her head up and down. "Yes, I know from what." However, she didn't know if she should thank him or yell at him. Part of her wanted nothing more than to join him, to become his wife in truth as well as in name, but the other part of her, the part still tormented by private demons, dreaded trading the sweet kisses for humiliation and pain.

She knew sharing a marriage bed with Bryce wouldn't be as horrible as it had been with Linley . . . not if Bryce's kisses were any indication.

"Are you hungry?" she asked brightly, changing the subject abruptly.

As she turned with Bryce's tray, she caught his knowing smile. "Starved."

The way he savored the word made her realize he wasn't speaking of food. Warmth flooded her cheeks as she bent down to place his tray on his lap.

"Thank you, darling," he said with a smile.

She gasped at his endearment.

Lifting one brow, he looked at her. "I see I've

been remiss in my duties if one soft word causes that reaction."

"It's quite all right," she mumbled.

"No." His smile faded. "It's not."

At a loss for words, Cassandra stared down at Bryce.

"But I will be certain to correct my behavior in the future." Waving to the tray, he asked, "Would you care to join me?" He hesitated for a moment. "That is unless you've peppered my food again."

Cassandra laughed at the memory. "I didn't add any spices this time."

"Thank God," he murmured in a heartfelt sigh. "I doubt if my tongue could stand another scorching."

"Come now, Bryce. You should know not to challenge me like that," she returned, placing her hands on her hips.

Chuckling, he shook his head. "I should indeed."

"Anyway, I thank you for your kind invitation, but I planned to breakfast with Elaina this morning. I want to hear how her evening went last night after we left her with my parents." And Cassandra doubted if she would be able to swallow a single bite if she sat on Bryce's bed, looking at his bare chest. Her breath fluttered out of her as she turned away from her all too appealing husband.

"I'll see you after breakfast then," he called to her.

"Of course," she returned as she slipped out the door. A few steps down the hallway, Cassandra realized that she'd forgotten to mention the incident with the Earl of Kingwood. Pausing, she hesitated in the hall, wondering if she should go back and tell Bryce.

If she told him, he would become annoyed and it would ruin his whole morning. Shaking her head, Cassandra resumed walking toward the dining room. Let Bryce enjoy his breakfast, dress, and prepare for his day . . . before she ruined it.

13

A lady must always bow to her husband's wishes.

Quoted from *A Lady's Guide to Proper Etiquette*,
written by Lady Cassandra Abbott

The desire simmering inside him flared when Cassandra walked into his study. Immediately abandoning his books, Bryce rose to greet his wife. "This *is* a pleasure."

"I fear you will not think so after you hear what I've come to tell you."

A finger of apprehension skimmed along his spine. "Surely it isn't so bad as all that."

Cassandra bit her lower lip. "Last night while at the ball, Lord Kingwood approached me."

The mere thought of Kingwood conversing with Cassandra made Bryce ill. "What did he say?"

Cassandra's expression didn't help to alleviate any of his anxiety. "To be truthful," she began softly, "I found many of his comments offensive."

"Go on," Bryce directed.

"He said he would like to get to know me better." Cassandra shivered, before admitting, "Though the words themselves seem innocuous, his tone of voice implied something far different."

Anger shook Bryce. "Why didn't you find me and tell me of Kingwood's insult?"

"I was going to after Lord Trinslow came to my aid—"

"Came to your aid?" Bryce's growing anger froze at her words. "Why would Trinslow have to come to your aid if Kingwood only spoke to you?"

He could tell by her expression that she hadn't meant to reveal so much. "As I turned to leave, Lord Kingwood grabbed my wrist and—"

Bryce was unable to contain the surge of raw fury raging through him. "What else did he do?"

"Nothing, Bryce," Cassandra said urgently, placing her hands upon his forearm. "I swear. After Lord Kingwood released me, I danced with Lord Trinslow and then he returned me to your side."

Reaching out, Bryce clasped her shoulders. "Why didn't you tell me immediately of Kingwood's insult?"

"I didn't wish to spoil the evening," she admitted softly. "I knew you'd react in this manner."

Though he was still annoyed that she hadn't come to him immediately, he understood her reason. "I don't want you or Elaina to step from this house until I return."

Alarm darkened her eyes as she grabbed hold of his lapels. "Are you going to track down Kingwood?"

"Of course," he confirmed. "He cannot insult and touch my wife without recourse for his actions."

"You won't do anything foolish like challenge him, will you?"

Since Bryce didn't wish to lie to his wife, he remained silent.

"Dueling is illegal, Bryce. If you don't end up dead from the foolishness, then you'll undoubtedly be placed in gaol."

"Only if an authority finds out about the duel," he pointed out.

"They always find out!" Cassandra tugged on his jacket. "Promise me you won't challenge him to a duel."

Concern had etched three tiny lines on Cassandra's forehead. "Very well," Bryce agreed reluctantly. "However, this is the last time I shall allow you to intervene."

From the sparkle in his wife's gaze, Bryce doubted she had any intention of heeding him. But he had no desire to continue the argument.

Tugging her hands off his jacket, Bryce absently bid her farewell as he left his study, his mind already focused on the confrontation with Kingwood.

"You *bastard!*" Bryce said an instant before his fist plowed into Kingwood's jaw. His muscles quivered with rage as he stood over his ex brother-in-law. All heads in the seedy Gaming Hell were turned to watch the action. "Get up," Bryce snarled, wanting nothing more than to knock the bastard back down again.

"I think not." Leaning back on one elbow, Kingwood fingered his jaw lightly. "Being punched once is enough for one day."

"Coward," Bryce sneered. "Unable to face me,

but perfectly content to sneak behind my back to insult my wife."

"The lovely Cassandra?"

Bryce saw red for a few moments, before he managed to tamp down his fury. "You will address my wife as Lady Amberville."

"I've never been much for titles," Kingwood returned blithely.

Grabbing the front of Kingwood's shirt, Bryce yanked him upward until he could glare into the bastard's eyes. "If you don't stay away from my wife, you shall soon possess the title of Dead Man."

Kingwood laughed bitterly. "Will you kill me as you did my sister, Amberville?"

"I won't stand here and listen to your rot," Bryce retorted. "Just be warned. If you dare bother my wife again, I will destroy you."

Turning on his heel, Bryce strode from the Hell before he did something foolish . . . like give in to his urge to beat Kingwood within an inch of his life.

"Need a hand up?"

Clive snarled at the outstretched arm. "Get the bloody Hell away from me."

"Don't be so quick to toss back my offer of assistance," urged the man, his blue eyes sparkling brilliantly. "I believe I can be of help in more ways than you could imagine."

Before Clive could send the man packing, the stranger bent down and pulled Clive to his feet. Tugging down his jacket, Clive stared at the stranger, taking in his fine clothes, neatly queued silver blond hair, and practiced smile. All in all, the man looked like a bloody dandy. "I rather doubt you could ever help me."

"I beg to differ," he argued. "For, you see, we have an enemy in common."

"Enemy?" Clive glanced toward the door. "Do you mean Amberville?"

The dandy's grin resembled a ghoulish mask. "Yes," he hissed vehemently. "Amberville killed the woman I love." The stranger's eyes filled with an odd light as he stared intensely at Clive. "Francesca."

Clive frowned at that bit of information. "You loved her as well? But she was with Hammond when she died."

"True, but she didn't love him," the man pronounced firmly. "Amberville's treatment forced her to seek love and affection in the arms of others." A muscle began to tick in the stranger's jaw. "While she might have shared the beds of others, I was the one she truly loved."

Staring at the man, Clive felt a chill race over him, but he pushed it away. He was willing to use anything or anyone, crazy or not, who would help him achieve his ultimate goal—to destroy Amberville.

Holding out his hand, Clive introduced himself. "Clive Milford, Earl of Kingwood."

The dandy nodded. "I know," he said, before holding out his own hand. "Evan Stanford, Marquess of Dranwyck, at your service."

Indeed he would be, Clive thought as he held back a smile. He'd make certain Stanford was at his service.

* * *

Having abandoned her book, Cassandra sat in her salon, staring out the window . . . and worrying. What was her husband going to do to Lord Kingwood when—

The sound of the front door opening caught Cassandra's attention. Leaping up from her chair, she rushed out into the foyer to greet her husband and very nearly ran right into Lord Trinslow.

The young man reached out to steady her. "My lady," he began as his cheeks flushed with embarrassment. "I do hope I haven't called at an inopportune moment."

"No, of course not," Cassandra hurried to reassure Lord Trinslow. "I am delighted you came to visit us."

His Adam's apple bobbed in his throat. "I am . . . that is . . . thank you for inviting me," he finished in an awkward rush.

Lord Trinslow appeared very, very young at that moment. Putting aside her worries about Bryce, Cassandra stepped forward to link arms with the nervous lord. "Might I offer you a—"

Before she could finish the sentence, Bryce strode into the foyer, his body practically vibrating with anger. "Bryce," she exclaimed, releasing her hold upon Lord Trinslow to rush to her husband's side. "I'm so glad you're home." Unable to stop herself, she ran her hands down his chest, reassuring herself that he was unharmed.

Capturing her hands in his, he drew her to his side as he turned toward their guest. "Lord Trinslow," Bryce said in greeting as he bowed to the young lord. "I am in your debt."

Lord Trinslow's mouth dropped open. "No need

for thanks, Your Grace," he said, his voice cracking. "I was merely aiding a lady in need, as any gentleman would in that situation."

"Perhaps, but it wasn't any gentleman; it was you, Trinslow," Bryce pointed out. "So it is to you that I am indebted."

Cassandra watched the young lord's chest puff up at Bryce's pronouncement. Despite her gratitude to Lord Trinslow, she wished he had called later in the day . . . after she'd had a chance to speak with Bryce in private and learn about his meeting with Lord Kingwood.

"If you'd told me we were having a family gathering in the foyer, I would have come down sooner," Elaina said with a laugh as she hurried down the stairs. "Why are you— Oh," she remarked, catching sight of Lord Trinslow. "Sorry. I didn't see you there."

Cassandra saw Bryce's jaw tighten at Elaina's offhand comment. "Elaina, I would like to introduce our guest to you." Reaching out, she wrapped her arm around Elaina's waist and drew her niece forward. "This is Andrew Polk, Viscount of Trinslow. May I present my niece, Lady Elaina Keene?"

Lord Trinslow bowed to Elaina, but he spoiled the elegant gesture by stumbling forward. Flushing deeply once more, he regained his balance and straightened.

Wanting to redirect Elaina's attention before she commented upon Lord Trinslow's awkwardness, Cassandra turned toward her niece. "Are you going riding in the park?" she asked, taking note of Elaina's elegant riding habit.

Though her eyes sparkled with ill-concealed

humor, Elaina thankfully refrained from any disparaging remarks about Lord Trinslow's awkwardness. "Indeed. I plan to take in a bit of fresh air," she replied after a moment.

Though surprised by her niece's restraint, Cassandra wasn't going to question her luck. "That sounds delightful," she murmured.

Lord Trinslow nodded enthusiastically. "It most certainly does. The weather is splendid today."

Inspiration struck Cassandra. "Since the idea strikes you as a fine one, my lord, why don't you join my niece on her ride?"

"Cassandra!" gasped Elaina. "You can't be serious."

"I most certainly am," she countered, leveling a stern look at her niece. "As a guest in our house, we must afford Lord Trinslow every opportunity to enjoy himself while here." Naturally, Cassandra didn't add that she wanted time alone with Bryce to question him.

Stepping forward, Lord Trinslow smiled tentatively at Elaina. "I truly would enjoy keeping you company . . . if you don't mind, that is."

In the face of such a heartfelt request, even Elaina couldn't turn him down. Hesitating only to send Cassandra a fierce glare, Elaina capitulated. "It would be my pleasure."

Bidding them farewell, Lord Trinslow escorted Elaina out the front door. As soon as they disappeared from sight, Cassandra rounded on her husband. "What happened in your meeting with Lord Kingwood?"

Amusement glittered in his eyes as he glanced

around the foyer. "I believe my study is a better lo-
cation for this discussion," he murmured as he led
her down the hallway.

The moment they reached the privacy of Bryce's
study, Cassandra again turned toward him. "Please,
Bryce, I wish to know what happened."

Lifting one shoulder, he trailed a finger along
her jawline. "Nothing much at all happened."

She allowed her doubt to show in her expression.

"Don't believe me?" Bryce asked with a laugh.
"Well, it's the truth. I merely warned Kingwood
against bothering you again."

"And that's all that happened?"

"Other than the fact that I knocked him to the
ground with a punch, yes."

His casual remark set her off. "You hit him?" At
Bryce's nod, she grasped his arms. "What if he chal-
lenges you?"

"Kingwood doesn't have the nerve," he scoffed
with a disgusted expression. "Don't worry anymore. Kingwood has slithered away from fights for
as long as I've known him. Now that he's aware I'll
ruin him if he so much as looks at you, I doubt
we'll be troubled by him again."

The fierceness of Bryce's reply troubled Cassandra.
"While Lord Kingwood's comments were offensive,
they didn't warrant such a vehement response."

"I know Kingwood and the man is a snake,"
Bryce rasped, his hands tightening upon her shoulders. "Trust me when I say he deserves every bit of
my anger."

As Cassandra tried to piece together the facts,
she couldn't help feeling there was something im-

portant that Bryce wasn't telling her. "What happened between you and Lord King—"

"What is between me and Kingwood is in the past and there it will remain."

"I believe it's already too late for that," Cassandra pointed out.

Thrusting a hand through his hair, Bryce rounded his desk. "Please, Cassandra, my day has been very trying and I have no desire to continue this discussion." He sat down and retrieved his quill. "Suffice it to say, Kingwood will no longer be an issue in our lives. Now, if you would excuse me, I've wasted enough time on this matter and really need to balance these ledgers."

His dismissal sent her staggering backward. "Sorry to have been a bother, my lord," she said tartly, before striding from the room.

Elaina tried not to laugh, but she wasn't certain if she could hold back any longer. Glancing over at her companion, she asked, "Have you ever ridden before?"

"Certainly," Lord Trinslow said firmly, before a sheepish grin split his face. "Once."

With that, she lost the battle. "I find your honesty most appealing," she admitted with a laugh, "and not at all what I would expect from a viscount."

An expression of chagrin twisted Lord Trinslow's features. "I realize that my blunt manner has caused me no small amount of problems." He wobbled on his saddle again and released the reins to grab hold of the saddle.

How well Elaina understood that problem, she thought, feeling a sense of empathy for the gawky viscount.

"I must say, though, that I am truly enjoying this ride with you, my lady," he added with a smile as he fumbled for the reins.

Eyeing his awkward movements, she couldn't help but laugh. "Perhaps you enjoy the company, Lord Trinslow, but I find it difficult to believe that you are enjoying the ride itself."

"You've found me out." His wide grin transformed his plain face, making him look surprisingly appealing. "Who would have thought a saddle could be so hard?"

"If you post, it makes the ride much smoother and easier on your posterior." As soon as the words slipped out of her mouth, Elaina wondered if Lord Trinslow would be offended by her reference to such an intimate body part. Heavens, all these rules could be very wearying.

"I'm certain you're correct," he acknowledged smoothly, obviously not offended in the least. "However, since I haven't the faintest clue as to how or even what posting is, I fear I am doomed to forgo sitting this evening." Wobbling on the saddle, he pointed toward an overgrown bush. "Be careful here, my lady," he warned as he reached out and pulled back the thick branch that hung over the path.

Charmed by his gallantry, Elaina nudged her horse forward, past Lord Trinslow, as he wrestled to hold back the branch. Turning in her saddle, she smiled at her escort. "With service such as that, I shall have to bring you riding with me all the time."

A groan escaped Lord Trinslow. "While I would enjoy the company, I fear my hindquarters couldn't stand the strain." He kneed his horse into sidestepping a few inches. "Careful while I release this branch."

Realizing her horse was too near the branch, Elaina shook her head. "No—"

But it was too late.

The offending branch whipped forward, catching her horse in the leg. Startled, the animal bolted forward in a full run, jerking the reins from Elaina's fingers and nearly tossing her from his back in the process. All she could do was hold on for dear life.

14

A lady must never address a gentleman without proper introduction.

Quoted from *A Lady's Guide to Proper Etiquette*,
written by Lady Cassandra Abbott

Well, well, well. Don't I have the devil's own luck?
Clive thought as he watched none other than Amberville's precious niece race past him on a runaway horse. He'd heard stories about the headstrong girl who drove her uncle to distraction with her wild antics.

It was precisely the opportunity Clive needed. If the girl were Hell-bent on behaving in a reckless manner, he was more than willing to escort her down the slippery path to dissoluteness. And, in the process, exact his revenge upon Amberville by completely corrupting his niece.

Absolutely perfect.

Kicking his horse into a gallop, he charged off to save the silly chit.

Like a knight from her girlhood fairytale books, a breathtaking man with his hair flying gloriously behind him pulled his horse even with hers. Reaching out, he grabbed hold of her dangling reins and slowed her horse's headlong race to a sedate walk and then to a stop. Elaina's heart pounded in her chest as she gazed at the gentleman.

White teeth flashed in his smile. "Are you all right, my lady?"

With his wicked good looks, he stole her breath, making it difficult to reply. "I . . . Yes, I am," she finally managed. "Thank you."

Sending his thick, dark hair off his forehead with a toss of his head, he returned the reins to her. "I am simply glad that I could be of assistance to a lady in need." He pressed his fingertips to his chest. "Allow me to introduce myself. I am Clive Milford, Earl of Kingwood."

She couldn't keep her gaze off his perfectly shaped mouth as he formed the words of introduction. Shaking her head, Elaina tried to regain a modicum of poise. "Lady Elaina Keene," she replied, holding out her hand to him. "It is a pleasure to make your acquaintance."

Accepting her hand, he kissed the back of her glove-encased fingers. "No, my lady," he whispered, glancing up at her from his bent position to gaze deeply into her eyes. "The pleasure is truly mine."

She felt something flutter inside of her. "Lord Kingwood, I am—"

"*Elaina!*"

Why did Lord Trinslow have to pick this moment to come crashing out of the underbrush? She wanted a few more minutes, no, a few more hours, to converse with the charming Lord Kingwood. Instead, she watched Lord Trinslow make his way toward them, barely clinging to his horse.

"Is that your escort?" murmured Lord Kingwood, a smile playing upon his fine lips.

She hastened to assure the handsome earl that there was nothing between her and the awkward Lord Trinslow. "My aunt asked him to ride with me."

"Ahhh." His small exclamation held a wealth of meaning. "I am relieved to hear you say that." Turning his head, he recaptured her gaze, hypnotizing her with an intense look. "I would hate to think your hand was already spoken for."

Speech was beyond her.

Shooting a quick glance at Lord Trinslow, who was slowly managing to close the distance between them, Lord Kingwood trailed his gloved hand along her cheek. "I shall leave you to your escort . . . for now," he added, his tone low and intimate. "I shall look forward to seeing you again, Lady Elaina Keene."

Excitement filled her at the very thought. "As shall I," she replied breathlessly.

Flashing her one more grin, he wheeled his horse around and galloped off with the skill of a master horseman. Sighing, she watched until he slipped through the trees and disappeared, before nudging her horse toward Lord Trinslow as he tried to guide his mount.

"You appear to be having a spot of trouble, my lord," Elaina called, finally able to breathe again now that the intriguing Lord Kingwood had left.

"Elaina, you are unhurt."

The relief in Lord Trinslow's voice made her smile. "Indeed, I am."

Yanking back on the reins, Lord Trinslow brought his horse to a halt. "I can't apologize enough for releasing that branch too soon. If anything had happened to you, I doubt I could have forgiven myself."

"Luckily for you, there is no need to concern yourself any longer on my behalf." Holding out her arm wide, Elaina offered him a reassuring smile. "As you can see, I am perfectly fine and completely unharmed." Warmth flooded her as she thought of Lord Kingwood. "Luckily for me, the Earl of Kingwood saw my plight and rescued me. Quite the brave gentleman," she finished, unable to keep her voice from softening.

Lord Trinslow's eyes narrowed, his gaze shifting toward the woods where Lord Kingwood had disappeared. "I have my doubts as to whether one could refer to Kingwood as a gentleman," he muttered under his breath.

His remark aroused her curiosity. How could anyone who was so courtly be anything less? "His lordship struck me as the perfect gentleman."

"I have no wish to disagree with you, Lady Elaina, so I shall simply refrain from discussing Kingwood at all."

Such a remark from a gentleman who struck her as mild-mannered deepened her curiosity about the all too intriguing Lord Kingwood.

"Are you ready to return home?" Lord Trinslow lifted a brow. "I've had quite enough of horseback riding for one day and I can only imagine that you feel the same after your wild ride."

If Lord Kingwood were here to accompany her, Elaina was quite certain she could have continued to ride for hours upon hours. However, one glance at Lord Trinslow's pained expression convinced her it was time to return home. "You are correct, my lord. I have had quite enough riding for today."

Watching Lord Trinslow attempt to turn his horse around spurred Elaina to make a rather unusual request. "My lord," she called to him, wincing as he pulled back on the horse's reins again. "I wonder if you might grant me a boon."

"If it is within my power," he replied immediately. "You have only to ask."

The viscount's gentle manner made her smile. "I'm afraid I'm a bit unnerved still and would prefer to lead the horses home."

"You wish to walk home?"

Hope mingled with relief in Lord Trinslow's gaze, telling Elaina that he appreciated her suggestion. "If you don't mind," she murmured.

"No, my lady. No, of course not," he stammered, unable to get the words out quickly enough. Awkwardly, he flung his right leg over the horse and slid off the saddle on the wrong side.

Elaina held her breath when Lord Trinslow walked behind the back of her horse, a foolish move for anyone who didn't wish to be kicked. She let loose a sigh of relief when he reached her unscathed. Grasping her waist, he gently lowered her to the ground, surprising her at his easy strength.

Again, he grinned in a friendly, appealing manner as he headed back around her mount to retrieve the reins of his horse. As he grabbed hold of the leather straps, Lord Trinslow stumbled over a rock, causing him to fall forward and tug sharply on the reins. His horse let out a whinny in protest.

Smiling bashfully at her, Lord Trinslow lifted one shoulder. "Oops."

Holding in a chuckle, Elaina wondered what other mishaps would befall him before they reached the Keene townhouse.

Bryce slammed the ledger shut with a sigh of disgust. He'd been staring at the blasted book for over an hour now and had yet to read one number. Thoughts of his wife continued to invade his peace of mind. Why couldn't she ever behave in a calm, deferring fashion like a proper wife? The way she'd stormed out of his study had spoken of her anger toward him, but he'd be damned before he'd apologize to her.

The worst part of it all was that he wanted to do precisely that. He'd sat here fighting the urge to chase after Cassandra, to apologize, to do anything necessary to make her smile at him again.

And it was that urge, that weakness, that kept him in his chair now.

Couldn't she see she was being impossible? Bryce thought, tossing down his pen. This matter with Kingwood was for him to handle . . . without her intrusion. But did his wife understand that? No! She expected to dictate his actions, to control him.

"Pardon the intrusion, Your Grace, but I wondered if I might have a moment of your time."

Shaking loose thoughts of Cassandra, Bryce waved Trinslow into his study. "Of course. Please come in," he bid the younger man. "Can I get you a brandy?" he offered as he rounded his desk.

"No, thank you, Your Grace."

"There is no need to address me so formally, Trinslow." Bryce laid a hand on the young man's shoulder. "When a man is indebted to you, Trinslow, you can call him any damn thing you want."

For an instant, Trinslow looked stunned, then a relaxed grin slid onto his face. "I suppose you are correct, Your—" He caught himself. ". . . Amberville."

"See? That wasn't so hard, was it?" Bryce slapped Trinslow's back in camaraderie, before moving toward the sideboard. "Are you certain you won't join me in a drink?"

"Positive." Lord Trinslow cleared his throat. "I wanted to inform you of an incident that occurred while I was riding with Lady Elaina."

Bryce unstopped the decanter and filled a glass to the top. A man needed fortification before hearing another humiliating tale of his niece. Taking a healthy swallow, Bryce braced himself before he turned back toward Trinslow. "What did she do now?"

"Do?" Trinslow's brows drew together as he shook his head in confusion. "You are mistaken if you believe Lady Elaina behaved in a less than decorous manner."

Well, that certainly wasn't what Bryce was expecting to hear. Some of the tension seeped out of his body. "Of course, I didn't mean to imply that," he said, lying smoothly. "I know my niece is a proper young lady." Lord, he couldn't believe God didn't strike him down where he stood for such a blatant lie.

"As do I, Your Grace," Trinslow agreed readily. "The matter I wished to discuss was what happened after Lady Elaina's horse bolted and—"

Brandy sloshed over the edge of his glass as Bryce started at the revelation. "Was she hurt?"

"No, Your Grace," Trinslow hurried to reassure him. "She is perfectly fine. I only mention the incident at all because of what happened afterward." Something in the viscount's tone made Bryce wary. "Lord Kingwood rescued your niece."

Bryce was surprised his glass didn't shatter within his grasp as fury raged through him. "What happened?"

Trinslow stiffened at the gruffness in Bryce's tone. "By the time I caught up with Lady Elaina, Kingwood had already departed, so I was unable to overhear their conversation. While Lady Elaina assured me nothing untoward was said, I felt it best to mention the incident to you."

"Yes, you did the right thing," Bryce replied, his anger abating as logic calmed him. "You say her horse bolted, so how did Kingwood know she'd be in that particular spot at that specific time?"

"He didn't; he couldn't possibly have known," Trinslow replied as he tugged down on his vest. "Which is precisely why I hesitated to mention this to you at all. It was simply rotten luck that brought him to Lady Elaina's rescue. Still, I felt it best that you knew of the chance meeting."

"I appreciate you keeping me informed." Bryce

lifted his glass to Trinslow. "I am now doubly indebted to you."

Trinslow's lips quirked upward. "As much as I'd like to accept your gratitude, I must inform you it is misplaced. After all, I'm the reason her horse bolted in the first place." He shook his head. "For some reason I'm clumsy and inept at everything whenever I'm around your niece. It's as if she's bewitched me and I can't even think straight when I'm around her."

"I empathize completely, my friend," Bryce murmured, thinking of his troubles with Cassandra. "Women can be the devil's own torment, can't they?"

Nodding firmly, Trinslow sank into one of the wing-backed chairs. "On second thought, I do believe I'll join you in a brandy. It might help steady my nerves."

Bryce didn't bother to conceal his grin as he poured Trinslow a drink.

Cassandra gazed out the window, lost in her thoughts. All afternoon, she'd been upset over Bryce's refusal to discuss the situation with Kingwood. Instead, he'd told her to stay out of the affair, to let him handle the matter as he saw fit, making her feel shut out, unwanted.

And yet wasn't she shutting him out as well?

Straightening, Cassandra sent Poco sliding off her lap as she realized the simple answer to her problem. Here she'd been upset with Bryce . . . instead of realizing she should be upset with herself, too.

She'd asked for a new beginning, yet she'd remained guarded, hiding behind the security of her provisions. She craved an intimacy with her husband, but was unwilling to face her fears.

That was it! Rising, Cassandra walked toward the connecting door and placed her hands upon the cool wood. Their lives would remain separate until one of them opened the way. For the past week, she'd grown to admire her husband for his strong sense of honor, his patience, even his cleverness. She'd also tasted passion for the first time in her life, lessening her fears of the marriage bed.

Yet she'd held herself back from him, not wanting to give ground, unwilling to share her innermost thoughts with him. So, because of this silly game they'd begun, they would be forever trapped in a marriage of convenience, neither side giving more than the other. And, surprisingly enough, she realized she *did* want more.

For the first time in her life, she wanted a husband to love . . . and for him to return her love.

Shaking at the notion, Cassandra dropped her forehead against the wooden panel, wondering if she was brave enough to take that first step toward true intimacy. A gasp broke from her as she heard Bryce enter his room. Undoubtedly he was changing into his evening clothes and would soon leave to pursue his nightly pleasures at White's.

It was now or never.

Taking a deep breath, Cassandra swallowed her fears and opened the door between their rooms.

15

A lady submits to her husband's intimate needs without complaint.

Quoted from *A Lady's Guide to Proper Etiquette*,
written by Lady Cassandra Abbott

Bryce's hands stilled upon his cravat as he turned to face Cassandra. Leaving herself no means of escape, she stepped farther into the room and shut the door firmly behind her. "Pardon the intrusion, Bryce, but I needed to speak with you before you leave for the evening."

Wearily, he tugged the silk from around his neck. "I don't know if I can handle another argument, Cassandra."

"I don't wish to argue with you," she hurried to assure him. "This afternoon, my anger toward you was unfair."

That admission captured his attention. Tossing aside his cravat, he urged her to continue. "I like the way *this* conversation is heading."

His remark did little to ease her nervousness. "I rather thought you would," she replied with a wavering smile. "You see, I was completely unjustified in my anger because I expected you to be open about your past . . . when I myself have not been."

Slowly, Bryce settled upon the arm of his settee.

"After all, how could I expect you to share when I've been hiding—"

"Cassandra," Bryce interrupted, cutting her off. "Why don't you sit down and make yourself comfortable before you tell me about your life with Linley?"

"Yes, why don't I?" she mumbled. Taking a calming breath, she perched on the opposite end of the settee and faced her husband. "My parents arranged my marriage to the duke, and though I had some misgivings because of his advanced age, I would never have dreamed of refusing their choice."

"You were expected to accept their match without demur," Bryce added softly.

"Exactly." Though his understanding should have relieved her, Cassandra tensed even further as she allowed dark memories to swamp her. "I'd always been told that if I followed the rules, I would have a perfect life." She shook her head. "But that wasn't true. My life with Alfred was horrible."

She saw Bryce's jaw tighten, but he remained silent, allowing her to continue. "On my wedding night, Alfred came to my room, tossed up my gown, and . . ." She trailed off, unable to voice the embarrassing moment.

"Consummated the marriage," Bryce supplied, his even tone helping her to regain her control.

"Yes," she whispered, unable to stop herself from twisting her hands together. "For the first few months, he would come to my room every few nights. Each encounter was painful, but blessedly short, taking no more than a few minutes. However, when I failed to become pregnant, Alfred became angry, blaming me . . . so, he berated me mercilessly. From that moment on, I was subjected to constant humiliation. He would speak of my failings in front of the servants, family, even the few guests who would call upon us. I was not allowed to leave the house without his permission and if I did, I was locked in my room for days until I begged for release."

Tears blurred her vision as she gazed up at Bryce. "I hated him."

Shifting onto the settee next to her, Bryce placed a comforting arm around her. "You don't need to say any more, Cassandra. That part of your life is over now."

"But it's not over," she replied fiercely, wiping the tears off her cheeks. "I'm allowing my fear from the past to shape my present. Why do you think I asked for all those provisions?"

Lifting his hand, he cupped her cheek. "There is nothing to fear between us, Cassandra," he whispered, his breath brushing against her lips.

"I-I realize that now." The desire simmering in his gaze burned away the last of her dark memories. "Your kisses make me feel things I never even imagined. You taught me the meaning of desire. You showed me passion."

"Let me show you more," Bryce rasped.

Looking into his eyes, Cassandra felt the rightness of this moment, of this man, wash over her . . . and she surrendered to her emotions.

"Yes," she murmured, closing the distance between them.

His mouth covered hers, capturing her lips in a hungry kiss that drew her into him. Sliding her arms around his neck, she fell into the embrace, pressing her body against his, eager for his caress. Bryce's hand slid onto the base of her neck, holding her steady for his deep kiss, while the other curved around her waist, lifting her until she lay upon his lap.

With skilled fingers, he plucked at the pins holding her hair in place, tossing them unheeded onto the floor until the entire length of her hair spilled down her back in glorious abandon. A groan rumbled from his throat as Bryce sent his tongue plunging inward, sweeping through her mouth in bone-shivering thoroughness.

She murmured softly in protest when he dragged his mouth from hers, but, as his lips descended onto the curve of her neck, she shivered in anticipation. Bryce sunk his fingers into the wealth of her hair, tugging gently, until she arched her neck to accommodate his devastating kisses.

"Cassandra," he rasped against her moistened flesh. Slowly, he traced the line of her back, reaching the fastenings on her dress. With practiced ease, he loosened her dress, undoing all the catches to her waist, allowing the garment to slip off her shoulders.

Welcoming the coolness to her heated flesh, Cassandra eagerly helped Bryce to remove the gown. Bryce recaptured her mouth in a hungry kiss, devouring her soft murmurs of delight as he trailed his fingers along the upper edge of her corset.

One tug released the ribbon on the boned garment, before he tossed it aside. Reeling from the heady sensation of freedom, Cassandra pressed herself against Bryce's hard chest, reveling in the feel of her near-naked body touching his.

For the first time, she felt desire lick at her, beckoning her forth toward the delights of the flesh. Heeding the call, she tugged in frustration at his shirt, wanting to touch him. Bryce broke off the kiss and tossed the garment over his head, flinging it aside without a care. Her hand shook as she ran the tips of her fingers along the curves she'd so longed to touch.

His gaze burned into hers, mesmerizing her, as he eased her chemise off her shoulders, pulling it down until it too lay about her waist. Her breath shuddered from her when he cupped the fullness of her breast, satisfying an ache inside of her. Moaning softly, she leaned forward, pressing into his palm.

Sliding his arm around her, Bryce arched her back until she lay open to him. He bent closer, pausing to kiss along her collar bone, then trailing a moist path downward onto the top of her breasts. Her fingers speared into his hair, holding onto him, as he captured her taut nipple between his lips. Swirling his tongue around the sensitive flesh, Bryce sent streaks of raw need racing through her. Nothing in her previous experience of awkward fumblings and humiliating gropings had prepared her for the earth-shattering sensations Bryce created within her.

"I need you," he rasped against her flesh.

"Bryce," she murmured, not even recognizing her own passion-laden voice.

Capturing her mouth once more, he continued to kiss her hungrily as he lifted her up into his arms and strode to his bed. Gently, he lowered her to the coverlet, sweeping his hand downward to push her dress and chemise off her body.

Bryce drew back to gaze at her. Laying before him in nothing more than her stockings, Cassandra suddenly felt completely vulnerable. Unbidden, a frisson of fear sparked inside of her and she instinctively covered her womanhood with one hand and crossed her other hand over her breasts.

Understanding softened Bryce's gaze as he stroked the backs of his fingers down her cheek. "I shall take care of you, Cassandra. You have no need to fear me."

In her heart she knew his words to be true, but dark memories of painful gropings held her still. Helplessly, she shook her head.

Rising from the bed, Bryce swiftly removed his breeches, straightening to stand in naked glory before her. "Look at me," he ordered softly. "You can trust me."

Slowly, she raised her eyes to meet his gaze. Trust him. He'd honored their agreement despite his anger, he'd treated her with respect, he'd even admitted his mistakes and apologized for them. The knot of fear began to ease as she realized she could indeed trust him.

Lifting her hand, she silently bid him forth.

His eyes flamed with banked fires as he accepted her invitation, lowering himself next to her. Cupping her face between his hands, he sealed their lips together, seeking and finding her desire that so perfectly matched his. Sliding her hands across his back, Cassandra savored the feel of his smooth, warm flesh against her palms. Caught up in a frenzy of need, she dipped her hands lower until her fingertips swept along the rise of his taut buttocks.

Bryce tore his mouth from hers to stare down at her, his expression fierce with desire. "Yes, Cassandra," he moaned as he lowered his head to her breasts once again. "Touch me."

Her fear burned away by his fiery caresses, Cassandra indulged in her every whim, her every desire, as she stroked along his muscular shoulders, down his defined arms, along the ridges of his ribs. And Bryce matched her every move, mirroring her boldness, accepting her intimate attentions and returning them with his own.

Cassandra shook with desire when Bryce shifted downward on the bed, his mouth making a foray toward her navel, taking soft love bites along her sensitized skin. Skimming his hand along her outer thigh, he pushed down her stocking to her knee. Bryce curved his hand under her calf and lifted her leg until it lay bent across his waist. One smooth stroke down the rest of her leg and onto her foot removed her stocking completely.

Trembling with need, Cassandra pushed off the other stocking before turning on her side and pressing herself fully against him. A perfect fit. A low moan reverberated deep in Bryce's chest as he rolled them over until he lay on top of her. Rejoicing in his weight, Cassandra wrapped her arms around his back, gasping as he rocked his lower body against hers. Without conscious thought, she parted her legs, welcoming him to seek her most intimate part.

Levering himself off to one side, Bryce curved his hand over her moistened womanhood, dipping one finger inward into her wetness. For an instant, she remembered the painful prodding of her first husband, but with one erotic swirl, Bryce destroyed that image and replaced it with his own beautiful memory. Unable to help herself, she lifted her hips, greeting his hand with a cry of pleasure.

Her eyes closed as passion pulsated through her, pushing her ever higher. Arching her back, she silently urged him to continue with his delicious caress. In response, he sent another finger curling into her.

Clutching at the coverlet, Cassandra could only ride the wonderful, unbelievable sensations thundering through her. A murmur of protest escaped her when Bryce removed his fingers. Opening her eyes, she fell still in shock as she saw Bryce settle his shoulders between her legs. "What are you doing?" she gasped, instinctively trying to draw her legs together.

"Trust me," he murmured, his hot breath rushing over her.

Without another word, he lowered his mouth to her most intimate of areas and gifted her with a very special kiss. White-hot streaks of desire coursed through her, draining Cassandra of her protests. Closing her eyes, she sank her fingers into his hair, holding onto him as he drove her passion harder, faster, higher.

Her entire body began to quiver with the overwhelming sensations he evoked in her while he continued to torment her with his wicked kisses. Cassandra forgot to breathe when Bryce deepened the kiss and she burst into flames beneath his touch.

Shivers raced along her skin as she trembled in the aftermath of passion fulfilled. Feeling Bryce work his way up her body, she opened her eyes to gaze at him in wonderment. "I've never . . ." She didn't even know how to put such incredible feelings into words.

A corner of his mouth turned upward. "I know."

Entwining their fingers together, Bryce lowered his weight onto Cassandra, allowing his masculine hardness to rest against her womanhood. She drew in a sharp breath when Bryce shifted his hips, inexorably pressing forward, melding their bodies into one. Her sense of satiation disappeared as an urgent need to bond with this man seared through her. Circling her hips upward, Cassandra sought to deepen Bryce's possession.

He smiled into her eyes as he thrust into her, completing their coupling, completing her. "Are you all right?" he rasped, his voice tight and raw.

Nodding frantically, she arched against him. "Please . . ." she begged, uncertain what her body craved even though she knew Bryce held the answer.

Shuddering at her entreaty, Bryce began to move in a slow, steady rhythm, bringing gasps of pleasure with each stroke. His tempo increased as he surged into her over and over again, thrusting her toward that glorious explosion of sensation.

"Bryce!" His name ripped from her.

With one last thrust, Bryce joined her, his every muscle tensing as he emptied his essence into her. Shaking with tiny tremors, Bryce slowly lowered himself onto her.

Releasing her hands, Bryce finally shifted to the side, tucking Cassandra against him. Contentment beyond any she'd ever known filled her near to bursting.

"Bryce, that was . . ." Adequate description escaped her. How could she possibly give voice to the incredible sensations that had torn through her?

"Beyond words," he finished for her in a perfect melding of their minds.

Resting her hand upon his chest, she sighed contentedly. "Exactly."

16

A lady should never question her husband's dictates.

Quoted from *A Lady's Guide to Proper Etiquette,*
written by Lady Cassandra Abbott

Stretching her arms above her head, Cassandra awoke with a delicious sense of well-being. Bryce. In one glance, she realized she was now alone in his bedchamber. Smiling like a well-fed cat, she snuggled into his bed, giving in to the urge to giggle.

She was in love.

Even in the bright morning light, that admission didn't frighten her. Not after last night. Not after Bryce showed her how he truly felt through his gentle touch and tender care. How wonderful it was to realize that her marriage of convenience had indeed turned into a love match.

Retrieving her husband's robe from the foot of the bed, Cassandra rose to face the glorious new day. Tightening the belt of the robe, she twirled around in a giddy circle, before hurrying toward her own room to dress.

Calling for her maid, Cassandra rushed through

her ablutions, eager to seek out Bryce. While checking the finishing touches to her hair, Cassandra heard a knock on her door. Thinking it was Bryce, she ran across the room and flung open the door.

"Elaina?" Cassandra asked, trying to keep the disappointment out of her voice.

Dropping her hands from her face, Elaina revealed her tear-stained cheeks. "He's *horrid!*"

Drawing her niece into the room, Cassandra dismissed her maid before seeking an explanation. Naturally, she didn't need to ask who *he* was. "What happened between you and your uncle this morning? It's early yet . . . even for the two of you," Cassandra remarked, hoping her levity would lessen Elaina's tears.

"This is not a matter for jest," Elaina cried. "He forbid me to leave this house without him by my side."

Confused, Cassandra shook her head. "Why would he do that? There have been no . . . incidents of late," she said, choosing her words carefully.

"He's upset with me for speaking with Lord Kingwood yesterday."

Lord Kingwood yet again, Cassandra thought with a frown, remembering Bryce's fierce reaction to the earl.

Elaina swiped at her tears. "Heavens, Cassandra, Lord Kingwood saved me yesterday. What would my uncle have me do? Completely ignore the man who stopped my runaway horse? He's being completely unreasonable."

Given the circumstances as Elaina explained them, Cassandra tended to agree with her niece.

Still, she refrained from expressing her opinion. "I shall speak to His Grace and discuss this matter with him," she offered instead.

"You'll make him realize he's being completely—"

"Unreasonable," Cassandra finished for her agitated niece. "However, until I speak with him, I don't know if his reaction is warranted or not."

Cassandra could tell from Elaina's expression that she wasn't happy with the reply. "I shall come around to your room as soon as I speak with your uncle."

Sighing, Elaina hugged Cassandra briefly. "Thank you," she murmured, before heading from the room.

Cassandra released her breath as she rubbed at her forehead. Dealing with this problem was the last thing she'd imagined herself doing this morning. Unfortunately, she'd been given no choice. Smoothing out her skirts, Cassandra went in search of her husband.

The moment she entered Bryce's study, Cassandra could see he was still upset. His expression remained cool as he gazed up at her. "What can I do for you this morning, Cassandra?"

His frosty reception chilled the glow of happiness inside of her. What had happened to the man from last night? Deciding to put aside her hurt, she forced a teasing note into her voice as she said, "I came for my good-morning kiss."

One brow lifted. "Pardon me?"

Trying to remain undaunted from his lack of welcome, she strolled farther into the room. "I believe it is customary to kiss your wife good morning."

He rubbed his hands across his face. "Forgive my foul mood, Cassandra. I've had a devil of a morning so far," he murmured, his apology soothing her. He rose from his desk, coming around to kiss her soundly. "Let's begin again, shall we?" he murmured when he finally pulled back. "Good morning."

Wrapping her arms around his back, she smiled up at him. "Good morning to you, too." She stroked her hand down his spine. "Are you upset because of your argument with Elaina?"

He jerked back to stare down at her. "How did you know?"

"Elaina came to my room this morning," Cassandra explained, allowing her arms to fall to her sides as Bryce stepped back. "She was very upset as well."

"She'll get over it."

Bryce's gruff response startled her. "Bryce, you need to make your peace with Elaina," Cassandra urged, purposely keeping her voice smooth and calm. "If you are going to banish her to this house, you should at least give her a sound explanation."

All traces of warmth left Bryce's expression. "I am her uncle and her guardian. I have my reasons for the request and should not have to explain my every action to a young girl."

"Of course not," Cassandra agreed readily. "But sometimes you do need to explain yourself, Bryce, even if only to keep the peace."

Bryce frowned down at her. "Kingwood is dangerous," he said firmly. "I thought I made myself quite clear during our discussion yesterday."

"If you'd only tell me why . . ."

His fingers flexed. "You trusted me last night,"

he pointed out. "Why can't you trust me in this matter as well and simply take my word for it?"

"Because I can't do that." Grasping his lapels, Cassandra implored him to understand. "I opened myself up to you last night. I told you about my marriage to Alfred, even about my childhood and how little control I had over my life. Please don't ask me to blindly follow your demands without understanding the reasons behind them." She gazed up at him. "I'm not your servant, Bryce. I'm your partner."

He looked at her as if she were spouting nonsense. "You are my *wife*, not my partner," he returned. "I thought you understood that since you surrendered to—"

"I did not *surrender*," she exclaimed, interrupting Bryce without a qualm. "When I came to you and told you of my past, I was merely making the first step. Now it is your turn to open to me as well, to let me into your life, both past and present."

His eyes widened. "I think not."

Those three words pierced her heart. "But you must, Bryce, if we are ever to have a true marriage between us."

"Our marriage is true," he said with a shake of his head. "We exchanged vows—"

"I'm not speaking of vows; I'm talking about exchanging hearts."

His expression softened. Reaching out, he tucked a loose tendril behind her ear. "If you fell in love with me, you wouldn't have to worry. I would protect your heart."

"As I would yours."

His hand dropped to his side and he fell suspiciously silent. The pain in her heart grew. "How foolish of me," she said, hating that her voice wavered. "If you won't even share your past, you certainly wouldn't share your heart."

"Cassandra . . ."

Holding up her hand, she stepped back, not wanting to hear his explanation. "I thought last night had changed things between us."

His eyes narrowed. "In other words, you thought that once I'd tasted that delectable body of yours I would be malleable to your ideas." He tilted his head to the side. "Do I understand you now?"

"No," she denied, pressing her hand to her throat. "I meant that we became man and wife in more than just words last night. I thought you would be willing, eager even, to share your life with me."

"You want to hear about my life before you?" At her nod, a bitter laugh escaped him. "Very well then, my dear wife, let me enlighten you. My first marriage made yours look like a stroll through Hyde Park."

The harshness in his voice startled her.

"Shall I start at the beginning?" Without awaiting her reply, he continued his story. "I'd offered for Francesca at the beginning of the Season and she accepted my proposal. However, she asked that we honor her parents' wishes and keep our betrothal a secret until after the Season." He shook his head. "I was a blind fool even then. You see, her parents never made such a request. No, it was all Francesca's idea to wait until the end of the Season to see if perhaps she could catch the eye of someone better than the second son of a duke. Unfortunately for me, she failed, so we wed at the end of the Season."

Cassandra found it difficult to fathom such deceit.

"Into nuptial bliss I fell . . . for precisely three hours." He gripped the back of a chair. "That was when I discovered my wild, exciting Francesca had already sampled the delights of the flesh outside the marriage bed. Though disappointed, I still believed the marriage would work because we loved each other." His fingers dug into the leather. "God, what a bloody idiot I was."

"Bryce," Cassandra murmured, reaching for him. "You don't need to—"

He pulled away from her touch. "Ah, but isn't this what you wanted, my sweet wife? Didn't you wish to learn the secrets of my past? Or have you changed your mind now that you realize how sordid and ugly those secrets are?"

Snatching her hand back, she lifted her chin. "I don't wish to cause you pain in the retelling."

"The pain I feel when speaking of those years with Francesca is nothing compared to the pain I felt while living them." Thrusting his hand through his hair, Bryce moved to the window, staring out into the sunny day. "We had terrible fights in public when I discovered her flirting with other men, but then we would return home and she would seduce me into forgiving her. She would use her charms to bend me to her will . . . and I let her." A sound of disgust rippled from his throat. "I began to hate her," he admitted softly.

And himself in the process, Cassandra realized, hurting for Bryce.

"But as much as she twisted me into doing as she wished, there was nothing she could say or do that would make me forgive her when I found her in bed with her lover. Once she realized I wouldn't bend, she taunted me, telling me of all the men she'd enjoyed, of all the ways she'd betrayed me. She mocked me for believing that she would ever fall in love with someone so worthless, someone who would always be second best. My love for her died completely that day." He rubbed the back of his neck. "After a while, I simply stopped caring who she was with, what she was doing. The only thing I felt when I learned of her death was relief. I'd vowed never again to marry, but when my brother died and I became Elaina's guardian, the decision was taken from me."

"So you offered me a marriage of convenience," Cassandra finished. "But don't you see we could have so much more?"

Bryce spun around to face her. "Of course I do, Cassandra, which is why I am asking you to cease this foolishness of yours and settle into being a proper wife."

"A proper wife," she repeated as the last tendrils of hope began to slip away. "What you want is for me to behave in a fashion befitting a duchess, teach Elaina to do the same, share your bed, and produce an heir."

His jaw tightened. "There is no need to make it sound as if it is a fate worse than death," he snapped. "You already trust me, so you know perfectly well I will care for you."

"While keeping your own emotions carefully locked within your heart," she whispered, her voice cracking on the last word, all hope dying. Still, she made one last try. "Last night I explained how powerless I felt while married to Alfred, how trapped I was beneath his control." Slowly, she shook her head. "What you are asking of me, Bryce, is something I can't give you. If we are ever to have a true marriage, one filled with love, then you need to trust me in return."

"I do trust you," he replied, frustration coloring his voice. "You have behaved with honor and—"

"I mean trust me with your heart."

His expression closed. "As you said, Cassandra, we could have so much, why can't that be enough?"

"Before last night, it was, Bryce," she admitted, blinking back the tears in her eyes. "But you changed all that when you touched me. You made me want more."

He thrust his hands into his pockets. "I can't give you more than I already have."

She couldn't hold back the tears. "I know," she whispered.

"So where does that leave us?"

"With a marriage of convenience." Pressing her fingers to her mouth, she left Bryce behind in his study. Alone.

As the door clicked shut behind Cassandra, Bryce lashed out, sending a vase crashing to the floor. Damn it to Hell, why did women have to be so bloody complicated? He'd woken this morning feeling he'd achieved more than he'd ever dreamed possible. He had a title, a solid financial standing, a growing understanding with his niece, and a sweet wife.

Those illusions were shattered one by one this morning. First with Elaina, when she railed at him for demanding she stay by his side whenever she left the house. Didn't the silly girl realize he was doing it for her own good? He knew in his gut that Milford was up to something, so it was only rational to keep close tabs on the ladies in his family.

Then, before he'd had a chance to inform Cassandra of the same restraints, she'd demanded to know his past, to have him open his heart. Lord, he'd been more than patient with her, putting up with her arguing, living with her damn ugly cat, yet it still wasn't enough. No, now she wanted him heart and soul.

Didn't the woman realize that he wasn't even certain if he possessed either one anymore?

She certainly should have after he'd spilled every dirty detail of his life with Francesca. But did she understand? Indeed not. Cassandra had demanded he explain his reasons behind his actions, yet when he did, when he told her why he couldn't relinquish control, she hadn't heard one word he'd said.

Well, fine then. She said they were left with a marriage of convenience, which is precisely where they'd started . . . and that was perfectly fine with him. After all, *he* wasn't the one who wanted more. He was extremely content with his marriage the way it was.

That thought calmed him. Glancing with regret at the broken vase, he turned to look out the window again. Taking a deep breath settled his nerves even more. After all, Cassandra had agreed to this marriage and he knew she would remain true to her vows . . . despite her feminine dramatics. In a matter of days, he was quite certain this entire incident would be forgotten and they'd settle back into a comfortable pattern.

And he was nothing if not a patient man.

17

A lady is duty-bound to ensure her household runs
smoothly.

Quoted from *A Lady's Guide to Proper Etiquette*,
written by Lady Cassandra Abbott

"*S*he what?"

Jacobson flinched at Bryce's shout. "I said she
asked me to transfer the funds in her account to another broker."

Slamming his hands on his desk, Bryce leaned
across the wooden expanse to glare at his man-of-
business. "I'm certain you refused her."

"N-n-no, Your Grace," stammered Jacobson. "I
couldn't deny her request; it is *her* private account."

"And I'm the fool who set it up that way," Bryce
muttered to himself.

Jacobson nodded glumly. "Provision number
fifty-one."

"Yes, I remember when I came to you about this
matter you told me I'd regret it," Bryce said, now
regretting his impulsive act. But what else could he
have done? When he'd read the provisions thoroughly, he'd seen the request and understood her

reasons behind it. She'd been left penniless upon the death of her first husband, so she would naturally want monies of her own, a personal nest egg to ease her mind.

Bryce tapped his fingers against his desk top. "Did she say why she wanted the monies moved?"

"She told me she didn't want my loyalties split."

His hand stilled. "Did she say anything else?"

Shaking his head, Jacobson hurried to reply. "Nothing, Your Grace."

What the devil was the woman up to? Bryce wondered, frustration streaming through him. It had been two whole days since those wretched arguments here in this very room and he hadn't seen Cassandra or Elaina since then. Not one bloody glimpse. The two of them were holed up in Elaina's room, receiving trays from the kitchen, ignoring his demands for entrance.

He knew perfectly well that he could simply find the master key and unlock the door, but it was the principle of the matter. He'd let the ladies sulk, acknowledge their fates, then accept their futures. Naturally everything would return to normal within a few more days.

If only he didn't crave the sight of his wife, it would be a tad easier to be patient.

But now it seemed that Cassandra had slipped out of the house when he wasn't looking, undoubtedly concocting some plan that would merely annoy him. Why couldn't the woman simply settle in?

Pushing back his frustration, Bryce focused on the matter at hand. "Which agent is she using?"

"Douglas Fairley." Jacobson shifted forward on

his chair. "He has a solid reputation as being honest and dependable."

"Well, at least that's some consolation." Rounding his desk, Bryce patted Jacobson on the back. "Thank you for coming to inform me of this matter."

Jacobson leapt to his feet, obviously eager to be on his way. Not that Bryce could blame the man. After all, who would wish to be in the middle of a marital spat?

"Let me know if anything else develops," Bryce asked before opening his door.

"Indeed, I shall, Your Grace." Bobbing his head, Jacobson hurried from the room.

Shutting the door, Bryce turned to lean against the wooden panels. This afternoon he would pay a visit to Douglas Fairley to see just what his headstrong wife was up to now.

My exotic beauty, my Elaina . . .

Sighing, Elaina tucked Clive's beloved note into her bodice, hiding it close to her heart. Little did she know when he stopped her runaway horse, he would then run away with her heart. Flushed with the knowledge that he returned her feelings, Elaina wished more than anything that she could tell Cassandra about Clive.

She'd known within moments of their second meeting that Clive had fallen in love with her at first sight. The romantic notion thrilled Elaina. To think that she inspired such devout emotions was almost more than she could bear. She wanted to tell everyone of her happiness, but Clive had asked her to keep it their secret until he could convince her uncle of the match. Remembering Uncle Bryce's reaction to the mere mention of the Earl of Kingwood, she regretfully acknowledged the wisdom of Clive's advice.

In the meantime, she would have to content herself with their furtive notes. Thankful that Cassandra was busy with the servants, Elaina took out a note card, sprinkled it with rose water, and began to pen her reply.

My darling Clive . . .

"I'm sorry, Your Grace, but I can't disclose any information about Her Grace's funds."

Lifting his chin, Bryce affected his most intimidating air. "I am the Duke of Amberville, Fairley. I should not need to ask permission in order to oversee my wife's monies."

"In this instance, Your Grace, I'm afraid you do." He picked up a document off his desk. "According to this agreement, which holds your signature, Your Grace, Lady Amberville is entitled to—"

"I know, I know," Bryce interrupted as he glared at the offensive document. If that blasted agreement taught him nothing else, it would certainly teach him not to be so accommodating to his far too clever wife in the future.

Setting the papers back down on his desk, Fairley fell silent for a moment. A heavy sigh escaped the broker as he rubbed a hand against his forehead. "While I am unable to discuss Lady Amberville in particular, Your Grace, I would appreciate if you would indulge me and listen to a story."

Bryce caught the underlying tones to Fairley's request. "By all means."

Watching the warring emotions in Fairley's expression, Bryce wondered if he would ever speak again. Finally, the broker began his tale. "In my business, I am privy to many private matters which would surprise most men . . . myself included. As a married man myself, I strongly believe in the sanctity of marriage. I also believe it is a wife's duty to bow to her husband's wishes."

A deep sense of foreboding settled upon Bryce.

"But, as I was saying, you would be shocked to know some of the requests I receive." Fairley glanced away, unable to meet Bryce's gaze. "For instance, there was once a lady who had monies of her own available and, though she was married, she wished to live in residence separate from her husband."

Bryce's heart stopped for a second.

"When I inquired if her husband had agreed to these . . . unorthodox plans, she calmly told me she didn't need her husband's permission as their marriage was simply a business arrangement."

A flush of anger heated his cheeks as Bryce struggled to remain calm in the face of Fairley's revelation.

"So, now you see my predicament," Fairley concluded, finally lifting his gaze to look at Bryce. "Legally, I am unable to tell the poor lord about his wife's reprehensible behavior."

Rising, Bryce nodded to Fairley. "I found your story most . . . edifying," he said, fighting to keep his voice calm and level. "Now if you'll excuse me, I have a few personal matters that require my attention."

Fairley nodded in agreement.

Humiliation washed over Bryce as he strode from the office, vowing with each step to make Cassandra regret her rash actions and convince her to repent her headstrong ways.

"Put that trunk—"

"Right back in Her Grace's room."

Stiffening, Cassandra turned to face her enraged husband. One glance at him and she realized he'd found out about her plans. "Pardon me, my lord, but I wish for the trunk—"

"I'm not interested in hearing about your wishes at the moment, madam." A muscle in his jaw twitched as he strode forward to grasp her elbow. Pausing to send a glare at the wide-eyed servant, Bryce tossed directions over his shoulder as he dragged his wife into his chamber. "Return that trunk to Her Grace's room immediately."

"Right away, my lord."

Refusing to engage in a public argument, Cassandra allowed Bryce to take her into his room, but once the door was shut, she jerked her arm out of his grasp. "I am your wife, sir, and should not be pulled about like a piece of furniture."

"Perhaps it would be easier for me to remember if you acted like my wife," he stormed back at her. "I discover you've leased your own townhouse, then come home to find you preparing to leave while my back was turned, and you have the nerve to reprimand *me*." He glared at her. "I've been more than patient with you, Cassandra. I've put up with your constant arguing, your defiant manner, and your misplaced belief that you could force me to your will. But with this little stunt, you've reached the end of my patience."

Apprehension quivered through her, but she refused to give into him. "Oh, poor Bryce," she scoffed softly. "Now if you are through with your threats, I have more to pack."

"Perhaps I have not made myself clear," he ground out through clenched teeth. "You are not going anywhere."

"I most certainly am." She set her hands upon her hips. "I'm afraid I don't find this marriage of convenience very *convenient* anymore."

Stepping forward, Bryce moved until he was mere inches from her. "I. Don't. Care."

Cassandra fought the urge to lean away from the raw fury radiating off her husband.

"I don't want to hear one more word about this matter. You will cease this foolishness and settle into the role of a proper wife!"

There was that infuriating word again—proper. Her anger rose to match his. "*No,*" she said simply.

His nostrils flared. "I'm sorry you feel that way, Cassandra, for you leave me with no choice but to confine you to your room until you've had a chance to reconsider your answer."

She couldn't believe her ears. "You can't be serious."

"Oh, but I am, my lady wife," he replied, steering her toward the connecting door. "You've spent most of your time these last two days locked in Elaina's room, so you should be well accustomed to it by now."

Opening the door, he spun her into her room. "I will not allow you to do this to me," Cassandra vowed quietly.

Bryce arched a brow at her. "I don't believe I'm leaving you any choice in the matter."

And with that he shut the door in her face. The key turned, clicking the lock.

Cassandra stared at the closed door for a long time, trying to contain her fury and ignore the ache in her heart. The man that she'd foolishly fallen in love with, the man who charmed his way into accomplishing his goals, was no more. In his place was a dictatorial ogre who thought to browbeat her into submission.

Well, that certainly was never going to happen.

Flicking a glance at the door that was locked from the outside, Cassandra spun around and strode to her window. She thrust up the pane and leaned out. No trellis rested nearby, but there was a narrow ledge that led toward the craggy stone edifice running down the side of the house. Leaning farther out, she looked at the long drop down to the ground, before glancing back at the ledge.

Pulling back into her room, Cassandra took a deep breath. She'd never even climbed a tree, yet here she was contemplating climbing down the side of her house. Trying to think logically, she weighed her options. She could either wait in her room until Bryce returned to see if she'd changed her mind, or she could gather up her courage and retake her freedom.

When put that way, Cassandra realized she didn't have much of a choice at all.

Hurrying to her armoire, she pulled out a large shawl and tied two of the points together, creating a carry-all. She retrieved Poco and tucked him carefully into the folds. With one meow in protest, he snuggled into the material, safe and sound. Gathering her skirts, she secured the material by tying a scarf around the bunched fabric.

Ready, Cassandra thought as she returned to the window. She dared to take one last look down to the ground. Or at least she prayed she was ready. Exhaling sharply, she swung her leg over the sill.

Pouring himself another brandy, Bryce tried to shake the guilt that had shadowed him all afternoon and evening. Ever since he'd locked Cassandra in her room, he'd had the overwhelming urge to go to her, to speak with her, to make her see reason. Their marriage had been going so well. He was still at a loss to understand how they had gone from finally consummating their marriage to this unguarded warfare.

"The Earl of Dunham to see you, Your Grace," announced his butler, Fibbs.

"Show him in."

With a bow, Fibbs left the library and Jonathan appeared a few moments later. "What happened to you this evening, Bryce?" Jonathan asked as he strolled into the book-lined room. "I've been waiting for you at White's. I thought we were playing cards tonight."

Bryce tapped the heel of his hand to his forehead. "Blast," he muttered, unable to believe that he'd forgotten the appointment. "I'm sorry, Jonathan. It slipped my mind."

Pouring himself a drink, Jonathan strolled toward Bryce. "Slipped your mind?" he murmured, a smile playing upon his lips. "Been taking rose-scented baths, perhaps?"

"No," Bryce replied shortly, his gut twisting.

Jonathan's smile faded away. "What's the matter, Bryce? You've lost that satisfied, almost smug, glow you've had ever since you wed the honorable Cassandra."

Part of Bryce wanted to confide in his friend, but the other part, the stronger part, wanted to keep the difficulties in his marriage confidential. He shook his head. "It's nothing really, just—"

A harried Fibbs burst into the library. "Your Grace," he said, interrupting in a manner completely unlike him. "I need a moment of your time."

Bryce set down his brandy. "Excuse me a moment, Jonathan," he murmured as he strode from the room into the hallway. "What is it, Fibbs?"

"The duchess is gone, Your Grace."

It took a moment for the words to sink in. "How could that be?"

Fibbs's gray hair flew around his head in disarray as he shook his head. "I don't know, Your Grace. I'd arranged for a dinner tray as you'd asked, then taken it personally to the duchess's room. When she didn't respond to my repeated knocks, I unlocked the door and brought in the tray, but the room was empty."

"Are you positive no one else unlocked the door?" Bryce demanded.

"Absolutely," Fibbs reassured him.

A sense of urgency pounded through Bryce as he took the stairs two at a time. Stepping around the food-laden tray left on the hallway floor, Bryce passed through the open door into Cassandra's room. He came to a halt in the middle of the empty room, wondering what could have happened to his wife.

Suddenly, a cool night breeze swept over him. "No," he whispered, a terrifying thought hitting him. In two swift steps, he reached the open window. Relief trembled through him when he saw nothing amiss outside. For one horrible moment, he'd imagined finding Cassandra lying in a crumpled heap upon the grass.

Looking closer, he eyed the ledge running beneath the window, leading toward the rough-cut stones decorating the side of the house. And there, trapped on one of the stones, fluttered a torn piece of blue fabric . . . the exact shade of his wife's dress.

A stone pinged off Elaina's window, distracting her from her note. As she looked toward the pane, another stone hit the window.

Clive.

Excitement rushed through her as she hurried across her room, throwing the window open wide . . . then ducking just in the nick of time as yet another stone soared past her. "I'm here," she called out, before again leaning out. "Is that you, my—Cassandra!"

"Shhhh," she whispered, glancing around her. "Come outside."

Elaina wondered at Cassandra's furtiveness. "Why do you want—"

Holding up her hand, Cassandra pressed a finger to her lips, before beckoning her down again. "Please, Elaina, just come now."

Always up for an adventure, Elaina nodded once, before ducking back into her room. Pausing only to retrieve her half-finished letter to Clive, she cracked open her door, peering out to ensure no one was around, then hurrying down the corridor to the servants' staircase.

She'd reached Cassandra a few minutes later. "Why did you want me to come out here?"

There was a peculiar gleam to Cassandra's eyes that Elaina had never seen before. "I am tired of following the dictates of others," Cassandra began, "so I have arranged for new lodgings here in town and would love to have you come live with me."

A multitude of questions lay upon Elaina's tongue, but she held them back when she realized that none of them truly mattered. The only question of importance was whether she wished to live with her overbearing uncle or with her new aunt. Answering that question was easy.

"When do we leave?"

18

A lady's reputation is her treasure.

Quoted from *A Lady's Guide to Proper Etiquette*,
written by Lady Cassandra Abbott

"I can't believe you lost your wife," Jonathan murmured as they left the Abbotts' townhouse.

"I didn't *lose* her," he snapped.

Placing a consoling hand on Bryce's shoulder, Jonathan shook his head slowly. "Sorry, I spoke without thinking," he apologized. "Since she's not at her parents', where should we check next?" Jonathan snapped his fingers. "Do you suppose she ran off to the country?"

Ran off. Bryce's stomach clenched at the words. His wife of less than a month had run away from him, taking his niece with her. Bryce cringed at the thought of them wandering through the dark streets of London alone. When he found Cassandra, he would tell her in no uncertain terms that she was never to do anything so dangerous again, then he would bring her home and keep her there.

And to think she believed she could lease a—

"That's it," Bryce exclaimed, turning toward Jonathan. "I know where they are. My wife recently leased another townhouse and was planning on residing there . . . without me," he admitted reluctantly.

His friend's eyes widened. "How did you go from receiving rose-scented baths to her arranging for separate households?"

Lord, if he had the answer to that question, he wouldn't be in this predicament in the first place. "It's complicated," he replied, dismissing the question altogether. "Right now, I need to focus on finding Cassandra and bringing her home where she belongs." Bryce slapped his friend on the shoulder. "The only one who knows where the townhouse is located is her broker, Douglas Fairley, so let's head to his offices."

"But it's near dawn," Jonathan protested as he fell into step beside Bryce. "No one is working at this hour."

"Then we'll simply have to retrieve the information without his help."

The sound of shattering glass pierced the silence.

"You just broke the window!" hissed Jonathan, twisting around to make certain no one else was around.

"How else am I supposed to get inside?"

Jonathan looked at him like he'd gone mad.

Whipping off his jacket, Bryce wound it around his arm as he began to clear away the shards of glass. "Don't worry, Jonathan. I'll send a man around in the morning to replace it."

"That is if we're not hauled off by the magistrates tonight."

"I'm willing to take my chances." Reaching inside the broken pane, Bryce unhooked the latch and shoved open the window. He grabbed hold of the edge of the frame and hoisted himself up through the opening. "Are you coming?" he asked Jonathan.

Shaking his head, Jonathan continued to glance about for onlookers. "I'll wait out here, thank you very much."

"Suit yourself." Not wasting another precious moment, Bryce wound his way through the offices until he reached Fairley's desk. Rifling through the orderly piles of papers, it only took him a moment to find a file with Cassandra's name printed neatly on the top.

"Here we go," he murmured to himself, flicking through the documents to find the address he sought. "Hello, my darling wife."

He tossed down the file and strode from the room. After all, he had a wife to retrieve.

"It's not quite as nice as the Amberville townhouse, but at least here I won't be kept a prisoner," Elaina remarked as she headed down the stairs.

Following her niece, Cassandra couldn't help but notice the layers of dust covering everything, the cobwebs spun around the furniture, and the alarming scratching of mice as they went skidding across the floor. "No, not quite as nice," she said weakly.

Elaina trailed her fingers along the banister, leaving a path in the dust. "I wish we'd taken a few of our clothes."

"I wish we'd taken clean bedding," Cassandra

returned, shuddering as she thought of the dirty sheets on the beds. Clutching Poco to her chest, she wandered through the lower rooms, wishing she'd also brought cleaning implements so she could at least make one room livable.

Elaina's nose wrinkled. "What is that unpleasant odor?"

Many possibilities ran through her mind, each one worse than the last. "I don't think I want to find out," Cassandra admitted.

Shrugging lightly, Elaina tugged back the curtains, sending up plumes of dust, and allowed the morning sunlight to peek into the room. If anything, the additional light only made the place look worse.

As a fat spider crawled across his web, Cassandra reminded herself that this was what she'd wanted. At least here, in this musty, moldy house, she wouldn't have a lord and master. She would be able to—

Breaking off her thoughts, Cassandra realized she could no longer lie to herself. To Bryce she'd spouted grand ideas of being his partner, of needing him to respect her, but what she'd really wanted was for him to open his heart to her. And that was why she'd left, why she'd *had* to leave.

Cassandra couldn't bear even the thought of looking at Bryce, day after day, with her heart aching with love for him and knowing, that to him, she was merely a convenience.

Surely anything, even this horrible house, was better than that unending pain. Taking a fortifying breath, Cassandra looked around the room with fresh eyes. It still looked as bad, but this time she looked past the dirt to see the possibilities. "First thing this morning we shall hire a few servants and, in no time at all, they will have this place shining." The frayed edge of the settee rubbed against her skirts. "Well, perhaps not shining, but we can always replace things as needed." Starting with the sheets.

Turning away from the window, Elaina clasped her hands together. "May we have a dinner party?"

A laugh broke from Cassandra. Here she was worrying about a rodent-free home and her niece was thinking of entertaining. "Don't you think we should clean before we invite guests into our new home? I highly doubt if anyone would appreciate sitting down upon a dusty chair that would leave a most embarrassing mark on their garments."

"You can be such a spoilsport," Elaina retorted with a chuckle.

Tucking Poco under one arm, Cassandra began to run through all the things that needed to be done. "We should hire at least three maids and we'll need a cook and let's not forget—"

"That you are married and already have a home."

A startled gasp escaped her as she spun to face Bryce who stood in the open doorway next to his friend, Jonathan. Before she could think twice, the one question burning inside of her popped out. "How did you find me?"

"You are hardly in the position to ask any questions," Bryce informed her coldly, before slicing his gaze toward Elaina. "Go out to the carriage, Elaina. Lord Dunham will escort you."

Though a mutinous expression darkened her face, Elaina stomped from the room.

"Have a care," Jonathan murmured softly to Bryce before following the younger girl.

"My friend seems to be worried that I shall lose control of my temper."

Bryce's smooth tone alarmed her far more than his yelling ever could. "So it seems," she agreed, pleased that her voice didn't reflect her jangling nerves.

Cassandra flinched as a vivid expletive ripped from Bryce moments before he strode forward. Grasping her by the shoulders, she met his wild gaze as he lowered his mouth to hers, capturing her lips in a fierce kiss that left no room for caution.

Unable to resist the temptation, Cassandra melted against him, offering him her mouth, her passion, her love. Bryce sent his tongue inward, laying claim to her mouth.

Abruptly, he broke off the kiss and laid his cheek against her hair. "Dear God, Cassandra," he murmured, his voice thickened with emotion. "I was so afraid that something might happen to you."

Tugging her back, he claimed her mouth once again in another short, but intense kiss. After a few moments, he pulled back to gaze down at her. "You could have broken your neck climbing out your window," he scolded her. "Do you realize that?"

But she didn't have time to answer before he gave her another swift kiss.

"All evening I've been torn between anger and fear. I didn't know if I would kiss you or throttle you when I finally found you."

Still awash with the feelings his kisses had invoked, Cassandra whispered, "Thank you for deciding to kiss me."

He scowled at her. "Don't thank me yet. After the night I've had, I still might do both." Releasing her shoulders, Bryce stepped back. "Now let's put an end to this nonsense."

His words chilled the warmth his kisses had created. "Have I inconvenienced you?" she asked softly.

"Do I even need to answer that question?"

"No," she finally replied. "No, I don't suppose you do."

Lifting her chin, she clutched Poco to her and walked from the house. After all, she could arrange for her new home to be cleaned just as easily from the comforts of her husband's abode.

His blasted carriage seat grew more uncomfortable with every passing hour, Evan decided as he shifted upon the stiff leather, but he would suffer any amount of discomfort to obtain revenge for his beloved Francesca. Glancing up and across the street, he silently cursed Amberville for remaining at home well past the noon hour.

Still, what was it to wait for a few more hours when he'd already waited so long? If only the seats weren't so blasted hard.

Wouldn't the man ever leave?

Bryce paused in the open doorway of the library. Ever since they'd arrived home, Cassandra had been sitting in the same chair, in the same position, reading quietly. A most ladylike pastime . . . and completely unlike his wife. Whenever she grew quiet was when he worried the most.

"Cassandra," he called to her, waiting until she calmly turned her head toward him. "I'm going to be gone for a few hours."

She continued to look at him in silence.

"Will you promise me you won't leave the house or do I need to lock you in a windowless room until I return?"

Though he would have thought it impossible, her expression grew even more distant. "I shall not step foot from the premises," she said finally.

Damn it to Hell, he hated her so subdued. The irony of the situation didn't escape him. He'd longed for her to behave so primly and sedate . . . and now that she was, he wished she'd return to her old, argumentative, clever self.

Thinking himself ten times the fool, he strode from the house to meet with his man-of-business.

After another interminable hour, Evan was rewarded for his patience when he saw Amberville's black stallion brought around front. Straightening on his seat, he watched closely, grinning broadly as Amberville came out his front door, mounted his horse, and galloped off.

Leaving the lovely Cassandra all alone.

Just to be on the safe side, Evan waited ten additional minutes before swinging his phaeton around. Whistling softly, he headed up the steps and knocked upon Amberville's door, bold as brass.

With Milford well on his way to seducing the

young Keene chit, it was time to put the next part of their plan into action.

"Your Grace?"

Starting guiltily at Fibbs's address, Cassandra prayed he hadn't seen her sending those four maids and two footmen off to clean her new townhouse. As Bryce's loyal butler, Fibbs would certainly report the incident to her husband. "Yes, Fibbs?" she replied, forcing a polite smile onto her face. "Do you need me for something?"

"Indeed, my lady." Lifting the small tray he held, Fibbs gestured toward the card. "Evan Stanford, Marquess of Dranwyck, has come calling."

She released the breath she'd been unconsciously holding. Though she didn't remember meeting the marquess, she would welcome anyone who would help distract Fibbs. "Please show him into the front parlor," she directed as she retrieved the card.

"Very well, Your Grace." Fibbs bowed to her before spinning on his heel and retracing his steps down the hall.

Her shoulders sagged forward in relief. The last thing she needed was for Bryce to discover that she intended to return to her new home as soon as it was cleaned. No, one confrontation per day with her husband was quite enough for her.

Steadying herself, Cassandra smoothed her skirts before heading for the front parlor. As she stepped into the room, an incredibly handsome gentleman moved toward her. "Lord Dranwyck, I presume," she said formally.

"Evan Stanford, Marquess of Dranwyck, at your

service, Your Grace," he replied, bowing to her. "Forgive my boldness in calling upon you without a proper introduction, but I had a most urgent matter to discuss with you."

Cassandra lifted her brows. "Since we've never met, my lord, how could you possibly need to discuss anything, urgent or otherwise, with me?"

"It is about your husband."

"My husband?" she asked.

Lord Dranwyck hurried to explain. "I overheard the duke threatening his ex brother-in-law."

Curiosity got the better of her. "His brother-in-law?"

Nodding, Lord Dranwyck provided the name. "Clive Milford, the Earl of Kingwood."

It took Cassandra a moment to regain her voice. "Lord Kingwood is Lady Francesca Keene's brother?"

"That is correct."

Did Bryce's strong emotions toward Kingwood mean he still had feelings for Francesca? Cassandra pressed a hand against her chest. "I know Lord Amberville disagreed with Lord Kingwood recently," she finally managed.

"Do you?" Cassandra heard the surprise in Lord Dranwyck's voice. "Then my visit here was for naught. I'd felt compelled to come because of the . . . passionate manner in which your husband delivered his threat."

Passionate manner. How well Cassandra knew about Bryce's virulent dislike for Lord Kingwood. In fact, Bryce could barely even speak the man's name . . . the man who was Francesca's brother.

Closing her eyes, she remembered how Bryce

had told her of his love for the wild Francesca, how he'd then grown to hate her. Yet, as everyone knew, the two emotions lay close in one's heart, and it was far too easy to hate someone even as you loved them.

Could it be true that Bryce loved Francesca still? Cassandra suddenly felt ill at the thought.

"Please forgive my intrusion," Lord Dranwyck said from behind her.

Hearing the uneasiness in his voice, she pushed aside her unbearable hurt and concentrated on more important matters. She wasn't foolish enough to think that Lord Dranwyck had been moved out of the goodness of his heart to inform her of Bryce's altercation with Kingwood.

No, she was well aware that he must have an ulterior motive . . . which is precisely why it would be perfectly fine to use him to help her out of this situation. "No intrusion at all, my lord," she said, purposely injecting a warmer tone into her voice. "In fact, I wonder if I might ask a favor of you."

The man's smile radiated warmth. "You need only to ask, Your Grace."

"Thank you." Dropping her hand to her side, she gestured Lord Dranwyck from the room. "I have a rather large trunk that I would like transported across town and I wondered if you might take care of that for me."

19

Outlandish behavior in public is most uncouth.

Quoted from *A Lady's Guide to Proper Etiquette*,
written by Lady Cassandra Abbott

"You lied to me."

Bryce's accusation didn't surprise her in the least. In fact, she'd been awaiting his arrival for the past hour. "No, my lord, I did not. If you remember, I promised not to set foot outside your house and I have not." She waved toward her legs currently resting on the settee. "As you can plainly see, my feet aren't touching the ground even now."

A corner of his mouth quirked upward and that action *did* surprise her. She'd been expecting his anger, not amusement. "Welcome back, my clever Cassandra. I'd wondered when you'd emerge again from your quiet, oh, so proper shell." Tossing his gloves onto a nearby table, he strolled farther into the now clean parlor of her leased townhouse. "Fibbs told me how you arranged for two footmen to carry you out to a carriage. Though it baffled me why you would do something like that, I now understand your reasoning. Poor Fibbs felt most guilty that he hadn't noticed the absence of five members of the staff until after you and Elaina left."

Growing warm with embarrassment, Cassandra picked at the threads hanging off the settee. "I'm sorry if I distressed Fibbs, but I didn't see any other way to accomplish my goals."

"Your goal being to live alone in this . . ." Bryce paused to glance around at the shabby interior, ". . . delightful house."

There was no way for her to explain her need to be apart from him without telling him of her love. "Yes."

Nodding slowly, Bryce rocked back on his heels. "And what of our marriage?"

"We shall continue onward with our arrangement." Her voice cracked.

"It's a marriage, Cassandra, not an *arrangement*," Bryce ground out, his eyes darkening.

"Come now, Bryce. You know as well as I do that our marriage has always been more of a business arrangement than anything else. You needed someone to help you with Elaina and I needed financial support." She shrugged one shoulder. "This change in living accommodations doesn't affect that arrangement at all."

He digested her argument for a moment. "What of an heir? It will be difficult to obtain a child with your plan."

Memories of their one glorious night of passion filled her, but Cassandra pushed them away. "Perhaps I am already with child," she murmured, unable to meet Bryce's gaze.

"And if not?"

"If not, we shall discuss the matter further." Swinging her feet to the ground, Cassandra rose to face her husband. "You've told me on more than one occasion that you find me argumentative and headstrong, so I don't understand why you wouldn't agree with my idea of separate residences."

"Because . . . it just isn't done," he finished finally.

His response confused her. "Of course it is, Bryce. Most ladies of my acquaintance live separate lives from their husbands, seeing them only at dinner parties or other affairs."

"Ah, but how many of them reside in an entirely different home when in town?"

She didn't know of one, so she remained silent.

"Precisely my point," he pronounced, satisfaction brightening his words. "So *now* will you cease this ridiculousness and return to our home?"

"No, Bryce, I won't." *I can't*, she thought, watching his expression tighten with anger. "And if you force me to return, I shall simply wait for an opportunity to return here."

Vibrating with pent-up emotions, Bryce thrust both hands through his hair. "Damn it, Cassandra," he railed, dropping his arms to his sides. "What happened to the proper lady I thought I was marrying, the one who believed in following the rules of polite society?" Leaning closer, he captured her gaze, allowing her to see the fury within him. "What happened to her?"

"She grew up."

A frustrated sigh ripped from him as Bryce stepped back, holding up both his hands. "I don't want to deal with this anymore," he said gruffly. "You're right, Cassandra; I *am* tired of all of your nonsense. You agree to the terms of our marriage, then you suddenly want to change them. You come to me and we make love, then the next morning you no longer wish to be married. How in God's name am I supposed to live with that?" Turning on his heel, he strode from the room, tossing one last comment over his shoulder. "Let me know when you finally remember how to behave like a proper wife."

Sinking back down onto her settee, Cassandra wondered if her tongue were bleeding from her biting it. Holding it between her teeth had been the only way she'd refrained from interrupting Bryce. When he'd said he didn't understand how she could agree to their terms of marriage one day, then want them changed the next, she'd ached to tell him that everything had changed when she'd fallen in love with him.

Her hands shook as she smoothed them along her skirts. At least she could take comfort in the fact that he hadn't dragged her back to the Amberville townhouse. With that struggle over, she only had one truly difficult problem before her.

Now she needed to devise a way to fall out of love with her husband.

"My darling Elaina," Clive murmured as he knelt at her feet. "You shouldn't have snuck away from your uncle. It would grieve me so to think I caused you trouble."

His concern melted her heart. Her beloved was

so gallant. "My uncle won't know anything, because I am no longer living with him."

Clive's head jerked upward. *"What?"*

"I've gone to live with Cassandra in her new home," Elaina explained.

Rising, Clive stared at her incredulously. "Are you telling me that Amberville's new wife left him already?"

The bluntness of his question was so unlike Clive that it surprised Elaina. "Well . . ." she began, reluctant to gossip about her family, ". . . yes."

His hoot of laughter made her frown.

"Really, Clive," she said sharply. "Your amusement is completely inappropriate and unappreciated."

"Why are you getting upset? I know there's no love lost between you and your uncle."

"Perhaps not," she acknowledged, "but he is family."

"That makes no difference to Amberville," Clive rasped, reaching out to grab hold of her shoulders. "He cares for nothing but himself."

The hardness darkening his gaze alarmed Elaina. It was as if her sweet, romantic Clive had suddenly become a stranger. "Clive," she protested, her voice thin and reedy. "You're frightening me."

Immediately, the scary mask slipped away and her Clive returned. Where his fingers had dug into her shoulders, he now caressed her skin. "Sorry, my love," he crooned softly. "It just upsets me to think that Amberville might be taking advantage of you."

Her unease began to fade away. "You needn't

concern yourself about that," she assured him. "I'm perfectly capable of dealing with my uncle."

"Of course you are," he murmured as he pulled her into his embrace. "I only worry about you because I love you so much and can't wait for the day until we can be together as one."

Winding her arms around his neck, she melted into him. "Oh, Clive," she sighed, unable to believe that this debonair gentleman had fallen in love with her at first glance.

He trailed the backs of his fingers along her cheek. "My beautiful Elaina," he murmured, before bending down to claim her lips.

The cards grew blurry. Blinking, Bryce tried to focus in on them, closing first one eye, then the next, yet they remained blurry patches of color.

"Do you fold, sir?"

Bryce lifted his head to glare at Lord Croft across the table, but when he saw two Crofts sitting there he didn't know where to look. "Will you stop moving?" he growled at the man. Reaching for his spinning brandy glass, Bryce managed to take a sip without spilling too much of the amber liquid on his jacket.

"You never were worth much when you're drunk," sneered Kingwood from somewhere behind Bryce.

The anger surging through him pierced the lovely alcoholic haze he'd spent most of the evening obtaining. Tossing down his cards, Bryce rose unsteadily to face Kingwood. "Perhaps, but you're never worth much drunk *or* sober," he retorted, pleased his voice hadn't slurred and ruined the effect.

Kingwood shoved at Bryce's chest, sending him stumbling backward. "You bastard," he snarled, advancing on Bryce. "It's time you received your comeuppance and I'm—"

"Hold on there, Kingwood," exclaimed Croft, grabbing hold of Kingwood's arm. "Amberville is barely able to stand upright, so it's hardly sporting of you to take advantage of him."

"You're a fine one to talk," Kingwood retorted. "I didn't see you having much of a problem fleecing Amberville at the gaming tables."

Croft stiffened, but he didn't release Kingwood's arm. "A gentleman's game is an entirely different matter than fisticuffs," he replied coldly.

"Leave off, Croft. This is none of your affair."

"It most certainly is. As a gentleman, I cannot allow this travesty to occur," Croft returned.

"It's all right, Croft," Bryce said as he released his steadying hold upon the table. "I can fight my own battles."

"But, Your Grace . . ."

Holding up his hand, Bryce wished the room would stop its dizzying spin. "I can—"

"Of course you can," Jonathan interrupted, joining their trio. "But not this evening, Bryce. Go home, Kingwood," Jonathan ordered in frigid tones. "I'm quite certain you will be hearing from Amberville on this matter."

Kingwood sniffed in disgust at Bryce. "When the drunkard sobers up?"

Pushing away from Jonathan's supporting arm,

Bryce forced himself to stand unaided. "You're an ass, Kingwood."

Kingwood's fist lashed out, catching him in the jaw, and it was a miracle that he remained upright. Jonathan rushed to his defense, but Bryce held him back. Lightly fingering his jaw, Bryce looked down his nose at Kingwood. "Is that all you have, Kingwood?" Bryce let loose a mocking laugh. "Hell, even your sister hit better than that."

Turning on his heel, Bryce heard Kingwood's enraged roar behind him. Knowing he'd scored a fine point, Bryce left the gaming hell on his own two feet . . . while he still could.

"Where have you been, Elaina?"

The young girl started at Cassandra's question. "I . . . I . . . was hungry," she explained in a rush. "So I went down to the kitchens for some food."

Cassandra didn't believe her niece for one moment. "And this took you two hours?"

"Well . . . yes," Elaina said firmly. Her niece's look of defiance was ruined only by the guilty flush staining her cheeks. "Not that it is any business of yours."

Cassandra rose from her chair to stand before the girl. "It most certainly is, Elaina, for in your uncle's absence, I am your guardian." Her smile faded away as she grew serious. "Now, please answer my question."

Elaina's mouth dropped open. "You're just as unreasonable as he is!"

"I hardly consider it unreasonable to demand an explanation for your absence. As a young, unmarried female, you should know better than to traipse off in the middle of the night without escort."

A sly expression slipped onto her niece's face. "But I did take escorts this—"

"No, you didn't," Cassandra interrupted, feeling her control on her anger begin to slip. "I've spoken to all of the servants and no one escorted you."

Abandoning that tactic, Elaina moved on to her next one. "Very well then, no one went with me," she admitted defiantly. "But I fail to see why that matters to you. After all, weren't you the one who said we needed to forge our own paths, make our own rules of acceptable behavior."

"Within reason," Cassandra countered, not about to be strung up by her own ideas. "I also told you that personal integrity and dignity were un-yielding rules of behavior. Disappearing from the house without an explanation, leaving me to worry about your safety, displays neither of those quali-ties."

When Elaina stuck out her chin, she looked more like a child of ten and two rather than a young lady of sixteen. "I'm too tired at the moment to argue with you, Cassandra. Please leave my room."

Trying to hold onto her temper, Cassandra pressed two fingers to her temple. "Please, Elaina. Please tell me where you were."

Elaina's chin lifted even higher. "No."

Any hope of controlling her annoyance with her stubborn niece disappeared. "Very well then, you leave me no choice but to confine you to your room until you are ready to explain your ac-tions."

Elaina's mouth flapped open. "Y-y-you can't be serious," she stammered.

"Oh, but I am," Cassandra retorted.

Tossing down her shawl, Elaina scowled at Cassandra. "You are just like my uncle. Completely unreasonable and overbearing."

There would be no reasoning with the girl, Cassandra realized, with sudden understanding for the problems Bryce had faced when trying to control his niece. Perhaps he had valid reasons for being so unyielding and controlling, after all.

"I don't know why you ever left him," Elaina continued, her voice raised. "It's obvious to me now that you were merely pretending to be my friend when all along you sided with *him.*"

Pulling Elaina's door closed behind her, Cassandra sagged against the nearest wall. She'd never before realized the full extent of what Bryce felt. And now that she did, Cassandra could only hope for one thing.

May the Lord give her strength.

"Are you sober yet?"

Moaning at the voice booming through his head, Bryce lifted his eyelids to look at Jonathan. "Unfortunately so."

Shaking his head, Jonathan sank down into a chair opposite Bryce. "What's happening to you?" he asked seriously. "The first week of your marriage you were the happiest I've seen you in many, many years, but now . . . well, now you're starting to act like you did when you were married to Francesca."

"What?" Bryce shouted, immediately regretting his outburst. Levering himself up into a sitting position, he forced himself to ignore the pounding in his head and tried to concentrate on the conversation. "Cassandra is *nothing* like Francesca."

"If that's the truth, then why are you in this condition?"

Bryce glanced down at himself, noting his ripped jacket, scuffed shoes, and stained breeches. "I was angry this evening," he said defensively.

"With Cassandra, I'll wager."

While that was the truth, Bryce wasn't about to admit it, not even to his friend. Instead, he chose to remain silent.

Leaning forward, Jonathan stared at him earnestly. "You're a good friend, Bryce, and I hate to see you torn again. After your marriage to Francesca, I watched you make a drunken fool out of yourself over and over, brawling publicly, embarrassing yourself. Then when you sobered, you simply withdrew, refusing to enjoy life at all."

Instinctively, Bryce shied away from memories of those dark days.

"And just when I thought you couldn't get any worse, you inherited the title and became even more rigid." Jonathan shivered lightly. "It was like you turned into your brother, Clayton. The humorless, self-righteous Clayton." He shook his head fiercely. "But I'll be damned before I sit back and watch helplessly as it happens all over again. This is exactly how it began with Francesca."

Bryce shook his head fiercely, ignoring the pain shooting through him. "Cassandra is nothing like

Francesca," he repeated. "While Cassandra might infuriate me, annoy me, drive me mad, she would never be unfaithful to me." He was as certain of that as he was that the sun would rise in the morning. "Francesca was a faithless, heartless woman who delighted in tormenting me, but Cassandra isn't like that at all. She's headstrong, infuriating, and stubborn, but she's also loyal, clever, and kind."

Confusion drew Jonathan's brows together. "Then why are you sitting here with a blazing headache instead of with her?"

"Because she doesn't want me," he rasped as pain raked through him.

"Oh, for God's sake, man, get over it."

Bryce blinked twice at Jonathan's scorn. "Excuse me?"

"Stop drowning your woes in brandy and convince your wife that she does indeed want you around." Thrusting to his feet, Jonathan paced across the room. "Seven years ago, you were a different man, Bryce. You were wild, fun, and charming. Hell, most of the ladies adored you even though they thought you a bit wicked. That's the man who became my best friend." Coming to a halt, Jonathan pointed at Bryce. "I hardly recognize you anymore."

A spark of annoyance burst to life within Bryce as he sat up even straighter, pulling down the sleeves of his jacket. "You have an odd way of demonstrating your friendship," he remarked dryly.

"I'm only saying this because I *am* your friend,

Bryce, and, if anything, I'm guilty of remaining silent too long. You need to let your past go if you are ever to find real happiness." Jonathan placed his hands on the back of his chair. "That first week of your marriage to Cassandra I saw glimmers of the man you once were . . . and I was overjoyed. Now you're sitting here telling me she doesn't want you. So what?" He leaned forward until his elbows rested on the chair. "Convince her she does want you. Seduce her. Charm her. Hell, Bryce, seven years ago you could have done that without batting an eye."

Seven years ago. Bryce rested his head on his hands. It seemed like a lifetime ago, before Francesca, before the burden of his title. What he wouldn't give to turn back time, to be the person he was when he'd teased the prim and proper Cassandra Abbott into a very improper outburst.

Lifting his head, Bryce wondered if he could become that man again.

Writing out the menu for the day, Cassandra paused at the commotion she heard out in the hallway. Setting down her quill, she went to investigate, only to pull up short at the sight of her husband.

"Take that trunk upstairs and place it in any one of the empty bedrooms," he directed two footmen, commanding them with ease from the middle of her foyer.

"Bryce?" She hurried toward him. "What is going on here?"

He turned toward her. "Good morn, my lady wife," he greeted brightly.

Gesturing toward the second trunk being carried up the stairs, she asked again, "What are you doing?"

Lifting a brow, he flashed her a wickedly appealing grin. "Why, my darling Cassandra, I'm moving in."

20

While a rake might appeal to your senses, he must be
avoided at all costs for he is certain to ruin your reputation.

Quoted from *A Lady's Guide to Proper Etiquette*,
written by Lady Cassandra Abbott

"You're *what?*"

"You heard me, Cass," he said, bending down to
press a quick kiss onto her mouth. "I've decided
you had the right of it and I'm running away as
well."

"Running away from what?" she asked, utterly
confused by Bryce's behavior.

Laughing softly, he chucked at her chin. "From
my responsibilities, of course."

"You can't do that," she protested, stepping back.

"Why not?" he asked, his grin widening. "You
did."

"I most certainly did not," she sputtered.

"Excuse me, but as the one left behind to manage everything from my business investments to
running the household, I beg to differ."

She didn't even bother to argue the point. "If
you've decided to *run away* from those responsibili-

ties, then who will take care of everything in your absence?"

"I don't know," he remarked brightly. "And to be perfectly honest, I don't really care at this point." He tilted his head to the side. "That's the lovely thing about running away, Cassie; it frees you from all those pesky details."

Flustered, she pressed a hand to her chest and gathered her composure. "What of Elaina? Have you freed yourself of all responsibility toward her?"

"No, you did that for me."

She opened her mouth to argue the point, then shut it again. He was right, darn him. When she'd removed Elaina from the Amberville townhouse, she had taken responsibility for the young girl's guidance. Remembering their disagreement last night, Cassandra wished she'd thought through that decision a bit more.

Propping her hands on her hips, Cassandra leveled a stern look at Bryce. "Even if you are serious about this running away nonsense, you can't stay here."

"Oh, I'm quite serious," he assured her as he tugged off his gloves. "And I am going to stay here whether you like it or not." He slapped his gloves against his thigh. "By the way, if you decide to do anything truly foolish like return to the Amberville townhouse, I shall simply follow you, Cass. I've recently discovered I'm amazingly mobile."

Panic at the thought of Bryce living with her sent an icy finger down her spine. "Why are you doing this?"

"Because, my darling wife," he murmured, tilting her chin up with his fingertips, "I plan to seduce you."

"So, ladies, where shall we go this evening?" Bryce asked cheerfully as he entered the dining room. Spreading his arms wide, he smiled at his wife and niece. "I am completely at your disposal."

"Disposing of *you* would suit my needs," Elaina said under her breath.

"My sweet Elaina," Bryce murmured as he moved behind the chair where his niece sat and, leaning down, pressed a kiss upon her cheek. "How I missed your dulcet tones."

He grinned when he saw her cheeks redden. Lifting his gaze to his wife, Bryce fought to keep an easy smile on his face. "And what of you, Cassie?" he asked, tacking on her nickname just to see her flush as well. The first time he'd called her Cassie today, he'd seen a heated flicker of memory in her eyes. Warmth coiled inside of him at the knowledge that every time he called her Cassie, she was remembering the first time he called her by that name, during their night of lovemaking. "What were your plans this evening?"

"I planned on staying in tonight." Cassandra paused for a moment, before staring at him with an odd intensity. "I thought it best to remain close to Elaina after the incident last night."

"Traitor."

"*Incident?*" Bryce asked, ignoring Elaina's remark as he wondered what the devil his niece had gotten into now. "What inci—" He broke off as he caught the satisfied gleam in his wife's eyes. Why, his clever Cassie was trying to trip him up, Bryce realized. She was just waiting for him to revert to his old ways. Though he burned to know what "the incident" was, he was unwilling to prove her right. He was finding it very difficult indeed not to react in his usual manner.

Shrugging, Bryce strolled casually across the room, leaning his elbow against the mantel. "I have every confidence you handled the situation perfectly, Cass."

Her look of chagrin made his efforts worthwhile. "So, would anyone care to play cards?"

Exhaling her breath in exasperation, Elaina rose from her chair. "I'm going to my room," she pronounced, pausing only to glare at Bryce, leaving little doubt she was retiring to be away from him. She flounced out of the room, slamming the door shut behind her.

His niece's dramatic exit suited him fine. Joining Cassandra upon the settee, Bryce laid his arm behind her. "What are you reading?"

"A book of sonnets."

Her frosty tones made him smile. He was getting to her indeed. "No need to be so snippy. I was simply trying to make pleasant conversation," he replied.

"It is difficult to read and converse at the same time." Lifting her book, she almost buried her face within the pages.

Falling silent, Bryce simply watched her, enjoying the way she squirmed on her seat every so often as if she were all too aware of his attention. After a few minutes, he shifted his gaze onto her hair, toying with the ringlets piled atop her head, remembering with hardening clarity how it had looked hanging free and wild around her naked breast.

"Leave me be!" she exclaimed, jumping to her feet. "I don't know what game you're playing now, Bryce, but it isn't going to work. No matter how annoying you are, I won't return to your house and be your convenient little wife anymore."

Cassandra tossed her book at him, hitting him square in the chest. Lifting her head, she marched from the room, slamming the door behind her.

My, my, my, Bryce thought, grinning to himself as he propped his feet onto the low table. He'd forgotten just how much fun life with Cassandra could be.

Yet, despite his best intentions, he found it hard to ignore the niggling worry in the back of his mind over what had happened with Elaina.

The moment she reached her room, Cassandra lay down on her bed, trying to calm her jagged nerves. She'd promised herself that he wouldn't upset her, but when he'd begun to weave his fingers in her hair, she'd been unable to bear it.

For whenever he touched her so gently, she wanted to turn, press into his arms, and kiss him until he made her believe he'd fallen in love with her.

"Fool that I am," she muttered. He'd told her in no uncertain terms that his heart wasn't available to her, so she would have to be a complete idiot to hope he'd changed his mind.

No, this new Bryce, charming, lighthearted, carefree, was simply another twist in their old game. Before, he'd virtually blackmailed her into being his "perfect wife," and now he was trying to charm his way into bending her to his will. *He'd said he planned to seduce me,* she thought, unable to keep a shiver of imagined delight from racing through her. Undoubtedly, he'd figured out that she was susceptible to his touch and planned on using her weakness to overcome her protests. Then, quick as he pleased, he'd have her back in his bed, arranging his household, and slotted back into his life.

Where her unrequited love for him would slowly destroy her.

If she were to safeguard her heart from further pain, she needed to get him out of her house as soon as possible. But how? Tonight, when she'd prodded him about Elaina, he'd revealed a crack in his new attitude before catching himself. Perhaps if she tested him, pushed him to his very limits of self-control, he would snap, lose his temper, and finally admit defeat.

Feeling calmer for the first time since she'd seen him standing in her foyer, Cassandra plotted the quickest way to send Bryce storming from her haven.

"Lord Dranwyck, I'm so glad you called," Cassandra said as she stepped into the parlor. "I can now thank you properly for your assistance the other morning."

"No need to thank me," Lord Dranwyck assured her as he bent and pressed a kiss to the back of her hand. "The pleasure was all mine."

She smiled at his polite response, for no one would consider lugging around trunks a pleasure. "Shall I call for some tea?"

"I—"

"Won't be staying," Bryce finished for Lord Dranwyck as he joined them.

Apparently her husband's good humor didn't even last through the night. "He most certainly will be staying. Might I remind you this is *my* house?"

Lord Dranwyck's smile didn't reach his eyes. "The lady is quite correct," he murmured. "She may entertain whomever she chooses." His expression grew mocking. "So, what are you doing here, Amberville?"

"I think you're forgetting one very important thing," Bryce countered as he placed his arm around Cassandra's shoulders and pulled her against his side. "This might be her house, but she is *my* wife."

Looking up at Bryce with her eyes wide, Cassandra kept her voice low so only he could hear her. "You are acting most possessive, Bryce. What happened to your new resolve to be carefree?"

Frustration flared briefly in his eyes, before he masked it. "My clever Cassandra," he murmured. "Pardon our rudeness," he said, turning back to Lord Dranwyck. "We are still quite newly wed."

"Quite all right," Lord Dranwyck replied in a jovial tone. "You should enjoy the attention while you can for, as you well know, it doesn't last long."

"*Lord Dranwyck*," gasped Cassandra.

"Don't upset yourself, Cassandra," Bryce replied in a cheerful voice that was at odds with the hard gleam in his eyes. "Dranwyck here is speaking nothing less than the truth . . . and he is quite knowledgeable about my first marriage because he was one of the many who enjoyed Francesca's favors."

"You bastard," hissed Lord Dranwyck, his hands fisting into tight knots. "How dare you speak of Francesca in that manner."

"I *dare* nothing," Bryce scoffed. "Like you, I am merely speaking the truth."

Cassandra was at a loss as to how she should handle this situation. Looking at Lord Dranwyck, she started at the fierce hatred twisting his angelic features.

"Luckily for me, I chose far better my second time around, for Cassandra is a loyal wife," Bryce pronounced, his arm tightening around her.

And like that, she was handed her weapon of vengeance. If she spent time with Lord Dranwyck, arousing Bryce's fury, she could easily drive him away.

Immediately she rejected that foul idea. As much as she wished to protect her own heart, she wouldn't destroy Bryce in the process.

Taking the matter in hand, Cassandra placed a hand upon her husband's chest. "Under the circumstances, my lord, I am quite certain you will understand if I ask you to depart. While I shall remain truly grateful for your assistance, I am afraid this revelation changes my previous invitation."

Lord Dranwyck stiffened and, after glaring at Bryce, he bowed in smooth motion. "Very well, Your Grace," he murmured, replacing his furious expression with one of calm understanding. "I apologize for this awkward situation and bid you good day."

Breathing a sigh of relief when Lord Dranwyck left the room, Cassandra sagged against her husband.

Placing a finger beneath her chin, Bryce tilted her face up to gaze down at her. "Thank you, Cass," he murmured softly, the words like a caress against her bruised soul.

"You're welcome."

He stroked the underside of her jaw with his thumb. "I knew I could count on your loyalty."

Like the good, proper, dutiful wife he wanted her to be. Lord, she was surprised he didn't pat her on the head like a faithful dog. Wishing things were different between them was a useless pastime, Cassandra knew, but there were times like this when it was impossible not to hope, to yearn, that Bryce would overcome his past and allow himself to fall in love again. But, she knew her dream was futile . . . especially when he was reminded of lessons learned at every turn. How often must he see a gentleman who was once Francesca's lover? She shivered at the thought.

Though she would never use Lord Dranwyck to drive Bryce away, the fact remained that she still needed to upset him to the point where he would leave her alone.

Her breath caught in her throat as Bryce slowly began to lower his head, his gaze fixed upon her lips with sensual promise, making her yearn to simply lose herself in his embrace, to accept what he offered without demanding more. Damning her heart for demanding more, Cassandra twisted out of Bryce's arms, stumbling backward, putting space between them. "This changes nothing between us,

Bryce," she said firmly, hoping he wouldn't notice the quiver in her voice.

"Ah, but it does, my sweet Cassie."

"Will you stop calling me that?" she exploded, pushing aside the erotic image it invoked. "My name is Cassandra."

"Not anymore." His smile had a decidedly sensual tilt to it. "Cassandra was the prim, proper lady who wrote that book on etiquette . . . and she no longer exists." Moving closer to her, he skimmed a finger along her arm. "Now Cassie, on the other hand, allows her headstrong nature and fiercely loyal heart to dictate her actions."

She forced herself to stand still beneath his soft touch, unwilling to let him see how deeply he affected her with one stroke of his hand. "But you wanted to marry Cassandra and settle down into a comfortable life," she pointed out.

"Yes, I did," he agreed, strolling around her, circling her like a tiger toying with its prey. "Yet, I have to admit that Cassie excites me terribly."

Heat spilled through her at his words, making it a struggle to hold onto her resolve. "You said that you'd had enough excitement with Francesca to last you a lifetime."

"That remains true," he said, leaning forward to press a kiss to the back of her neck. "But you're forgetting one very important difference."

"And what would that be?" she asked a bit frantically.

"You just proved your unswerving loyalty to me." Sliding his hands along her ribcage, he tilted his head to nibble on her earlobe. "However this game between us plays out, I know for certain that you and I will be the only players involved," he whispered in her ear, before kissing the base of her neck.

Finally, Bryce slid around to face her. "Just you, my darling Cass, and I," he murmured an instant before claiming her lips in a leg-melting, heart-stopping kiss.

When he'd destroyed all of her resolve, just moments before she wrapped her arms around him and begged him to take her to his bed, Bryce broke off the kiss and released her. Flashing her a knowing grin, he strode from the room like a man confident in his ability to seduce her.

Cassandra waited for him to leave, before collapsing onto a nearby chair, knowing full well Bryce thought it only days before she gave in to him.

Damn him for being right.

Whistling, Bryce vaulted up the stairs two at a time. He'd been right about Cassie all along. She was nothing like Francesca. He'd never return home to find another man in his bed, Bryce knew with a certainty that surprised him.

For the first time in seven years, Bryce allowed himself to feel a glimmer of hope that he could indeed become the trusting, carefree man he once was . . . instead of forcing himself into simply *acting* that way.

But would he ever be willing to open himself up to love again?

A few weeks ago the mere question would have made him freeze over, but now it simply caused a mild chill. Instead of hearing a resounding *no* in his head, this time he heard his heart whisper a hesitant *perhaps*. The thought startled him into stopping in the middle of the corridor.

Feeling a brush against his leg, Bryce glanced down to find Cassie's cat winding himself against him. He retrieved the mangy animal and tucked the cat against his chest. Stroking the purring cat behind the ears, Bryce looked down at his wife's beloved pet, remembering how furious he'd been when he'd first seen the animal.

The cat tilted his face up toward Bryce. "I think you're starting to grow on me, Poco," he said to the satisfied feline. "You aren't half as ugly as I thought you were."

Poco dug his claws into Bryce's chest.

Bryce laughed at the reaction. "You're just as clever as your mistress, aren't you?"

Not deigning to answer, Poco closed his eyes and began to knead Bryce's chest.

Grinning like a fool, Bryce headed down the corridor to his room . . . with the cat he'd once despised tucked firmly against his chest.

21

It is a vulgar display of emotion for a married lady to dance
with her husband more than twice in one evening.

Quoted from *A Lady's Guide to Proper Etiquette*,
written by Lady Cassandra Abbott

The moment Lord Conover claimed Elaina for a
dance, Cassandra breathed a sigh of relief. All
evening, Elaina had refused to say one word to her.
Instead, her niece had retreated behind frosty
glares and deafening silence. Elaina's cold fury had
stretched Cassandra's nerves to the breaking point.

At present, Elaina was waltzing around the
room with her skirts lifted, flashing her lower legs
for anyone to see . . . and Cassandra couldn't gar-
ner enough energy to even get upset. Luckily,
Bryce had left for his club earlier in the day and he
hadn't returned by the time she and Elaina headed
off for this affair. Relaxing for the first time all day,
Cassandra sipped at her punch and watched the
dancers.

"Lovely party," remarked Lady Perth as she
joined Cassandra. "But then Emmaline always did
know how to plan a marvelous ball."

"Lady Hallerton never disappoints," Cassandra agreed politely.

"Speaking of disappointment," began Lady Perth, fixing her piercing gaze upon Cassandra, "where is that young man of yours?"

"He's—"

"—right behind you," Bryce finished with a smile.

Stunned, Cassandra was speechless as she watched Bryce bow to Lady Perth. "Would you mind if I borrowed my wife for this dance?"

Beaming at them, Lady Perth assured Bryce, "Not at all. If you'll remember, Your Grace, it was I who recommended this match many years ago."

"Would that I had listened to you," he replied in heartfelt tones. "Shall we, Cass?"

She opened her mouth to decline, but before she could utter a word, Bryce slipped his arm around her and swept her onto the dance floor. Just as he had the very first time he'd danced with her, he pressed her far too close for convention. As a prim and virginal young lady, she'd been shocked by the closeness, by the way his body rubbed against hers, but now, as a woman who had tasted the delights of passion, she grew warm at the intimacy.

"I believe we are attracting quite a bit of attention," she said, hoping he would think her breathlessness was due to the energetic dance.

One glance at his wicked grin and she realized he knew precisely why she was finding it difficult to breathe. "Perhaps Cassandra would mind," he murmured, bending his head closer, "but my Cassie will revel in the excitement of the moment."

Lord help her, she did.

"Your cheeks are flushed," he said softly, his breath brushing over her like a warm caress.

She didn't want to admit to anything, to let him know how he made her long to toss caution to the devil. "It's warm in here."

His chuckle feathered along her flesh. "Liar." Molding her closer still, he twirled them across the floor, leaving Cassandra breathless and clinging to him.

"Bryce, you're making me dizzy," she said when he finally slowed their steps.

"Good." Leaning closer, he kissed her full on the mouth for all and sundry to see. "You deserve to be dizzy every once and a while."

Lord, did he appeal to her.

Finally, thankfully, the music came to a stop. Sliding her hand off his shoulder, Cassandra tried to move out of his arms, but Bryce held her firmly against him. "The dance is over, Bryce," she murmured, aware of the amused gazes resting upon them.

"Only if we wish it to be," he returned, continuing to waltz her slowly around the dance floor.

How did she respond to a comment like that?

A corner of his mouth tilted upward. "Come on, Cass," he urged her, amusement coloring his voice. "Live dangerously."

How could she ever resist someone so utterly charming?

The musicians must have seen them for they struck up another waltz.

"See? Even the musicians wish to continue the waltz."

"Two in a row?" Cassandra murmured, glancing around to see everyone's shocked expressions. "It's simply not done."

Bryce laughed softly, before capturing her mouth for yet another kiss. "Haven't you realized, my clever Cassie, that the bold make their own rules?"

Gazing up into his smiling eyes, she felt her heart slide deeper in love with this mercurial man. May God help her now, she prayed silently, for when she uncovered his game, he wouldn't simply bruise her heart.

No, this time, he would shatter it completely.

Clive kicked at a rock, sending it crashing into a nearby garden bed.

"You appear a bit perturbed, Kingwood," Evan observed as he strode down the path from the Hallertons' well-lit house. "I take it you've seen Amberville cooing inside with the beautiful Cassandra."

"How could I miss it?" Thrusting back his jacket, Clive fisted his hands upon his hips. "What the devil is all that about? I thought you said she'd asked you to help her move out of Amberville's townhouse yesterday."

"She did."

"Then why in the name of Christ is she pressed up against him in a public display that would shock the most libertine of rakes?" Clive exclaimed loudly.

"Shhhh," Evan hissed, glancing around the dark gardens. "Do you want someone to hear you?"

"Who's out here to overhear a word I say?" Shaking his head, Clive flicked a hand toward the house. "Everyone is crowded around the dance floor, watching Amberville seduce his wife."

Evan snickered loudly.

"I fail to see what is so amusing about this situation," Clive growled. "If you'd done your part, Amberville's wife would have been hanging on you."

Lifting one shoulder, Evan didn't appear in the least bothered by the comment. "I tried my best to entice the lady, but she proved immune to my charms."

"Then you didn't try hard enough."

"It was a bit difficult to seduce the lady with her husband standing by her side, now wasn't it?" Evan scowled at that memory. "There I was, all ready to begin my grand seduction, when in walks Amberville, confident as can be. While I rattled him a bit, he didn't react at all like he has in the past." He shook his head. "Instead of yelling and ordering me from the house, he wrapped an arm around his wife and proceeded to introduce me as Francesca's lover."

Clive couldn't believe his ears. "He did *what?*"

"You heard me," Evan retorted. "Afterward, I was indeed tossed from the house . . . but not by Amberville."

"Are you telling me that the woman you set out to seduce threw you out of her house?" Clive asked incredulously.

"Yes," muttered Evan. "And all the while, Amberville stood there touting his wife's loyalty, holding that cold bitch above my beloved Francesca."

Stroking his chin, Clive tried to think of a way to use Evan against Bryce. "So Amberville claims his wife is loyal, does he?" murmured Clive softly. "I wonder if he would retain his faith in the proper Cassandra if he were faced with proof of her infidelity."

"I just told you she didn't give any indication that she was interested in me personally."

"Yes, I heard," Clive remarked, casually slinging an arm around Evan's shoulders. "But that's the beauty of my new plan. She doesn't have to be interested in you at all."

Evan lifted an eyebrow. "I'm not following your logic, Kingwood. How can we strike Amberville through his wife if she has no interest in becoming my lover?"

"Quite easily, my friend," Clive replied, almost purring over the words. "What you're forgetting, Dranwyck, is that appearances can be deceiving."

Comprehension dawned in Evan's eyes a moment before he began to chuckle in a low, delightfully evil tone. "From what I've seen, Amberville is infatuated with his new bride."

"Wonderful news," Clive pronounced, "for it shall only sweeten our revenge."

"And we mustn't forget his overbearing protectiveness toward his niece." Evan shifted out from beneath Clive's hold. "When are you going to finish with that bit of goods?"

"Soon," Clive promised, shivering at the thought of taking Elaina's innocence. "I'm simply savoring the dénouement."

Rubbing his hands together, Evan grinned at Clive. "Amberville once destroyed Francesca, a woman we both loved," he murmured, hatred darkening his voice. "I wonder how he will feel when we turn the tables on him and destroy the two ladies *he* loves."

This time Clive chuckled at the dark imagery as the sweet sensation of revenge flowed through him. "I've waited years for this moment to arrive, for Amberville to let down his guard and allow someone to matter to him." The power of his hatred burned into him. "For him to love someone, so we could strip him of his happiness, forcing him to watch as the woman he loves betrays him, destroying his dreams and illusions one by one until he wishes we'd just killed him."

Parting the fronds of the large fern, Cassandra peered between the greenery, searching for Bryce. Lord, she hoped she'd finally escaped him. Unable to see him, she sighed in relief, released the fern, and leaned back against the pillar beside her. How had she gone from asserting her independence to being forced to seek shelter behind a fern? She pressed two fingers against her forehead.

Bryce had claimed four dances in a row, refusing to allow her to leave the floor. The entire room was abuzz with shocked whispers at their unconventional behavior. Who would have thought the epitome of a well-bred lady capable of such licentious behavior? If they'd spent a few days in her husband's all too enticing company, Cassandra was quite certain anyone would understand.

But, at least for now, she'd escaped the prying eyes of the ton and the enticing company of her husband. Yet, even though she'd managed to elude Bryce, he was still disturbing her peace of mind, heating her blood. Pressing against him all evening had made every inch of her tingle with desire, making her wish that his attentions weren't simply another ploy in their game.

The problem was that even though her head cautioned logic, her heart urged her to give in to her own feelings, to surrender to Bryce's seduction, to tell him of her love. Only the raw memory of his rejection held her back. To give all—heart, body, and soul—and receive only passion and duty in return would eventually destroy her. She had to remember that, Cassandra knew, but it was so blasted difficult to remember anything when Bryce held her close.

"There you are."

Fighting the urge to knock her head against the pillar in frustration, Cassandra forced herself to straighten and face her husband.

"I didn't know where you'd gotten off to," he remarked, his eyes gleaming with a knowing look. "Here is your punch." A smile played upon his lips as he held out the cup. "After the way you disappeared the moment we left the dance floor, I got the impression that you weren't so much thirsty as you were tired of dancing."

Accepting the punch, she took a sip before answering, "Come now, Bryce. Even you must admit that four waltzes in a row was truly excessive. I'm quite certain everyone breathed a sigh of relief when we left the dance floor."

Bryce shrugged lightly. "The musicians didn't need to play four waltzes in a row."

She gave him a level look. "When a duke of the realm remains waltzing upon a dance floor, it leaves the hostess and her entertainment little choice but to accede to his wishes."

Tilting his head to the side, Bryce seemed to consider her point. "I always knew this bloody title would be useful someday."

Cassandra couldn't hold back her laugh. Smiling, she gazed up at Bryce . . . and proceeded to lose her ability to breathe as his eyes darkened with unconcealed desire. She'd seen that intense light in his gaze before, Cassandra realized, her lips parting in response. Bryce was going to kiss her . . . and, Lord help her, she was going to let him.

"Thank you for the dance, my lady." Bending over Elaina's hand, Lord Trinslow pressed a kiss onto the back of her gloved fingers.

As he straightened, she gave him her first smile in two days. "You are quite welcome, my lord," she returned, dipping her head downward. "I must say, Lord Trinslow, you dance far better than you ride."

Once again, his grin gave his plain features an appealing quality. "Lucky for me, I do most things far better than riding."

"You should hire an instructor," Elaina recommended. "With your natural coordination, I'm certain you would quickly learn to ride as if you were born to the saddle."

His cheeks grew flush. "I thank you for the advice, Lady Elaina, and for the compliment as well." He glanced away. "Most people find me somewhat . . . awkward."

"I . . . I . . ." She didn't know how to respond to that remark without hurting his feelings.

He placed a hand lightly upon her arm. "It's quite all right, my lady. I assure you I've long grown accustomed to my failings."

Elaina drew her brows together as she swept her gaze over his tall, thin body. Perhaps he could use a bit of filling out, but in a few years time, after he'd grown into his body, Lord Trinslow would be a most dashing figure. "I believe you know me well enough to realize that I am painfully blunt, my lord, so you must believe me when I say I don't understand why anyone would consider you awkward."

His light blue eyes darkened into an intense sapphire. "Lady Elaina, I find you most—"

Breaking off abruptly, Lord Trinslow stiffened, redirecting his gaze over her shoulder.

"Elaina, my love."

A happy exclamation broke from Elaina as she spun to face her exciting Clive. Turning her back on Lord Trinslow, Elaina clasped Clive's forearm with both her hands. "Clive," she said breathlessly. "I'd hoped you would come this evening."

"I came for you, my darling Elaina," he murmured softly. "One night apart was far too long for me."

His intense gaze sent her heart fluttering. "For me as well," she agreed with a smile. Remembering Lord Trinslow, she stepped back until the three of them faced each other. "Clive, allow me to introduce—"

"We've met," Clive interrupted, rudely cutting off her introduction. "I need to speak with you privately."

Torn, Elaina didn't know how to handle the

awkward situation. She considered Lord Trinslow a friend, a friend who had just received a direct cut from the man she loved.

"I don't believe you should leave the ballroom," Lord Trinslow said stiffly.

"But I—"

Before Elaina could reassure her friend that she would be perfectly fine, Clive cut her off. "You don't have to answer to this toad."

"*Clive,*" she exclaimed angrily. "Lord Trinslow is a gentleman and I insist you apologize to him for that insult."

For a moment, Elaina didn't think Clive was going to honor her request. "Sorry," he finally muttered, before returning the full force of his attention onto her. "Please come with me," he urged her softly, brushing a finger along her lip, destroying her annoyance and any notion of resisting his charms with one touch.

"Yes," she murmured, already anticipating Clive's soul-shattering kisses. Sending Lord Trinslow an apologetic look over her shoulder, she allowed Clive to tug her out through the glass doors and into the moonlight-kissed gardens.

Savoring the moment, Bryce gazed down at his wife, delighting in her heightened color and parted lips. He could feel the desire pulsating through her, calling to his own barely checked needs. Tonight, he would reclaim his wife.

Holding her gaze, he lowered his head.

"Your Grace."

Snapping his head up, Bryce glared over his

shoulder to see who had disturbed their private moment. The distress on Lord Trinslow's face cut through his annoyance. Immediately, Bryce turned toward the young man. "What's wrong, Trinslow?"

Trinslow leaned closer. "Your niece just went into the gardens with Kingwood. I tried to dissuade her, but she wouldn't listen to me." An angry flush stained his cheeks. "From their casual address, I got the impression that their relationship is far more intimate than you suspect, Your Grace."

Frustration rushed through Bryce as he glanced back at Cassie. He'd vowed to turn his back on responsibility, to become the fun-loving, carefree gentleman of his youth. If he remained true to that vow, he would leave Elaina to make her own mistakes and lose himself within his wife's warm embrace. Lord knew, he wanted to taste Cassie's passion once again, wanted it more than he wanted his next breath, but at what cost? It was far too high a price to pay.

Damning himself for a fool, Bryce strode from the private alcove . . . to cheerfully throttle Kingwood.

22

A well-bred lady never shirks her duty.

Quoted from *A Lady's Guide to Proper Etiquette*,
written by Lady Cassandra Abbott

The sight of Elaina wrapped in Kingwood's arms only added to Bryce's rage. *"Elaina!"* he called out sharply as he stormed toward them.

Immediately Kingwood released Elaina and, placing her in front of him, stepped backward.

"Coward," Bryce sneered as he reached his niece.

"No, merely cautious," countered Kingwood. He fingered his jaw, obviously remembering the last time Bryce hit him.

Struggling to break away from Bryce's hold, Elaina pulled at the hand he'd wrapped around her arm. "Let go of me," she demanded. "You can't keep me from the man I love."

"I beg to differ." Glancing back, Bryce saw Trinslow and Cassie heading toward them. Having his wife look on while he taught Kingwood a well-deserved lesson held little appeal for Bryce.

"You are horrid!" Elaina cried, before bursting into tears.

Unable to handle his niece's feminine hysterics, Bryce pushed her toward Cassie, who now stood at his side. "Hold onto her for a moment," he ordered as he strode over to Kingwood. Grasping the younger man's lapels, Bryce dragged him forward until he was mere inches away. "I gave you fair warning that I would destroy you if you dared come near my family again," he hissed, his voice vibrating with fury. "And now you will pay for your foolish actions."

Kingwood sneered at Bryce. "You can't touch me, Amberville."

"You personally? No," Bryce agreed, shaking his head. "But what I can touch is your fortune." Satisfaction roared through Bryce as Kingwood's eyes widened in alarm. "Indeed, I shall make it my goal to see that your fortune is decimated within the year."

"You bloody bastard." Kingwood's features twisted with hatred. "Wasn't destroying my sister enough for you?"

Bryce's fingers tightened upon Kingwood's jacket. *"For the last time, your sister destroyed herself,"* he ground out. "I've tolerated your ill-will and misplaced anger for far too long, Kingwood. You've broken my patience with your actions toward my wife and my niece, so now you will pay dearly." Thrusting Kingwood away, Bryce wiped his hands on his breeches. "Perhaps now you'll be too busy trying to save your fortune to bother me anymore."

Turning his back on Kingwood, Bryce stalked toward Elaina and Cassie. Grabbing hold of Elaina's arm, he ignored her shrieks of protest. Calmly, he placed his hand over his niece's mouth as he gestured toward the side entrance to Hallerton's garden. "We'll leave through there as I don't relish the idea of dragging our lovely niece through the ballroom with my hand clamped over her mouth."

Nodding in understanding, Cassie moved ahead of him. "I shall open the door for you."

At her offer of help, Elaina let loose another muffled screech. "Will you make our excuses, Trinslow?"

"I would be honored to help," he said, pausing to glare at Kingwood. "And I shall make certain I spin a tale that will discredit Kingwood here if he attempts to rejoin Hallerton's ball to spread rumors."

"Excellent thinking," Bryce commended Trinslow. "I do appreciate your help once again."

Trinslow's expression hardened as he looked first at Elaina, then back at Kingwood. "No need to thank me for discrediting Kingwood here," he said in a low, tight voice. "This time it truly is my pleasure." Turning on his heel, Trinslow headed back to the ballroom.

"As for you, Kingwood," Bryce began softly, "you'll hear from me soon."

Kingwood's arrogance had returned in full force as he bowed mockingly. "Then I shall have to return the favor."

Hearing the threat beneath Kingwood's response reaffirmed for Bryce his decision to financially ruin Kingwood. Without another word, Bryce pulled his struggling niece down the path, leaving Kingwood standing alone in the dark.

* * *

Dawn broke through the night, sending streaks of light through the window. Dressed in nothing but his breeches and open shirt, Bryce watched the sun brighten the morning sky. He'd been awake all night with only his churning thoughts for company.

Furious at both him and Cassandra, Elaina had marched up to her room last night and locked them both out. He rubbed both hands over his face. When was the turmoil going to subside? Would she ever learn to trust him, to believe in his advice? He saw no end in sight.

When he'd first married Cassandra, he'd been so relieved to see Elaina bond with her, but their relationship now seemed strained. Whatever "the incident" was, it had been enough to cause a break between Elaina and Cassie.

But it hadn't only been his ongoing troubles with Elaina that had kept him awake. No, his nagging desire for his wife had fueled his surging emotions. He'd been so close to seducing Cassie last night; he'd felt her hunger when he'd held her in his arms. He'd wanted to taste her passion once again, to bring an end to this game of hers.

Yet his responsibility toward his niece had overridden his desire for his wife.

And *that* realization was what had kept him standing before the window all night. He'd vowed to shake free of his burdens, to enjoy life with careless abandon, but at the first true test, he'd failed.

But had he really?

How could he have lived with himself knowing that he'd sacrificed Elaina for his own personal gain? Bryce scowled at that thought. He wouldn't be much of a man if he put himself and his desires above everyone else's needs, now would he? Like the sun breaking over the rooftops, understanding grew inside of him.

Of course he couldn't be the man he once was; he wouldn't want to be, Bryce realized as his heart began to pound. No, indeed not. He'd been shallow and self-absorbed in his pursuits of pleasure. True, he'd had fun, but he'd never held himself accountable for anything. Suddenly all of the lectures he'd received from his father and brother made sense.

But they'd been wrong in their assertion that he needed to put aside his zest for life and face his duty with somber respect. Last night when he'd danced with Cassie over and over again, setting many tongues wagging with his scandalous behavior, he hadn't harmed anyone with his actions. Yet, when he'd been called upon to assert himself as Elaina's guardian, he'd assumed that responsibility immediately.

All this time he'd believed he had to be either completely carefree or staid and proper . . . never realizing that he was meant to be a blend of both.

Elation crashed through him at his epiphany. Striding across the room, he opened his door, wanting to share his realization with Cass, only to pull himself up short. She was still abed, undoubtedly exhausted by the emotional drain of Elaina's dramatic outburst last night. It would be utterly thoughtless of him to awaken his wife to share news that could easily wait.

Returning to his room, Bryce began to refasten his shirt. Perhaps he couldn't wake his wife at present, but there was nothing to stop him from doing something he'd wanted to do for days.

He wanted to look over his accounting ledgers.

Tossing on his coat, Bryce headed off to his familial townhouse wearing wrinkled clothes and a huge grin.

Evan couldn't believe his luck when he saw Amberville stride briskly away from his wife's townhouse. Perhaps his good fortune was finally arriving. With a hop in his step, he headed around to the kitchen entrance and rapped on the door.

"Good morn," he greeted the young maid. "I have something from your master."

"The duke?" The maid's eyes widened. "Perhaps you'd like me to fetch Cook, my lord?"

"No need to trouble her," Evan reassured the sweet thing. "I'm certain she is quite busy." And not as gullible as this pretty little maid.

"She's preparing Her Grace's tea, but I don't know if I should be accepting things from the master." Uncertain, the maid glanced behind her in the kitchen. "I'm new here, my lord," she confided in Evan.

Perfect. Offering her a reassuring smile, he waved away her concerns. "I quite understand," he said smoothly. "Then why don't you fetch Cook? I shall wait right here."

As the maid scurried away, Evan easily slipped into the now empty kitchen and slipped up the servants' staircase to the second floor. Positioning himself where he could see down the entire hallway, Evan waited until the maid appeared carrying the tea. Knowing she would lead him straight to

Cassandra's bedchamber, Evan fought back a chuckle at his cleverness.

The maid paused in the hallway, setting down the tray, and knocked on a doorway. "Lady Elaina?" she whispered through the closed door. "I have a message for ye."

Taking a risk, Evan stepped closer to hear the exchange more clearly.

"Go away."

As the maid glanced down the hallway once again, Evan pressed into one of the doorways, praying she would not spy him. His luck held for she said, "No one's about, my lady, and this missive's from the gent you told me about."

In an instant, the door opened, allowing the maid to slip inside . . . leaving the tray untended upon the table. Unable to believe his good fortune, Evan didn't waste another minute. Instead, he lunged forward, dumped the contents of the sleeping draught into the teapot, and darted back to his hiding spot.

Not one moment too soon either, he realized, as the maid slipped back out into the hallway. Retrieving the tray, she hurried a few doors down and knocked again. "Your Grace?" the maid called out, waiting until she received a reply before heading into the room with the tray.

Easing into the room behind him, Evan noted his watch . . . and waited for the drug to take effect.

Having finished her tea, Cassandra swayed in her chair and tried to focus on her book. She'd only been awake for a few hours, so she didn't understand why she was having a hard time keeping her eyes open. Still, it seemed useless to fight it. Fatigue weighed heavily upon her as she made her way back upstairs to her bedchamber.

Laying atop her blankets, Cassandra promised herself she would simply close her eyes for a few minutes until this wave of sleepiness passed . . . and that was her last thought as she sank into the darkness of sleep.

Signing his name with a flourish, Bryce finished his note to his steward overseeing the Amberville Scottish holdings. It was gratifying to see that he'd taken those unproductive lands, invested in sheep, and turned that estate into a profitable holding. Having heard his father declare the lands worthless, Bryce savored the success that much more.

As he placed his wax seal on the missive, Bryce realized he'd increased his inheritance thrice over. Whistling softly, he set aside the ledgers from Scotland and placed the books from his holdings in Wales on the middle of his desk. He'd only just opened the first ledger when a knock disturbed the quiet.

"Come in, Fibbs," he called out, glancing up at the door.

"Pardon the intrusion, Your Grace, but I thought you would like this delivered immediately." Holding out a note, Fibbs moved into the room. "The messenger said it was from Her Grace."

Bryce accepted the note with a smile. "Thank you," he murmured to Fibbs as the butler left the room. Eagerly, he broke the seal and quickly scanned the letter.

The desire humming along his veins for the past

few days began to race through him. His wife
wanted him to come home as soon as possible . . . and attend her in her bedchamber. Though
he wondered at the unusual request, Bryce wasn't
about to question his good fortune.

With any luck, he would have his wife back
where she belonged—here in his bed in the Amberville townhouse. Grinning with satisfaction,
Bryce hurried from his study.

Elaina's hands trembled as she reread the note
that a maid had just delivered to her. Dear God in
Heaven, Clive wanted her to run away with him.
Did she dare?

Once she left, there could be no coming back,
and while she would dearly love to escape her
overbearing uncle, she still hesitated. He was, after
all, the only family she had left. Would he completely turn his back on her if she did run away
with Clive? After seeing his reaction last night,
there was no doubt in Elaina's mind that her uncle
would never abide her marrying Clive.

And did she really want to?

Insidious doubts crept into her thoughts. Clive's
behavior last night had disturbed her far more than
she wanted to admit. He'd been so rude to Lord
Trinslow that she still winced thinking back on it.
Every now and then, she would catch a glimpse of
a darker side to her charming Clive. But, like last
night, before she could ask him about her misgivings, he began to kiss her, his touch burning away
her questions and doubts.

Was her apprehension merely fear over leaving

the life she now knew and heading off into the unknown?

A shiver raced through Elaina as she sat down on her bed, hugging her knees into her chest. A mewing sound to her right startled her. "Poco," she exclaimed, picking up the lazy cat. "You scared me."

Purring loudly, the cat rubbed his head against Elaina's chest, giving her comfort with his affection. "What do you think I should do?" she asked the homely animal.

He simply closed his eyes and arched his neck to her touch. "A lot of help you are," she muttered even as she continued to stroke his fur. "You see, Poco, I need to decide if I should run away with the man I think I love or stay here with my uncle." Spoken out loud, her choices somehow became clearer. "While Clive may be rude occasionally, at least he doesn't treat me like a child. Isn't that right?"

Poco thumped his tail against her arm.

"I think it is, too," Elaina said, hugging the cat. "I wouldn't be so afraid to leave if I didn't have to go alone," she admitted softly. Hugging Poco into her chest, she suddenly had an idea. "What if you came with me, Poco? I know Cassandra would miss you, but I need you far more than she does at the moment." As the idea took hold, Elaina felt the nervous tension inside of her ease. "You would only have to come for a little while, just until I felt comfortable in my new home. And it would also be a reason for Cassandra to come to see me . . . even if she is furious with me for running away."

Excitement streaked through Elaina as she gently laid the cat on the bed. "It shall be a grand adventure, Poco," she assured him as she rose from the bed. Retrieving her satchel, Elaina began to pack for her trip.

Taking the stairs two at a time, Bryce bounded upward, anticipation sizzling through him. He'd finally made peace with himself . . . and now he would do the same with Cassie. When he mended the rift in their marriage, all would be right with the world, Bryce thought with a grin. At Cassandra's door, he knocked once, before pushing it open.

"Cass?" he called out, looking around her sitting room. Noticing the adjoining door was ajar, Bryce smiled at the thought that she was waiting for him in her bed. He walked over and pushed open the last remaining barrier between them. "I'm surprised to find . . . *Good God!*"

Stumbling back, Bryce grabbed hold of the doorjamb to keep himself from falling. Pain drove through him, fierce, pounding, as he tried to make sense of what his eyes told him.

There, in Cassandra's bed, lay his wife . . . with none other than Dranwyck laying on top of her.

Suddenly, Dranwyck lifted his head and gave Bryce a smug smile. "What an unexpected surprise, Amberville," he drawled lazily. "Come to join us?"

His shock gave way to a burning fury. Blinded by a haze of hatred, Bryce started forward with a roar.

23

A lady never allows herself to be placed in a compromising
position.

Quoted from *A Lady's Guide to Proper Etiquette*,
written by Lady Cassandra Abbott

Dranwyck's smug expression shifted into one of
fear as Bryce charged toward the bed. Sliding to the
opposite side of the bed, he held up a hand. "Your
wife invited me into her bed."

Uncertain if he could bear to look at his wife,
Bryce glanced down at her, before looking away.
But something nudged at him, making Bryce look
down at her again. Pain pierced his heart as he took
in her beauty.

The intense emotion overtook his blind fury,
clearing his mind to allow logic to prevail. This was
Cassie, his loyal, headstrong, stubborn wife. She
would never betray him. Of that, Bryce had not
one doubt . . . even when faced with evidence to
the contrary.

True, his wife was lying naked in a bed with
Dranwyck, but there had to be an explanation.
Leaning down to look at her closer, Bryce touched

his hand to her heated forehead. Her eyes were open, but they were glazed and unfocused.

She'd been drugged.

"You bastard," Bryce growled, reaching across his wife to knock Dranwyck off her bed.

Falling backward, Dranwyck tugged the top blanket off Cassandra's bed to wrap around his nakedness. "Calm down, Amberville," he said, backing up against the wall. "You can't expect me to resist a beautiful woman like your wife when she literally throws herself at me."

"You're a bloody liar." His fist met Dranwyck's face with a satisfying crack. Stepping back, Bryce allowed the dandy to slide to the floor. "What did you give my wife?" he demanded.

"Nothing," moaned Dranwyck as he cradled his jaw.

Drawing back his fist to convince Dranwyck to tell the truth, Bryce held himself in check when Cassie began to moan softly. Though he vibrated with rage at the bastard lying at his feet, Bryce knew his wife needed him and she was far more important than satisfying his need for vengeance.

Bryce grabbed hold of Dranwyck's arm and dragged him from the room. In the hallway, Bryce bellowed for the servants, who came running in response. Pointing to a footman, he snapped out orders. "I'm putting you in charge until you can arrange for my man, Fibbs, to come and handle this matter. For now, I want you to take this piece of offal and lock him up, then send someone to fetch both the magistrate and Fibbs. When my butler arrives, tell him to keep the household calm and this man under lock. Notify me when the magistrate arrives." Bryce released Dranwyck and stepped over the body to return to his wife.

"Are you feeling better, Cassie?"

Keeping her eyes closed, she nodded slowly, not wanting to make any sudden movement that would upset her stomach yet again. It was embarrassing enough to have lost the contents of her stomach twice in front of Bryce.

When he began to stroke back her hair, she almost purred. Hoping the room wasn't still spinning, she opened one eye. "What happened?" she croaked, her throat still tight.

"Dranwyck drugged you somehow." Though Bryce's voice remained level, his gaze heated into molten fury. "I am going to have to leave you in a few moments to speak with the magistrate."

She fought back a sense of panic at the thought of him leaving her alone. "Why did he do it?" she asked, trying to focus on their discussion.

"Because he wanted me to walk in and find the two of you in bed together . . . which I did."

This time there was no holding her panic at bay. "I swear to you, Bryce, I had nothing to do with—"

"Shhhh," he murmured, leaning forward to press a kiss upon her forehead. "I know that, Cass." A corner of his mouth tilted upward. "I knew it from the first. Even though I was looking at what appeared to be proof of your infidelity, I knew there had to be another explanation."

Her heart tightened at his unwavering faith. "Oh, Bryce," she whispered.

"You are many things, Cass, but unfaithful isn't one of them." This time his smile reached his eyes. "Now, I want you to rest while I speak with the magistrate." He leveled a finger at her. "Promise?"

She blinked back her tears. "Promise."

Leaning forward again, he kissed her cheeks, her eyelids, and her nose, before rising from the bed. She watched him leave her room, feeling her emotions swell. Lord, she loved that man.

As the door clicked shut behind him, she closed her eyes and sent a prayer of thanks winging upward. With his past, Bryce could have easily been blinded to the truth and thought she'd welcomed Dranwyck to her bed. Instead, he'd trusted his heart and not his eyes.

His unshakable faith humbled her, leaving her path clear. The time for games had passed. Cassie didn't understand what had caused Bryce's new outlook on life, his sudden decision to seduce her, or even his tender touches, but tonight she would uncover his secrets. For surely if Bryce could learn to trust again, then he could learn to love again, as well.

So, this evening, she would gather her courage and tell Bryce that she loved him.

". . . so there you have it, Mr. Clancy," Bryce said to the magistrate, informing him of Dranwyck's vile actions against Cassie.

"With your pardon, Your Grace," Fibbs said as Bryce returned to his seat next to Mr. Clancy. "I have spoken with the staff and have uncovered some information you will find useful."

"Go on," Bryce urged his butler.

Tugging down on his vest, Fibbs cleared his throat. "This morning, one of Her Grace's new kitchen maids said a man wished to deliver a package from his lordship. Wisely, she refused it and fetched Cook instead. However, by the time she returned, the gentleman had already left. Neither the maid nor Cook realized he must have slipped into the house."

"So, he came into my house and somehow managed to drug Her Grace's tea," Bryce concluded. Controlling his temper, he turned toward the magistrate. "I believe you have all the information necessary, Mr. Clancy, to charge Lord Dranwyck."

"Indeed, I do." Nodding briskly, Mr. Clancy rose from the chair. "I'll collect his lordship and be about my business."

"Certainly." Gesturing toward his butler, Bryce said, "Fibbs here will show you where we put Dranwyck."

Fibbs shifted on his feet. "Might I remind you, Your Grace, that Lord Dranwyck is still in a state of undress."

"Thank you, Fibbs. I am aware of that." Turning toward Mr. Clancy, Bryce smiled slightly. "I'm certain you will agree with me that any man bold enough to break into my home and accost my wife in her private chambers soundly deserves to be tossed into gaol wearing nothing but a blanket."

Mr. Clancy chuckled loudly. "I'd say it'd be *more* than he deserves."

"I knew you were a man of sound judgment the moment I met you," Bryce murmured as he gestured toward the door. "If you require anything else, please feel free to contact me."

Tipping his hat, the magistrate followed Fibbs from the room. Within a matter of minutes, Mr. Clancy was calmly dragging Dranwyck from the house. The sound of Dranwyck's protests over not being allowed to clothe himself rang loudly through the hall.

As soon as the door shut behind the two men, Bryce mounted the stairs and checked on his wife, who lay in a peaceful slumber. Pacing down the hallway, he tried to rid himself of the rage still steaming within him, but found little release within the confines of the hall. While he'd wanted to vent his anger upon Dranwyck, Bryce had restrained himself, disposing of the odious Dranwyck like a gentleman . . . which did nothing to ease the anger.

Leaving strict orders that Cassandra wasn't to be disturbed under any circumstances, Bryce headed for the stables, choosing the fiercest mount, and thundered away, allowing the pounding ride to shake loose the last vestiges of his fury.

Elaina jumped at the knock on her door. "Come in," she called, hoping her voice didn't reveal her nervousness.

Moments later, a maid entered with a dinner tray. "Here you are, my lady," she said brightly, as if Elaina should be pleased to eat yet another meal alone in her room.

"Thank you," she returned, hiding her emotions. "Before you leave, Harriet, I would like you to lay out my clothes for tomorrow."

Dipping into a curtsey, the maid hurried over to the large wardrobe and began to sort through the clothes. Elaina snatched up her satchel with one hand and Poco with the other, then rushed from the room. Gently, she closed the door, locking it as well. Even if Harriet did begin to beat on the door and call out, the servants would undoubtedly ignore the maid . . . just as they'd ignored her pleading for days.

Listening for anyone approaching, Elaina hurried along the hallway, down the stairs, and out the front door. She didn't understand where all the servants were or why the house seemed to be in disarray, but she simply accepted it as good fortune.

In the waning afternoon sun, Elaina took a bolstering breath before disappearing down the street.

Cassandra awoke revived . . . but with no clear memory of Lord Dranwyck's assault upon her person. She remembered feeling a heavy weight on top of her, then hearing Bryce shout, but she had no recollection of her clothes being removed or of Lord Dranwyck joining her in bed. A shiver wracked her body at the awful thought, making her doubly thankful of her foggy memory.

What she did remember clearly was Bryce's tender care after he'd tossed Lord Dranwyck from her room. A sudden urge to see her husband overtook Cassandra. Rising from her bed, she rang for her maid. She busied herself with picking out her dress, but when Harriet didn't arrive, she rang a second time. Still, her maid failed to answer the summons, leaving Cassandra no option but to dress herself.

After struggling into her gown, Cassandra left

her room in search of Bryce. Heading downstairs, she blinked in surprise when she saw the Amberville butler. "Fibbs," she exclaimed. "What brings you here?"

"His Grace requested my assistance in restoring order to your household, milady," Fibbs replied formally.

She smoothed her hands down her ribs. "Yes, well, thank you for your help."

"I am pleased I could be of assistance." Bowing in deference, Fibbs continued across the foyer.

"Oh, Fibbs," she called out to him, remembering Harriet's odd behavior. "Would you mind checking on my maid, Harriet, for me? She didn't answer my summons."

"Immediately, Your Grace," Fibbs said with another bow.

"Oh, and Fibbs," she hailed him again. "Have you seen His Grace?"

Fibbs nodded once. "Indeed, milady. His Grace has gone riding."

She doubted she hid her disappointment from Bryce's butler. "Thank you again, Fibbs," she murmured, keeping her voice level. "Please inform me of His Grace's return."

"At once, Your Grace."

Cassandra wandered into her parlor, amazed by the fact that she missed Bryce's presence. When she'd first married him, she'd been happy that he'd ignored her for days; now she hated to be apart from him for mere hours. Smiling over her fanciful thoughts, Cassandra retrieved her book and tried in vain to lose herself in the story.

Giving up, she shut the leather tome and lost herself in thoughts of Bryce instead.

Having driven his horse into a lather, Bryce finally felt calm ease into him, so he headed for home. He tossed the reins to a groom and strode into his wife's house.

"Bryce!"

The sight of Cassie standing in the doorway nearly sent him to his knees. "Cass," he rasped, his voice dark with emotion. "You're all right."

As if she did it every day, Cassie stepped into his arms, wrapping him in her embrace. "I'm fine," she assured him.

Shuddering, he held her tightly against him, thanking God, the angels, and anyone else who cared to listen for his wife's well-being. Pulling back, he clasped her face between his hands, gazing down at her beauty. "Cass, I—"

"*My lord!*" Fibbs shouted as he ran into the foyer. "Your niece, Lady Elaina! She's missing!"

"She's probably just hiding in her room somewhere," Bryce countered, reluctantly releasing his hold on Cassie.

"I personally searched Lady Elaina's room, Your Grace, but found no one other than Her Grace's maid, Harriet." Fibbs smoothed back his ruffled hair. "According to the maid, Lady Elaina directed her to retrieve a dress and while Harriet's back was turned, Lady Elaina left the room, locking the maid inside."

After dealing with Dranwyck, this was the last thing he needed. "Have you searched the house?"

"The house, the gardens, and the stables, Your

Grace." Fibbs shook his head. "Other than Harriet, no one saw Lady Elaina this afternoon."

A finger of panic slithered down his spine. "Are you certain you've searched everywhere?"

"Yes, Your Grace," Fibbs replied swiftly. "But I do have an idea as to where Lady Elaina might have gone." Without another word offered, Fibbs held out a crumpled missive.

Snatching it from his butler's hand, Bryce read through it quickly . . . then again, for he couldn't believe his own eyes. "Dear God, no."

"What is it, Bryce?" Cassandra asked, gripping his arm. "What does the note say?"

Lifting his gaze, Bryce looked at his wife. "She's run away . . . with Kingwood."

A gasp broke from Cassandra. "Surely not," she said, shaking her head in disbelief. "Even Elaina wouldn't do something so foolhardy."

"If she's nowhere to be found and there is a letter from Kingwood asking her to run away with him, then I can only conclude that she is indeed that foolish." His fingers tightened, crumpling the note into a ball. "And if he's already ruined Elaina, I'll kill him."

24

An unmarried lady should never be without proper escort.

Quoted from *A Lady's Guide to Proper Etiquette*,
written by Lady Cassandra Abbott

*B*ryce, Cassandra, Fibbs, and four servants headed over to Lord Kingwood's townhouse. Feeling the anger radiating from her husband, Cassandra stayed close to ensure he didn't do something foolish . . . like actually kill Lord Kingwood.

Without bothering to knock, Bryce stepped into the townhouse like the avenging uncle he was. *"Kingwood!"*

His bellow shook the rafters and brought servants running from four different directions. "Please, my lord," exclaimed Lord Kingwood's butler. "You cannot simply burst into—"

Grabbing the man's lapels, Bryce lifted him up until he was mere inches from Bryce. "Where is she?"

All color drained from the butler's face as his eyes flicked toward the stairs. "I-I-I don't—"

But Bryce already had his answer. Releasing the

butler, he vaulted up the stairs. Afraid they were already too late, Cassandra hurried after him. Greeted by a long corridor of doors, Bryce paused only for an instant, before he began to shove open each one, peering in to see if Elaina was inside. As Bryce opened the fourth door, he discovered Lord Kingwood belting his robe.

"I say, what is the meaning—Amberville!" Lord Kingwood hissed as the person in the bed let loose a feminine squeal before diving beneath the covers. "What the devil are you doing in my home?"

"Retrieving what is mine," Bryce ground out as he strode to the bed.

Lord Kingwood grabbed hold of Bryce's arm. "Now see here—"

Jerking his arm free, Bryce rounded on Lord Kingwood. "I am so close to shooting you where you stand, Kingwood, that I wouldn't press your luck."

The hatred between the two men was a palpable thing. Knowing she needed to get Bryce away from Lord Kingwood as quickly as possible, Cassandra moved toward the bed to collect Elaina, but halfway to the blanket, she froze at the sight of blond hair sticking out from beneath the covering. "Bryce," Cassandra said urgently. "This isn't Elaina."

Immediately, Bryce spun around. "What?" With a flick of his hand, he sent the blanket fluttering back. "Who the devil are you?"

"Georgette Amrand," she squeaked, clutching the blanket beneath her chin.

Bryce's eyes narrowed. "The Duke of Clovingham's daughter?"

Feeling sorry for the girl, who couldn't have

been older than fifteen, Cassandra reached out to pat the girl's shaking hand. "There now," she said soothingly. "Everything will be just fine."

Bryce shook his head in disgust. "Not if her father finds out," he predicted gruffly. "Clovingham is one of the meanest bast—" He broke off at Cassandra's sharp look. Shrugging in dismissal, he returned his attention to Lord Kingwood. "Where is Elaina?"

"I haven't the foggiest."

"You're lying to me, Kingwood. I saw the note you sent her, asking her to run away with you."

Ignoring the cry of shock from Georgette, Lord Kingwood lifted one shoulder. "When she failed to reply I assumed she'd decided against it."

Bryce jerked his head toward the bed. "So you didn't waste any time seducing another innocent young girl."

"What is the point of having a vice if you don't indulge it?" Lord Kingwood asked with a practiced smile.

"Your days of indulging are over, Kingwood!" boomed a large, gray-haired gentleman from the doorway.

"Clovingham," Bryce murmured. "What marvelous timing you have."

Stepping back, Bryce folded his arms across his chest and gazed with unabashed pleasure as Lord Kingwood grew pale. "Your Grace," he stammered as he stumbled backward. "I can explain all this."

Lord Clovingham shook a finger at Lord Kingwood. "I'm not looking for your explanation, Kingwood. All I want to know is the wedding date."

"Wedding date!" Kingwood choked out.

Narrowing his gaze, Lord Clovingham grew still. "You were planning to marry my little girl, weren't you, Kingwood? If you were only dallying with her, then I'd be a trifle upset. So upset, in fact, that I might just have to break off that piece in your pants that you're so proud of."

Instinctively, Lord Kingwood crossed his legs and swallowed. Hard.

Turning his attention onto Georgette, he nodded to Cassandra. "I appreciate your concern about my daughter, Lady Amberville, but if you'll excuse us, I'll see to her now."

Hesitating, Cassandra slowly straightened. "Will you be all right?" she asked Georgette.

Cassandra blinked at the young girl's cheerful smile.

"Don't worry about her, my lady," Clovingham assured her. "What you don't understand is that Georgette here is the one who left me a note telling me where to find her."

"*What?*" Lord Kingwood yelped as fury mottled his skin. "You . . . you tricked me!"

Georgette didn't look quite so young or innocent as she sent Lord Kingwood a fierce look. "No more than you were trying to trick me," she countered. "You thought to lure me into your bed without any care for my reputation." She smiled brightly. "Lucky for you, I decided you would make a splendid husband."

Bryce laughed out loud as Lord Kingwood's mouth opened and closed, emitting only little squawks of protest. "Come along, Cass," he said finally, gesturing her toward him. "Let's leave Kingwood in Clovingham's capable hands."

As Cassandra took Bryce's arm, she glanced back at Lord Kingwood and realized, much to her surprise, that he wasn't paying them any attention. Indeed, all of his fury was directed toward Georgette, who continued to smile up at him.

"I do believe we owe the less than innocent Georgette a measure of gratitude."

Bryce lifted his brows. "And why is that?"

"Because she has ensured that Lord Kingwood won't trouble you anymore."

"How do you come to that conclusion?"

"Quite logically, Bryce." Cassandra paused at the top of the stairs. "From the look on Lord Kingwood's face, I'd say he'll be far too occupied seeking revenge on his calculating young wife to even give you a second thought."

Bryce nodded in agreement. "With Kingwood out of the way, we only have one problem remaining," he said, looking down at Fibbs and the other servants who peered anxiously up at them. "Where the devil is Elaina?"

Shadows began to claim the park, but still Elaina sat upon a rock, looking at the spot where she'd first seen Clive. Lord, she was a coward, she thought, burying her face in Poco's soft fur. She'd stood outside Clive's townhouse for at least an hour, just staring at it, yet unable to walk up the steps and knock on the door. For she'd known that once she'd crossed that doorway, all attachments to her uncle would be severed. She'd seen the hatred between Clive and her uncle at Hallerton's ball and as furious as she herself was with her uncle, she couldn't forget that he was all the family she had left.

So, in the end, she hadn't been capable of destroying any hope of affection between her and her only relative. Now she sat here in the waning light wondering how to begin the long road home.

"Cor, what 'ave we 'ere?"

Startled, Elaina slid off the rock, landing in a heap upon the grass. Gazing up at the filthy man standing over her, Elaina instinctively knew she was in danger. "S-s-stay away," she stuttered, trying to scramble to her feet, but unable to untangle her legs from her long skirts.

"No need to get up, lovey," he crooned, showing his rotting teeth. "I'll join ye."

As he leaned over her, Poco hissed loudly, striking out with his paw and catching the man on the cheek. "Bugger," he swore, pressing a hand to his injury. "The bloody cat made me bleed."

The man's expression twisted into an ugly mask of anger. "I'll teach ye and yer cat a lesson, lovey," he promised. "Damned if I—"

"*E-L-A-I-N-A!*"

At the cry, the man swore viciously before lunging to his feet. Nearly sobbing in relief, she looked around for her rescuer. There, galloping across the field, was Lord Trinslow. His legs flailed out to the sides, his arms flapped like a dying chicken, and his body slid from side to side on the saddle.

She'd never seen such a beautiful sight.

Another curse escaped the beast masquerading

as a man before he spun on his heel and raced toward the trees. Scrambling to her feet, Elaina held Poco tight as she raced toward Lord Trinslow.

Dismounting in an awkward sprawl, he reached for her. "Are you hurt, my lady?"

She burst into tears as she lunged into his arms. Immediately, Lord Trinslow wrapped her into a tight embrace. After a moment of giving in to her emotions, Elaina lifted her head and looked around the clearing, afraid the man might still be lurking in the trees.

Lifting her gaze to her hero, she smiled up into his now dear face. "Please . . . Take me home."

"She can't just have disappeared," Bryce snapped at Cassie as he paced the length of the parlor. "We need to think of places she enjoyed to visit. We also need to make a list of her friends. Perhaps she called upon one of them." He stopped abruptly in front of the window. "It's getting dark." And his niece was out there alone.

Fear clutched at him, making it nearly impossible to concentrate. *When had it happened?* he wondered to himself. When had he grown to love that argumentative, irritable niece of his? Yet he did. He loved her so much he felt the terror of possibly losing her right through his bones. He'd thought her an inconvenience, a duty, but never a necessity.

But this godforsaken, bone-chilling fear cut through to the heart of his emotions, making him realize how utterly foolish he had been to cut himself off from his own feelings.

Shaking free of his thoughts, he tried to refocus

on how to find Elaina. "I shall send Fibbs to fetch a dozen Bow Street Runners and arrange for them to find her."

Cassie came up behind him and rested her cheek against his back. "We shall find her, Bryce."

Her soft reassurance helped keep the mind-numbing terror at bay. "I drove her away," he said softly, feeling the sting of guilt. "Instead of explaining my reasons for not wanting her near Kingwood, I simply allowed her to lock herself in her room." A painful scrape of laughter escaped him. "I should have refused to leave her alone until she heard why I feared her relationship with him."

"Don't be too harsh on yourself," Cassandra scolded him. "Her behavior didn't reflect that of a mature young lady, so it was only befitting that you treat her like a child. If you remember, Bryce, when left alone with Elaina, I ended up confining her to her room as well." She rubbed her cheek against his back. "She's still in pain over losing her parents and her home all at once, so she's acting out in a childish fashion. As soon as she realizes she's safe and that we aren't going away, I truly believe she will settle down." A groan escaped Cassie. "I can't believe I just used that awful term—'settle down.'"

Bryce smiled at his wife's disgust. "I rather like it myself."

"You would."

"Your Grace!" Fibbs shouted from the foyer in a most un-Fibbs-like manner. "Come quick! Lady Elaina has returned."

Racing across the room, Bryce came to an abrupt halt in the foyer. "Elaina," he whispered, unashamed by the tears blinding him. "Elaina," he said again as he ran forward, picked her up in his arms, and whirled her around the room. "I was so worried."

His confession brought fresh sobs from his niece, so he held her close until the storm had passed. Looking up at him with tear-smudged eyes, she had never looked so young or so precious to him. "I'm so, so, so sorry."

He shook his head. "As am I," he countered as he pressed a kiss upon her forehead. "But from this moment forward, we shall begin anew . . . as soon as I explain a few things about Kingwood."

Her smile was one of the sweetest things he'd ever received from her. "I knew you'd manage to qualify your promise somehow."

Laughing, Bryce hugged Elaina once more, before stretching out his hand to Trinslow. "I can only assume from your presence that you are in some way responsible for the safe return of my niece."

Though Trinslow opened his mouth to reply, Elaina pulled back and answered for him. "He most certainly is," she exclaimed, moving to Trinslow's side to place a hand upon his arm. "A dreadful man had come upon me in the park where I was sitting trying to collect my thoughts, when along comes Lord Trinslow, charging forth on his white horse like a bold knight of old." She pressed a hand to her chest. "I am indebted to him."

"And, so it seems, am I," Bryce murmured. "Once again."

"I am always pleased to be of assistance to Lady Elaina." Flushing, Trinslow shook his head. "Though despite what she might say, I assure you,

Your Grace, I hardly present the romantic figure on horseback."

"Don't say that, my lord," Elaina chided him gently. "You and Poco were my saviors."

"Poco?" Bryce drew his brows together. "The cat?"

"Not just any cat, a most heroic one." Elaina sent Cassie an apologetic look. "When I left, I took your cat with me, Cassandra. I know how much you love him, but I, well, I didn't wish to leave alone. I'd planned to return him as soon as I felt comfortable as Lady Kingwood."

Just the mention of Kingwood's name made Bryce frown. "Speaking of Kingwood," he began, promising himself he would not lose his temper, "what happened this evening? Did you or did you not run away to be with him?"

"I did," she admitted in a small voice, sending a glance up at Trinslow, "but I couldn't go through with it. I stood in front of his townhouse and realized that if I entered I would be losing you, Uncle Bryce."

The affection in her voice pierced his heart. "I'm just thankful you showed some sense," he replied gruffly, taken aback by his emotions.

She smiled at him. "I love you, too."

Clearing his throat, Bryce clapped his hands together. "Well, now that we have this settled, why don't we adjourn to the parlor for some refreshments?" He looked at Trinslow. "Please join us for supper this evening."

The young lord flicked a glance down at Elaina, who remained at his side. "I'd be honored, Your Grace."

Escorting his wife into the parlor, Bryce heard

Elaina ask Trinslow, "What *were* you doing riding in the park?"

"I'm trying to improve my equestrian skills," he admitted bashfully. "I think I'm getting quite good, don't you?"

"No," replied his niece, ever blunt. "Though you were the most beautiful thing I'd ever seen riding toward me tonight, technically speaking, your form was positively dreadful, my lord. You need to remember to keep your legs tucked against the horse and . . ."

Bryce found himself grinning like a perfect idiot as he listened to his niece dole out advice. Despite her sweetness when she'd first returned, Bryce knew that she would soon return to her own brazen self.

Thank God.

25

A lady should accept her mother's guidance without
question.

Quoted from *A Lady's Guide to Proper Etiquette*,
written by Lady Cassandra Abbott

"I simply had to call upon you despite the embar-
rassingly early hour," Lady Darwood said to Cassandra.

Though she didn't want to be uncharitable, Cassandra wished her mother had waited a while before coming to call. After yesterday's tumultuous
events, everyone had retired to bed early, so she
hadn't been given an opportunity to speak privately with Bryce. This morning, she'd risen early,
hoping to find him still in his room, but he hadn't
answered her knock.

She'd been terribly disappointed, as the need to
confess her love to him grew by the very minute. Especially after seeing the tenderness he showed Elaina
yesterday, Bryce had become an easy man to love.

"Why, all of polite society is agog over your behavior at the Hallertons' ball," her mother continued, recapturing Cassandra's attention.

The Hallertons' ball. Cassandra smiled to herself at the delightful memories of being waltzed around the room over and over again, held tightly in her husband's arms. "I fail to see why everyone would be so shocked. I only danced with my husband."

"Which is precisely my point," said her mother, leaning forward to tap Cassandra on the knee. "You showed an inordinate amount of attention to your husband, Cassandra. It simply isn't done."

"Nonsense."

Her mother's mouth flapped open. "What did you say?"

Though her immediate response stunned her as much as it did her mother, Cassandra knew it was how she truly felt. "I said nonsense, Mother." She smiled at her mother's shock. "As a married lady, I am free to dance with whomever I wish and if the only man I wish to dance with happens to be my husband, then that should be perfectly acceptable to everyone else. And if it's not . . ." Cassandra lifted one shoulder to show her utter disregard.

Lady Darwood fanned herself frantically. "Why, Cassandra, that is positively . . ."

". . . reassuring to hear," Bryce finished for her mother, strolling into the room. Coming up behind Cassandra, he placed his hand upon her shoulder. "How are you this fine morning, Lady Darwood?"

"Positively scandalized," she whispered. "Surely you do not wish for my daughter to be gossiped about, do you?"

Bryce smiled down at her mother. "Of course

not," he said, causing her mother to nod in relief. "Unfortunately, I have no intention of limiting the number of dances I enjoy with my wife." He ran a finger along Cassandra's cheek. "So, if that causes people to gossip about me and Cassie, it is an unavoidable situation."

Cassandra watched as her mother struggled to decide which issue to tackle first. *"Cassie?"* Lady Darwood finally said. "You've begun to call her Cassie?"

"Yes, and I rather like it," he admitted as he leaned down to place a kiss upon Cassandra's cheek. "Besides, it fits my headstrong wife."

"Oh, dear Lord." Lady Darwood fanned herself. "Cassandra, I love you dearly, but you know better than most how completely unacceptable that nickname is. My goodness, Cassandra, what are you thinking, darling? You even wrote the book on proper etiquette."

Before Cassandra could reply to her mother, Bryce responded for her. "Then it is time for her to rewrite it, for your darling Cassandra has become my beloved Cassie, who breaks more of her own rules than she follows."

My beloved Cassie. Cassandra turned the phrase over in her head, wondering if he'd said it as an offhand comment or if he truly meant it.

Rising, her mother reached out a hand to Cassandra. "Please, darling. You know that this will cause people to gossip about you."

Cassandra stood as well, meeting her mother as an equal. "I truly regret if that will cause you any embarrassment, Mother," she said sincerely. "But I can't go back to being your prim, staid daughter, Cassandra. I've changed, for the better I think, so if you find it difficult to accept these changes, I'll understand."

Her mother leaned forward to give Cassandra a quick hug. "It might take me some time to acclimate myself," she admitted with a smile, "but I'll adjust."

"Thank you," Cassandra murmured, returning her mother's embrace. "I love you, Mama."

Pulling back, her mother dabbed at her eyes. "Well, all I have to say is if anyone dare speak poorly of you, they shall have to answer to me," she remarked, straightening her shoulders.

"And to me," Bryce interjected.

"You're both wrong," Cassandra corrected them. "As much as I appreciate your support, I am perfectly capable of handling a few gossips." She gazed over her shoulder at Bryce. "After all, I am Lady Cassie Keene, Duchess of Amberville."

Her mother laughed brightly, before pressing a kiss upon Cassandra's cheek and leaving the room. Cassie barely noticed her mother's departure; she was too absorbed in the warm approval shining out of her husband's gaze.

"The best thing I ever did in my life was arrange to marry you," he said with a smile.

His words gave her hope and the strength to forge onward. "I'm glad you feel that way, because I feel the same way." Walking around the chair, she moved to stand in front of Bryce. "Did you mean what you said to my mother?"

"Every last word of it."

She shook her head. "I thought you wanted

me to settle in, to become a proper, convenient wife."

"I was an ass," he said with a laugh. Reaching out, he tucked a strand of her hair behind her ear. "I've recently realized that I've been wrong about a number of things. I thought I needed to be forever serious and in control as the duke, but I don't. I can enjoy my life, breaking rules that don't hurt anyone, yet also gain pleasure from handling the multitude of responsibilities that come with the title."

"Like dancing four waltzes in a row with your wife," she murmured with a smile.

"Precisely," he agreed, tapping her chin with his index finger. "After my disastrous marriage to Francesca, I never wanted to marry again, but then I became Elaina's guardian and knew I needed help to guide her. I decided to marry someone who was prim and a stickler for the rules, someone who would settle into a comfortable, convenient life. I wanted my marriage to be a most proper affair." He paused, tilting his head to the side. "Did I already tell you I was an ass?"

Cassandra laughed at his remark.

"Then I married you and got far more than I bargained for. You made me crazed from the first, but you also made me feel alive. I now realize that you are precisely what I need in a wife. You're loyal, generous, warm, and tender-hearted. But after Francesca, I was afraid to trust you with my heart." Cupping her face between his hands, he gazed into her eyes. "Again, here's where the ass part comes in, for I didn't realize that by the time I sought to protect myself from further hurt, it was already too late. I began to fall in love with you from the moment I walked into your chamber and found out about those ridiculous provisions."

If she hadn't been so touched by his words, she would have been embarrassed by the memory.

Leaning forward, he placed a soft, sweet kiss upon her lips. "I love you, Cassie Keene, Duchess of Amberville."

And with that one simple phrase, he granted her dearest wish.

"Oh, Bryce, I love you too," she murmured, blinking back her tears.

"Then why did you leave me?"

Hearing the pain in his question, she gave him a tremulous smile. "Because I loved you far too much to accept being a 'proper' wife."

"Well, thank God you did, for it would have taken me a few extra days to realize that I love you," he returned lightly, before kissing her again. "One more thing, darling, can we return to the Amberville townhouse?" Lifting his head, he gave her a look of chagrin. "I miss Fibbs."

Bursting into laughter, Cassie wrapped her arms around Bryce's neck and held him tight. "I'll set the servants to packing immediately."

Slowly, Bryce shook his head. "There's no rush," he murmured, leading her around to the settee. "I have plans for your immediate future."

Desire flooded her as she saw the sensual promise in her husband's gaze. It amazed her how hot passion burned when driven by love. With a smile, she held onto Bryce as he lowered her onto the cushions. Clinging to him, she offered herself to him, heart, body, and soul.

"My one-of-a-kind Cassie," he whispered before capturing her lips with his.

The need for words disappeared as they began to speak with their bodies, each stroke, every touch, conveying a message of love.

Epilogue

A lady should be an equal helpmate to her husband.

Quoted from *The Revised Lady's Guide to Proper Etiquette*,
written by Lady Cassie Keene, Duchess of Amberville

One year later

"You know, Robert, I do believe you are taking far too much of Her Grace's time," Bryce said as he plucked the playful baby from Cassie's lap. "While I understand she's your mother, you really do need to share her every now and then."

Laughing at Bryce's silliness, Cassie refastened her gown. Again, she'd gone against convention and had declined using a wet nurse. "He's only three months old," Cassie reminded her husband. "You've had me for far longer, so I believe you're the one who needs to learn to share."

Cradling Robert in one arm, Bryce looped the other around her waist, pulling her against him. "If you ask me, I think you're perfectly capable of meeting both of our needs." He leaned over and lightly nipped at Cassie's neck. "After all, Robert and I have very different needs."

The low, sensual note in her husband's voice reminded Cassie of just how long it had been since they'd shared a bed. A shiver ran through her as she lifted her face and met Bryce's ravenous kiss with matching hunger. An urgent need rushed through her, making her turn her body fully into his, pressing herself against him.

As if sensing their growing involvement, Robert began to protest his lack of attention. Loudly.

A groan broke from Bryce as he pulled back. Seeing the disappointment in his gaze, Cassie took Robert from him and walked to the parlor door. Calling for her son's nurse, she handed him off with a tender kiss. "He's ready for bed," she told the nurse as she placed Robert in her arms.

Stepping back into the room, Cassie shut the door and leaned against it. "Now where were we?" she asked playfully.

A grin split Bryce's face as he strode over to her and gathered her back into his embrace. Like a conquering lord, he claimed her mouth for his own. Hunger too long denied raged between them as Bryce pressed her back against the door, rubbing his body into hers.

"Aunt Cassie? Uncle Bryce?" Elaina called through the door. "I need to speak to you immediately," she added, knocking on the wooden panels. "Is this door locked?"

When Bryce lifted his mouth from hers, he sighed like a man long denied his last meal. "Tell her we're busy," he hissed under his breath.

"I can't do that," she returned. "It sounds urgent."

Grinding his hips forward, he rasped, "I'll show you something urgent."

Lord, how she wanted to revel in pleasurable pursuits with her husband, but at the moment, their niece needed them. "As soon as she leaves, Bryce, I promise you we'll have an intimate discussion about your urgent matter."

"Promises, promises, promises," he retorted. With a resigned sigh, he shifted them away from the door, careful to position himself behind Cassie's full skirts. "Come in, Elaina."

Flouncing into the room, she held her arms out at her sides. "Andrew is refusing to take me to the Perths' ball if I wear this gown."

"I most certainly am," Trinslow stated firmly as he joined them. "That gown is positively indecent, Elaina."

Bryce eyed his niece. "I've got to side with Trinslow on this one, Elaina. You're fair to bursting out of the bodice."

"It's all the rage," she protested, shifting her gaze to Cassie in hopes of finding an ally. "What do you think, Aunt Cassie?"

The bodice dipped so low that she could almost see the color of her niece's nipples. "I'm going to agree with your uncle and affianced, Elaina."

Crossing his arms, Andrew rocked back on his heels. "Just because I adore you, Elaina, don't believe for one moment that I will allow you to lead me around by my nose."

Her eyes sparkled as she reached out to pat Andrew's cheek. "You're unspeakably adorable when you act all stiff and proper, Andrew."

"Why, thank you . . . I think," he said, unable to

keep from smiling over Elaina's teasing. "But your compliment doesn't alter a thing."

"Fine," she snapped, drawing her skirts back. "Then I shall accede to your odious wishes."

After Elaina stomped out of the room, Andrew shook his head. "She can be as upset with me as she'd like, just as long as she changes that gown." He smoothed his hands down his jacket front. "I'd like to apologize for not heading Elaina off before she bothered you."

"It's quite all right," Cassie reassured him. "Isn't that right, Bryce?"

"Most certainly." Bryce offered Andrew a sympathetic smile. "I'm still grateful to you for helping Elaina."

"It was . . . is . . . my pleasure." Andrew blew out his breath, sending a lock of his hair sailing upward. "Well, most of the time, that is. Though I love Elaina dearly, she can be very wearying."

"The best women are," Bryce agreed, earning an elbow in his ribs. "Ouch!"

"That was for calling me wearying," she informed him with a pleasant smile. "I'm confident Elaina would be as offended as I am."

Andrew stumbled over his apology. "I meant no disrespect, my lady," he murmured. "I apologize for speaking out of turn."

"Don't trouble yourself over the matter," she replied with a wave of her hand. "And whenever you think Elaina is difficult to manage, remember the lovely Georgette and how she's busy making Lord Kingwood dance to her whims."

Bryce's laughter filled the room. "When I saw

Kingwood last week at White's, he certainly had the look of a haunted man."

"Well, that bit of news brightens my day," Andrew remarked with a grin. "Kingwood deserves every torment his wife can inflict upon him."

"True," Bryce agreed, "but I'd wager there are times when he envies Dranwyck his solitary prison cell."

"I wouldn't doubt it." Hearing Elaina come down the stairs, Andrew turned toward the doorway to watch her rejoin them. He pressed a hand upon his heart. "If you grow any more beautiful, my darling Elaina, I vow I shall perish from the shock."

Bryce's snort earned him another sharp elbow in the stomach. "I hope you enjoy the Perths' ball," Cassie said with a warm smile. "Please give Lady Perth my regards."

"I shall," Elaina promised as she waved to them while Andrew led her out of the house.

Placing his hand on the small of her back, Bryce turned Cassie to face him. "Would you like to go to the Perths' ball this evening as well?"

Cassie shook her head. "I most prefer quiet evenings at home with you and Robert. Besides," she began with a grin, "I'd probably spend more than half the night defending my new book."

"Come now, darling, do you really blame the ton for being set on its proverbial ear with your latest etiquette guide?" Bryce chuckled lightly. "You can't urge young ladies to be independent, self-sufficient, and unmalleable without raising a few hackles. Hell, every time I walk into White's, I'm surrounded by gentlemen complaining that their wives are beginning to rebel."

"Poor dears," Cassie murmured in a dry tone. "I suppose they're now forced to treat their wives like equals rather than a convenient possession."

"You, Cassie, shall undoubtedly be the downfall of gentlemen everywhere," Bryce remarked, tapping his finger on the tip of her nose.

"If a gentleman cannot handle a strong-willed lady, then he can't be much of a man, can he?"

Bryce snorted in laughter. "According to your theory, I must be a paragon among men."

"Quite true," she retorted, lifting on her toes to press a quick kiss upon his mouth. "And you can dance, as well."

"If you value my dancing ability above all else, perhaps I should refresh your memory." Bryce held out his arms in the waltz position. "May I have this dance, Your Grace?"

Giggling at their foolishness, Cassie dipped into a curtsey. "Most certainly, Your Grace," she murmured in return before launching herself into his arms.

Caught off guard by her exuberant acceptance, Bryce stumbled backward a few steps before catching his balance. Glancing down at her legs wrapped around his waist, he lifted an eyebrow. "Is this proper, my lady?"

"For us, Bryce, it most certainly is," she countered, feeling more complete than she'd ever dreamed possible. "And I should know. After all, I wrote the book."

Their laughter blended into joyous music as Bryce waltzed her around the room.

Return to
a time of romance...

SONNET
BOOKS

Where today's

hottest romance authors

bring you vibrant

and vivid love stories

with a dash of history.

PUBLISHED BY POCKET BOOKS